EÞANDUN

EÞANDUN

EPIC POEM

WILLIAM G. CARPENTER

Edited by Kellie M. Hultgren
Jacket and interior artwork by Miko Simmons
Book design and typesetting by Jim Handrigan
Managing Editor: Laurie Buss Herrmann

ISBN-13: 978-1-64343-959-4
Library of Congress Catalog Number: 2019905606
Printed in the United States of America
First Printing: 2020
24 23 22 21 20   5 4 3 2 1

Beaver's Pond Press, Inc.
939 Seventh Street West
Saint Paul, MN 55102
(952) 829-8818
www.BeaversPondPress.com

To order, visit www.williamgcarpenter.com. Reseller discounts available.

Contact the author at www.williamgcarpenter.com for interviews, speaking engagements, and school visits.

Quid enim Hinieldus cum Christo?
What has Ingeld to do with Christ?

—Alcuin

He was our king just as much as yours.

—A. P. Rockwell

✝

∽ Contents ∾

⟶ Abbreviations ⟵

★ . . . . conjectural		emp. . . . . emperor		
abd . . . . . abdicated		estab. . . . . established		
abp. . . . . . archbishop		exp. . . . . . expelled		
acc. . . . . . acceded		f. . . . . . . father		
ald. . . . . . alderman		G . . . . . . Gothic		
a.m . . . . . Anno Mundi		gdf. . . . . . grandfather		
br . . . . . . brother		gdm. . . . . grandmother		
bap . . . . . baptized		gt.-gdf . . . great-grandfather		
bk . . . . . . book		gt.-gdm . . great-grandmother		
bp . . . . . . bishop		k . . . . . . king		
c . . . . century		L . . . . . . Latin		
ca . . . . . . circa		OE . . . . . Old English		
ch . . . . . . chapter		OEN. . . . Old East Norse		
co-k. . . . . co-king		r . . . . river		
cons. . . . . consecrated		s . . . . son		
ct. . . . . . . count		sis . . . . . . sister		
d. . . . . . . died		ss . . . . . . sons		
da . . . . . . daughter		w . . . . . . wife		
dep . . . . . deposed		wid . . . . . widow		

EÞANDUN

I.

The Wiltshire Front

⁊

The Danes' conquest of Northumbria, East Anglia, and Mercia has left West Saxon Alfred the sole independent native king. Alfred and his thanes are discussing whether to pay an agreed indemnity when a guardsman announces a visitor. Athelnoth and Wulfhere interview the newcomer, who breaks free and attacks the king. Alfred orders Ealhswith to take their children to Frome for safekeeping.

Pour your glory, Lord, on the struggling king,
who by your hand ransomed the ravaged land;
illuminate the faces of your people,
who bled for you on every slaughterfield;
and kindle, Comforter, our uncouth hearts
that we may burn to do your will and earn
the blessings, not the curses, of our ancestors.
The pagan Danes had conquered the four kingdoms.
Clerics and kings, churls and thanes they'd slain,
while the living they plundered and enslaved.
Alfred, caked with the blood of friend and foe,   *k. of West Saxons*
tasted the dregs of that envenomed horn,   *acc. 871*
but granted faith and craft by our dear Savior
he steeped old Godrum's host in faith and fear   *Godrum / Guthrum*
and steered the stubborn oarsmen from our soil.   *Guþormr / Gormr*

Long years the heathens raged, led by strong kings.
They splashed ashore and seized Northumbria   *866–867*
and crowned a puppet king, who purchased peace.

They martyred Edmund *rex* and set a puppet
on the East Anglian seat. He purchased peace.
They maimed the Mercian host at holy Repton;
their new-made puppet, quaking, purchased peace.
Alone the West Saxons kept their *cyning*,
whose throne Woden-descended Cerdic reared
when Arian Theodoric ruled Rome.
Alone the tender mercies of our Father
spared Alfred's people from the sword of Gorm,
though Alfred too had purchased peace at Wilton,
at Wareham, and again at Exeter.

K. Edmund of E.
Angles d. 870
874

king (OE)
K. Cerdic d. 534
K. Theodoric d. 526

871
876, 877

After seeing the Danes across his border,
trailing them up the Fosse Way to the Thames,
King Alfred, pious Athulf's youngest son,
retired with his troops to Chippenham,
where Athelwulf had built a hunting lodge.
The Saxon captain loved that timbered den
surrounded by tall trees, where as a boy,
when Osburh lived, his godly Jutish dam,
he'd seen his sister marry Mercian Burgred,
and where his own brood now scrapped and scrabbled.
The meadows round about fed browsing cattle,
the neighboring woodlands pastured deer and swine,
and brown hares could be taken everywhere.

K. Athelwulf d. 858 f. of
K. Athelbald d. 860, K.
Athelbert d. 865, K.
Athelred d. 871, K.
Alfred d. 899

Athelswith d. 888

"industrius venator
laborat non in vanum,"
Asser 22

Standing at ease in his scriptorium,
a beechwood fire crackling at his back,
West Saxon Alfred beamed at Athelnoth,
his minister in Somerton, and said,
"*Carissime,* companion in our wars,
whose war-lamp lighted heathen fiends to hell,
I plan to put you up for alderman
of Somerset, our land of milk and must.
These slopes and moors that nourish sheeted cattle,

these harbors, markets, turbaries, and mines,
all these we lease to you, which you'll confirm
with lump amounts I don't doubt you'll find.
Werwulf has prepared this charter, here,
which only lacks your handwrit or cross."

As Athelnoth imbibed these heady words
Lord Wulfhere, long-time alderman of Wiltshire,
glared at the king from under tangled brows.
"*Illustrissime rector,*" Wulfhere said,
"son of Athelwulf and seed of Ingeld,
the silver you exact from this young thane
to execute these kingly, lavish grants
will sap the very lifeblood of his office.
Consider sending flooded Somerset
a prince unfettered by such debts and rents,
to wit, my son, the uncle of your nephews."

"dilectus et venerabilis
dux"; ealdormann (OE)

Alfred's gt.-gt.-gt.-gt.-
gdf., br. of K. Ini; þegn
(OE)

Wulfhere's da. is K.
Athelred's wid.

King Alfred eyed the graduated candle
as a hound gnawed a loud bone at his feet.
A widow and two sons survived his brother,
King Athelred, who perished after Merton.
She was Wulfhere's daughter, they his grandsons—
her brother thus was quasi-royalty.
"*Eala,* these heathen fiends," said Alfred,
"even in victory, I'm still their slave.
Their lying chief, who breached the peace at Wareham,
punctiliously expects his promised pence.
And I have thirty growing guards to feed."

Wulfthryth; Athelhelm
and Athelwold

876

"Send twenty of them home," said prudent Wulfhere.
"And let my Wiltshiremen depart in peace.
As for your payment due, wet Somerset
encompasses the Glastonbury hoard,
including Saint David's giant sapphire."

The Saxon captain turned to Athelnoth,
a native of the yearly flooded moors.
"Shall we lay hands," he asked, "on means amassed
for seven centuries by Joseph's monks?   *Joseph of Arimathea*
Demand a gift from Abbot Herefrith?
A *sportula* to prove his loyalty?"

But Athelnoth was in no mood for jokes.
"Do we defend our altars with our arms,"
he asked, "or yield their riches on demand?
Come spring, old Godrum's crews will gather here
with whetted shares to plow our people's flesh.
So why augment the coffers of the devils
with silver you can use to feed your sheep?
Is my lord more honorable than God?"

His features darkening, one finger pointing
upwards like an apostle's, Alfred said,
"The Romans, hedged about with strangers, found
a haven in their fathers' treasury.
The Hebrew kings, we read, likewise appeased   *2 Kings 12:18, 18:15-*
the Syrians and fierce Assyrians   *16*
with precious metals fetched from the Lord's temple.
Men pay the stipulated price of peace
to spare themselves the punishments of war."

"The peace of Wilton," Wulfhere said, "endured
four priceless years. However much we spent,   *871–875*
the men whose blood we bought must count it cheap."

Here entered the senior hoard-guard and bowed.
"An East Angle is come from Lundenburg
with gifts, he says, for our anointed king."

The Athulfing (that's Alfred) gave a smile.
"Ask and you shall have," he said. "A wise man

from the east. Invite him back tonight to feast
the first appearance of our living Lord." *Epiphany, Jan. 6*

The guardsman paused, then stammered out,
                    "The Angle,
the Angle begs an audience with my lord.
He has a plan to magnify your throne."

"Don't see him, Lord," the Somersetan warned.
(That's Athelnoth.) "The town is thick with Danes."
But Wulfhere welcomed gifts from wheresoever
to resupply the king's depleted means.

"All of you, go, and grill this visitor,"
the Saxon chief impatiently replied.
"But if it's just another dun from Gorm—
just promise him his patron will be paid."

The monarch—Alfred—gestured at his candle.
"Now we turn to spiritual things.
Orosius' first book is almost done.
He says, before our longed-for Savior came,
perpetual war raged among the nations,
at least since bloody Ninus and his queen *Semiramis*
first bred the lust for conquest in the earth.
He claims that wars grew less calamitous
when God the Son assumed our human form.
I find that doctrine hard to understand.
The Rome he claims the Lord of Heaven shielded
the Huns subdued, the Moors and Vandals stripped, *452; 455*
and Odovacar ruled, a foreign king. *476–493*
Our worthy fathers worshiped ghosts and devils.
Yet in our time we Christian men have seen
wars as fierce as any our fathers waged.

"All thanks and praise for the Lord's tender mercy
in ousting cornered Gorm from Exeter, *877*

7

but we may yet see Godfred's grandson bring
ruin and death on the West Saxon folk."
He looked at Athelnoth with kind regard.
"Do read his book, my friend, when you learn to read,
as all our judges must who expound our laws."

The westerner inclined his head and said,
"The erudition of our lord is known
and would adorn a bishop or a monk."

"Send in the bishop," Alfred said to Werwulf   *Athelheah 9th bp.*
as the scribe closed and stowed the scribbled quire.   *of Sherborne cons. 871*
"You'll find His Stoutness camped out in the kitchen,
interpreting the wheeling flocks of cooks."

☙

An ivory crucifix; a silver scourge;
a reliquary clad in ivory tiles,
each panel crammed with goggling eyes and drawn-out,
knotted, disunited limbs; a glass cup;
a silver dish on which bare shepherds pranced
and women lolled on double-bodied monsters—
these and other works of men, which men
in honor of our Father's workmanship
have added to his intricate creation,
were spread out on a plain deal table
in the sunken shed the house-guards called the gatehouse,
though Alfred's lodge had neither gate nor wall.
Two guardsmen eyed the envoy from the east,
a burly champion with raven hair
and features uglier than any man's.

"Our misery still rings in all men's ears,"
the self-styled Anglian began,
"how Ingwar caught our king and held him prisoner.   *Ingwar s. of Ragnar*

At breakfast, Ingwar offered him a berth
as regent while he toured his other holdings,
but Edmund said he'd only take that post
if Ingwar burned his wooden gods and drowned
his sins beneath the Savior's healing wave.
Nonplussed, the fiend delivered Wuffa's seed
to the untender mercy of his earls,
who made our holy, Woden-sired lord
a butt for their barbaric bowmanship
and dragged him back to Ingwar to be judged.

"The heathen king intoned a prayer to Grim,
uncaged the eagle in brave Edmund's back,
then, for good measure, cut off his head.
A huge wolf guided us to the place
where our king's blood cried to us from the earth.
We fetched his head, still muttering prayers in which
we heard our names, to Bedricworth estate,
where the Most High has worked wonders by it."

As the great thane spoke, he drew a comb
of horn through the bright wavelets of his mane.
Undazzled, Athelnoth was studying
the steep-sided, transparent chalice
as Wulfhere, Wiltshire's alderman, drank in
the drollery unfolding in the dish.

"This scene," said Wulfhere, "lacks the quinotaur,
the spawn or fry of fishy Neptune by
Salacia or Venilia, his consorts.
One foggy day on Gaul's low-roaring shore,
said misfit, wriggling up from the abyss,
begot Meroveus on a Frankish frow
and thus fathered the Merovingian kings—
whose spines, they say, sprouted a golden pile.
Their blood excited Eadbald of Kent,
who got it from his godly Frankish dam,

Lodbrok; 870

Edmund k. of E. Angles
d. Nov. 20, 870

Wuffa 6th c. k. of E.
Angles

Woden

Basina w. of Clodius
gt.-gdf. of K. Clovis I d.
511
K. Eadbald s. of
K. Athelbert d. 616 and

9

to wed his father's widow, spurn our Lord,   *Bertha da. of K.*
and offer sacrifice to Jutish Thunor.   *Charibert d. 567; K.*
At least when Alfred's brother Athelbald   *Athelbald d. 860;*
embraced their buried father's Frankish bride,   *Judith da. of Emp.*
he didn't rebuff our West Saxon bishop."   *Charles d. 877*

The giant's eyes flared darkly. He declared,
"Thus much of Edmund's hoard we grabbed and fled
and hid in Lundenburg, gnawing our grief,
until we heard that Athulf's youngest son,
alone among the island's Christian kings,
had forced the fiends to fear the Christian sword.
We also heard he'd welcomed Edmund's brother,   *Eadwald*
preserving him from bloodthirsty Grim."

"Our king's progenitor," said Athelnoth,
raising the glass cup to the gray-lit doorway.
"He doesn't drink the blood of Christian princes."
He passed the chalice to a guard, who peered
through its thick foot as through a plate of ice.

"The Angles beg your king," the man concluded,
"to drive the devils from our soil and plant
our exiled atheling on Edmund's throne.   *æþeling* (OE)
There's precedent for this request, my friends.
When sturdy Ecgbert freed us from the Mercians,   *K. Ecgbert d. 839*
he installed Athelstan, young Alfred's brother,   *825; K. Athelstan*
as king over Wuffa's widowed folk.
Come back, Saxons. Give us Athelstan."

The Somersetan nodded to the swordsmen,
who seized the enormous envoy by the arms.
"You've got it wrong, my friend," said Athelnoth.
"The prince who governed the gull-eating Angles
was Ecgbert's second son, our Alfred's uncle—
as any genuine Anglian would know."

"Unhand the man!" cried Wulfhere, Wulfheard's son.
"Why vex our guest with genealogy?
Alfred will keep his peace! Gorm will be paid!"

Half-grinning as the hall-guards eased their grip,
the traveler replied, "So say you now,
but in what coin, the self-stamped gold of kings   *kunukar (OEN)
or the blood-debt owed for a thousand men?"   *mæn (OEN)

Abruptly roaring in a whirl of hair,
the rower tore his elbows from the guardsmen
and swiftly drew their dragon-patterned swords,
which leapt, as if enchanted, from their sheaths,
uncorking both white throats in that ascent.
As suddenly, he sprang across the room
and lighted like an *alf on the high threshold.   elf (OEN)
Blotting out the day for half a breath,
his grisly features buried in his shadow,
he vanished, troll-like, in the cloudy light.

⌒∞⌒

Stunned, the Saxons stumbled into the yard,
where thanes and ladies decked in winter pelts
arrived to celebrate Epiphany.
"Invader! Pagan! Dane!" cried Athelnoth,
but his voice fell short in the frozen air.
The devil's tresses trailing like a banner,
a blooded blade upraised in either hand,
he drove among the nobles like a nightmare.
A guardsman flung a flashing one-edged knife
that struck his back flat-bladed and just hung there,
pointing at the ground, as he beat down
the sentries' wavering, worm-tinted weapons.
Passing the marshaled tables and high folk,
the Dane raised his eyes to the blackened dragon
that overlooked the hall as blackened hams

11

and flitches hang from beams like butchered fiends
to frighten famine from a churl's board.
The oarsman galloped past the bolted storerooms
and suddenly appeared before the king.

He knew him from the Wilton slaughterfield   871
and Exeter's and Wareham's treaty sessions,   876, 877
and now found him coiled over a table
on which a graduated candle burned.
Lifting his head, the Athulfing disclosed—   *Alfred*
or so his foe inferred in the warm gloom—
the dread not only of a beast condemned
to death by bestial enemies or hunters,
but of a dying spearman who conceives
his memory will perish with his breath.
A deerhound, growling, leapt to her four paws
as Alfred's bishop, known from former fights,   *Athelheah bp. of*
inclined his bulk against a cherry chest   *Sherborne*
atop which stood a honeycomb of stone.
Against the wall, a monk shook like a sapling,
as if afraid of his own shivering blade.

"Alfred, son of Saxon Athelwulf,"
the stranger cried, "I summon you for murder,
peculation, sorcery, and fraud!"
Before he said it thrice, the deerhound sprang
and clamped the giant's elbow in her jaws.
His other arm hurled a sword at Alfred,
who ducked behind the shield he yanked upwards,
though the steel boss caught on the table's rim.

"Heathen!" cried the king. The pirate jeered.
The bishop found his axe behind the chest.

"Behold," he said, "a people from the north   *Jer. 5:15, 6:22, 50:41*
will come, whose tongue you will not understand—"
The hero howled, flinging flying Frec,

whipping through willow lamina like water
and splitting mitered oak with the strength of ten.
Unfrightened by the fiend's inhuman fury,
the bishop sank his axe in an outstretched arm.
It gripped an instant in the living bone.

"They ride the earth on horses," he declaimed,   *Jer. 6:23, 50:42*
"a company whose cries roar like the ocean—"
The potent form, contracting, twisted free
and halted, sap spilling from his sleeve.

"You breached my peace," averred the Saxon king,
menacing the fiend with unstained blade.   *K. Edmund d. 870;*
"King Edmund sent me," said the sailor, panting.   *★Yatmutr,*
"Wuffa's heir, it seems, is short a head."   *★arfi, ★hofoþ* (OEN)

Now Athelnoth and two fresh guards appeared.
Bawling, the brigand wove his watered wand,
which king and bishop shunned, while Sigewulf
and Wulf went in forthwith. Poor Wulf was fined
a foot, but soon the Somersetan swung
south of Sigewulf's stroke, which, Sherborne's shield   *Athelheah*
discerning, drove his troll-wife down the toll-road
cleared by the killer's ward as careful Alfred
aimed his edge and nicked the bristled neck. Wulf
lobbed his limb at the snout, Sigewulf struck
brawn, and the bitch chomped the carl's calf.

He bellowed now, a bear enraged by spears,
while wary Werwulf, who recalled the Danes'
demonic devastation of his house—
a fief of Offa's line, on Breedon rise,   *Breedon on the Hill 870*
where Abbot Hædda was the first to rule
and Abbot Eanmund unraveled verse—
the monk approached the sailor, blade held close.
A voice exclaimed, "My lord! My lord!" outside

the shuttered window, or a lull allowed it
to be heard. The voice was the voice of Wulfhere,
who'd thrown a ring of spears around the lodge.

The rower's glower balked the blood-mad Saxons.
A storm-struck ship, each strake a spouting spring,
he trained his oar on Alfred and declared,

Thoughtful, the thrasher   of thick-set thorn-groves
waddled the whale-road   to the worm's home.   **hualiarþ, *ormr*
Whom will they hail   the high horseman's *kunur   (OEN); *women* (OEN)
to gnaw with the named ones?   No one knows.

When the Dane sank, the Saxons hacked his shape
beside the cherry-spattered plaster wall
until the soul receded from his eyes
and martial virtue failed in their arms.
Exhausted, they surveyed their outsized foe,
who now sagged like an ox stunned in the shambles,
his brow bent by the honeycomb of stone.
As Frec, the deerhound, sniffed the creeping gore,
the Athulfing caressed her wiry pelage   *Alfred*
but quickly hid his unsteady hand.
The bishop bowed and bound Wulf's footloose stump,
then parted the marauder's tattered tunic,
uncovering his bloody bearskin vest.

"It's Attila," he said. "We should have known   *Wilton 871; Wareham*
this face from Wareham, Exeter, and Wilton.   *876; Exeter 877*
The Lord, in his wisdom, blinded our eyes."

"Perhaps King Edmund truly sent this devil,"
the monk said shakily, "to warn our king."

Alfred answered, eyes fixed on the corpse,
"King Cwichelm sent Lord Eomer to slay   *K. Cwichelm d. 636*
Edwin, Northumbria's then-pagan king.   *Easter 626; Bede,*

This was in early days. We too were pagans. Ecclesiastical Hist. *bk.*
Feigning an embassy at Eastertide, *ii ch. 9*
Eomer thrust clear through Lord Lilla's flank
and pricked the warlord with his poisoned blade.
Bedridden with a fever, Edwin swore
to serve the Lord if he might right that crime,
and the Lord God agreed. Great Edwin whipped us. *fenglas, æftergenga*
Five West Saxon kings fell in one fight. (OE)*; K. Oswald*
But Edwin's blest successor, holy Oswald, *acc. 633*
sponsored our King Cynegils at the font, *K. Cynegils bap.*
since when we Saxons serve the one true Ruler." *635*

⌀

In the unlit abutment of the passage
that ran along the north wing of the lodge,
the seed of Ingeld faced the studded door. *Alfred*
"It's me," he called, his man's voice immured
by the close wattle walls and pented roof.
He'd scrubbed his hands and hurried through the hall,
but a fresh terror shook him where he stood.
What if another devil, a berserker,
had dropped into his bower through the thatch?
What an imprudent, giddy fool he'd been
to bring his wife and pups to Chippenham!
He heard a muffled bump as one within
unset the wooden bar. "Come in, O king,"
he heard his helpmeet utter, his blood still
thumping in his ears. The stiff hinges squealed,
and there, lit by twilight from the smoke hole,
stood Ealhswith, his hardy Mercian darling.

She aimed a one-edged blade a forearm long
straight at his throat and squinted past his ear.
With eyes of wintry blue, a brow of cloud,

and resolution blazoned in her port;
with mane the tint of stripped woods in the distance
curtained by a screen of blowing snow;
with chalk-white shift that hid the fruitful corpus
from which their youngest guzzler sucked his substance,
she seemed the incarnation of that Wisdom
Boethius, the senator, adored
before Theodoric, the Gothic king,
the savior and the conqueror of Rome,
disposed of him for loving his own country—
though long before young Alfred heard the name
of that afflicted, steady matron, Wisdom,
the daughter and the handmaid of the Father,
this daughter of a Mercian alderman
and a Mercian lady sprung from royal blood,
by the sole grace of him who brought him to her,
had purified his disreputable youth.

Boethius d. 524
K. Theodoric d. 526

Reluctantly, she angled down her blade
as Hilda, her companion, lowered her bow
and Alfred's elder children sheathed their knives
and grimaced at the king, portraying courage.
Meanwhile, Alfred's guileless younger girls
struggled, sniffling, out from under the bed
and the babe bawled on Athelflaed's small breast.
She was anxious Alfred's eldest child.

"Just so, my cubs," the Athulfing affirmed,
caressing fragrant heads and narrow shoulders,
"just so, my little thanes, you'll guard and shield
your mother, and each other, from the devils."
Hot tears of pity started in his eyes
for the miserable wilderness of ills
that lay in wait to ravage their young lives.

Alfred

"Our Lady loves you yet," said Ealhswith,
stitching a quick cross to her gem-strewn chest.
"Are all the devils dead and damned?" asked Hilda.

"There was only one," the Saxon captain said.
"He called, 'I come, Lord Woden,' as he fell—
in that he spoke the truth—then flew to hell."
He grinned to reassure the staring children.
"Our Savior's offered grace astonished him,"
he said, "as when the Lombard giant raised   *Gregory,* Dialogues *bk.*
his sword to slaughter Sanctulus of Norsia.   *iii*
The heathen strangers gathered in the square,
expecting to enjoy a good beheading,
but when the giant's weapon ripped the sky
the Benedictine bellowed, 'Hold, Saint John!'
The eagle-eyed apostle, peering earthwards,
inhibited the foreign ogre's stroke.
He strained, he shook, he groaned to heave his steel,
but the keen blade just glittered in the sky,
like Joshua's sun glorying over Gibeon.   *Josh. 10:12-13*
The monk refused to loose the Lombard's limb
until he swore to injure no more Christians.
He swore, and his rigidity was healed."

Thus earnest Alfred entertained his issue,
relating lore from Gregory the Great,
then held his lady's forearms in his palms.
"Ealhswith," he said, "the mailed Danes
could strike this market town at any hour.   *Chippenham*
Accompany these little ones to Frome,
where Aldhelm's abbey walls will shelter them."   *estab. 7th c.*

His bride replied, "If pagan Godrum comes,
won't we be safer here in Chippenham?
The devils feed on feebleness, not strength."

"*Leof*," Hilda said, "you've got your levies.   *sir* (OE)
You've got your guardsmen, paid to shield your hide."

"We want to stay with you," said Athelflaed.
"We want to slaughter sailors," Edward cried.

The Saxon chief confessed to Ealhswith,
"A grievous sin it was to bring you here.
I'll meet you at the Feast of the Conversion.   *Conversion of Saul,*
If I don't show, you get this crew to Sherborne.   *Jan. 25*
Lord Athelheah will ship you overseas."   *bp. of Sherborne*

How changed she was, the Mercian girl he loved,
with thinning cheeks and smaller, harder limbs.
He saw her search his face for a reprieve.
"I would go with you, if I could," he said.
"Together we could pray in holy Romeburg,
where Leo crowned me consul of Britannia—   *Leo IV 847–855*
where the Romans still show the ship that bore
Father Aeneas up the muddy Tiber."
His sister lived at Rome, where Mercian Burgred   *Athelswith d. 888*
absconded on a hurried pilgrimage
when Halfdan's rowers maimed the Mercian host.   *Repton 874*
"Or we could sail to Jerusalem,"
he said, "our mother, bride of our dear Lord,
to venerate his empty sepulcher."

The king recalled that Saxon Willibald,
a Hampshire monk, had roamed the Holy Land   *ca. 725–732*
when Athelheard was king, succeeding Ini.   *acc. 726*
He'd seen the low cave where Christ was born,
the riverbank where John acknowledged him,
the hill on which he died so hideously,
and the new tomb in which he was interred.
After a ten-year stint in Subiaco,
that brother served Archbishop Boniface,

himself a Devon monk, Wynfrith by name,
who placed him in a new Bavarian see. *Eichstätt ca. 741*
Before the heathen Frisians murdered him, *June 5, 754*
Saint Boniface, a friend of Charles the Hammer,
had set the Frankish crown on Pippin's brow *K. Pippin acc. 752*
(the shamming Childeric having been deposed), *s. of Charles Martel*
who left it to his son, a greater Charles, *d. 741; K. Childeric*
whom grateful poets glorify as David. *III dep. 751; K.*
And so a lad from Saxon Crediton *Charles acc. 768*
was midwife to a resurrected empire. *emp. 800*

As Ealhswith studied her husband's features,
her scalding feelings overflowed her eyes.
His robe hung slack on his scarecrow shoulders,
even after seven years as king.
"My precious boy," she said to boost his spirits,
"we pray the almighty Thunderer for courage."

Thus spoke his wife, to whom the king replied,
"By my age, Ceadwalla was dead in Rome, *K. Ceadwalla d. 689;*
where Sergius the First baptized him Peter. *Sergius I 687–701*
Besides recovering our Chiltern lands,
where the pale, leafless ghost orchid grows,
he built on our inheritance from Cerdic *K. Cerdic d. 534*
by overrunning Sussex, Wight, and Kent." *686*

He stopped, his poor spirit drained of words.
His *cwene* clutched clumsily at his fingers. *woman (OE)*

II.

Enemy Courts

ℭℴ

The scene turns to the Danes. Halga says farewell to his Frankish concubine.
In his speech to the army at Cirencester, Guthrum assigns the earls their
roles in the invasion and prays for victory in the name of his slain son. Back
in Chippenham, Alfred celebrates Epiphany. After giving thanks for the
Lord's protection, he warns his guests of a likely attack.

Now tell us, Ghost, of the cold, seaborne Danes,
your children, out of Noah, like ourselves.
You gave them breath and places on the earth
from which to brave the bird-nurturing waves.
You gave them sun and moon and heaven's weather
so they might know their Maker cares for them   *Metod (Measurer)* (OE)
and seek him out with overflowing hearts.
And though their kings claim Woden as their forebear,
as ours who stem from Father Cerdic do,
you delegated captains from your host
(not just the fallen ones, as some have grumbled)
to train them in the ways of peace and war
and lead them, in good time, into your kingdom.

In Roman Cirencester, beside the Churn,   *"Siziter"*
Caer Ceri to the Welsh, where three roads meet,
beneath a Hwiccan noble's frozen thatch,
good Halga, Eric's nephew, Hemming's seed,   *Halga s. of Harold s. of*
attempted to console his Frankish girl   *K. Hemming; Eric ct. of*
for staying put while he campaigned with Gorm.   *Dorestad by grant of*
Riding without camp followers or baggage,   *Emp. Lothar d. 855*
they planned to fall like lightning on the foe,
and she was now in no fit state to gallop.

21

Halga therefore said to thickening Ymme,
"I'll send for you before your childbed.
But if I don't, this purse of gold dinars
will underwrite your place among the Danes.
I bought a heifer we shall offer Freya
and masses for the saints you specified,
Elizabeth and John and holy Mary.
My lands I leave to my surviving young,
but while you live, you'll share the fruits thereof.
So eat your fill of eggs and cream, my dear,
and steer clear of Hwiccan cunning men."

Kneeling, Ymme poured warm streams of tears
on Halga's callused palms and rubbed her cheek,
her sodden cheek, against his knucklebones.
"May the good Lord," she murmured, "shield my lord—"

Good Halga pulled her up. A gem she was,
a slaughtered burgher's daughter Gorm had bought
for thirty *solidi* in Colchester—   *shillings* (L)
she might have fetched ten times that much in Spain.
If Hemming's scion lived, he might yet win
a royal Anglian or Saxon dame
or one of King Sigfred's landed nieces
or a gilt princess sprung from Karli's loins,
but for the time this virgin and her child
would ease the tedium of camp and teach
a northern lord to govern Christian nations.

"May the Lord speed our scheme," Lord Halga countered.
"If we succeed, this lamb will be a great one
in the land, mastering the fat Saxon nobs.
Now dry your chin," he said, wiping his eyes.

"And I may be a queen someday," she added,   *regent after K. Clovis II*
"like Saint Baldhild, the thrall who ruled the Franks." *d. 656*

Below, where worried Hwiccans waited on him,
with hand as hard as iron tongs that clamp
the hot work aglow in the forge's maw,
bold Halga gripped the shoulder of his host.

"Pamper my Imi, Mercian," Halga said,
"or Earl Hrut's sons will flay you alive."
The Frankess frowned to show that she concurred
in the fierce menace uttered by the sailor.

∽∞∾

A moot or pack or fellowship of earls
awaited Hemming's grandson in the street.   *Halga*
Lord Hrut of Hedeby was first to hail him:
it was Hrut who'd first approached the kings   *K. Halfdan &*
to vouch for exiled Gorm's benign intent   *K. Sigfred*
in gathering men and ships to pillage Britain.
The earl's gray wolf cloak revealed a jacket
of watered leaf-green silk; atop his brows
his bald crown blazed like a baby's bottom.

Next in rank (not counting Gorm) came Wiga,
a noble Ringsted man the kings had sent
with twenty crews of mailed Zealanders.
His ancestors had fought at Bravellir,
where the best men of the era stress-tested
War-tooth's overlordship of the north.   *K. Harald*
His silken coat or vest, of Grecian make,   *Wartooth*
glowed like a raft of daffodils in spring
beneath his glossy black marten cope.

Beside him lingered Siward, Smala's son,
a Scanian from Lund who'd raised ten crews
of fishermen and husbandmen who'd never
pulled an oar for any raiding chieftain.

Both man and woman, thrall and thane esteemed
Lord Siward's kindliness and sense of justice.
His otter cape revealed a tunic dyed
the welling blue of the All-Father's hood.

Behind him, Wan, from Limfjord's northern shore,
rested his famous axe against his thigh.   *øhs (OEN)
Of East Frankish work, enchased with silver,
that gift from Ingwar had delivered Grim's
eagle from Aella's and Saint Edmund's backs.   K. Aelle d. Mar. 21,
His crews included one of true berserkers,   867; K. Edmund d. Nov.
captained by Attila, his fastest friend.   20, 870
The rough pelt of a bear engrossed his form,   *biarn (OEN)
brushing his hips and knees with its hooked claws.

Next, there came two enterprising earls
Gorm had enrolled from the stripped Frankish towns:
Lord Froda, with six western companies—
his seal coat concealed a purple shirt—
and Toca, Toca's son, of Himmerland,
who led five crews of veterans from Orbaek.
The Himmerlanders claimed to be the first—
under the Cimbrian name, which Caesar mentions—   Gallic Wars bk. ii
the first far northerners to challenge Rome.
His copper locks still burned with summer's fire
above a cape patched up of hare and stoat.

The gang of chiefs included Theodric,
Gormr's Nordalbingian Saxon ally,
who'd fought with him in Eric's thrust at Eric,
the son of Hemming versus Godfred's son,
and Nyklot, Halga's Abotritan friend.
The Abotrites abhorred their northern neighbors.

Surrounded by his earls, Godfred's grandson,   Godrum / Gormr
their *dux bellorum* and their acting king,

who traced his parentage to royal Dan,
whom the Danes first raised on the shield at Viborg,
displayed a grin amidst his salted beard,
a shred of breath drifting across his features
as tenuous as whispered prayers to Grim.
His sable mantle marked his shoulders' strength,
his scarlet tunic flamed with heartfelt fire,
and links of reddish gold flared on his chest,
outglistening the morning's muffled light.

Old Gorm had wrested tribute from young Alfred
despite the ruin of his fleet off Swanage;   *877*
he'd slipped a leaguered army out of Wareham,   *876*
leaving his only son in Saxon hands;
he'd shared in Halfdan's victories at Repton   *874*
and Wilton, where they'd routed Alfred's host;   *871*
he'd piloted three covered longships north,
beyond where fur-clad Finns and Terfinns dwell,
through the White Sea to cold Beormaland;
but none of his achievements blared so loud
in northern ears as when, to avenge his father,
while fighting beside the above-referenced Eric,
he cut down Eric his father-brother,   **faþurbruþur* (OEN);
who'd long ruled the Danes with a rod of iron.   *ca. 854*
No matter what adventures he confronted,
what lands and fame he racked up for his crews,
the world accounted Godrum Eric's bane,
the killer of his own royal uncle.

The earls' women followed close behind,
of Danish, Anglian, and Jutish blood,
their open capes exposing polished gauds.
All greeted Halga, Hemming's seed, and Ymme,
the images of Freya and her twin.
The party then proceeded towards the church,
significantly named for John the Baptist.
"A splendid day for raiding," Gormr said.

"The earth is iron," Earl Hrut confirmed.
But Halga walked in silence by his thrall   *þral (OEN)
along the empty stalls that lined the street.
"Long years it is since I fathered a child,"   *barn (OEN)
the seed of Dan conceded carelessly.   Godrum / Gormr

Stopping by another timbered lodgment,
the king sent Wan to summon Halga's son,
Hrothulf, an able captain and tactician.
The earl found the hero with his handmaids
adjusting his immoderate fox-fur wrap.
"Dear ladies, as I'll call you from now on,"   *snotir (OEN)
young Hrothulf prophesied to Night and Day,
the names he gave his Irish concubines,
"soon you shall outrank the Saxon queen,
and though you never shall be more than slaves,
you'll have Saxon slaves to do your bidding,
as will your children and your children's children."

The newly minted ladies seized his hands
and pressed them roughly to their anxious lips.
"But don't go fooling with Hrut's handsome sons,
and steer clear of the slinking Hwiccan swains,"
King Hemming's glaring great-grandson warned,
"and do not mock our army's watchful gods,
or you shall lose those childish ears and noses
and earn your bread cavorting in a hedge."
Contented with his wit, Hrothulf reflected
on Huneric the Vandal's Gothic bride,   da. of K. Theodoric
sent home from Vandal country, thus disfigured.   I d. 451

The girls, recoiling as if stung, let fall
the foreign prince's ring-encrusted fingers.
He laughed and turned to follow Earl Wan,
whose raven crown protruded through the floor.
"Come, *kunur," Hrothulf ordered with a smile.   women (OEN)

They watched the gorgeous bunches of his cloak
slide opulently through the open hatchway.

The earls and their consorts welcomed Hrothulf
with zeal aimed to please a would-be king.
The Limfjord earl asked his foster-son,   *Wan; Hrothulf*
"What will you call the whelps of Day and Night?"
"I think I'll call them Dusk and Dawn," he said,
"though men will just say, 'Hey, slave,' if we fail."

Hearing a steersman's summons roil the air
above the smoke and murmur of the camp,
the men set down their whetstones and their combs
and left the Roman theater to fill
the forum facing St. John the Baptist's temple.
They now saw old Gormr mount the doorstep,
his arms in hand, his earls at his heels.
Wholeheartedly, the rowers cheered the lord
who'd guided them to signal victories
in three ferocious trials with their foes.   *Merton 871; Wilton*
The sailors knew it was their part to shout,   *871; Repton 874*
not clog their hearts with dread of ills to come,
and knew it was his part to stoke their ire,
not beg forgiveness for the miseries
they'd suffered circumscribed by native steel.

Now Godfred's grandson raised his implements.
An oxhide hung behind him on the door,
daubed with the rough outlines of the shires.
"My friends," cried Gorm, "tonight we call on Alfred,
the mean and fearful West Saxon queen."
The Danes guffawed, jeering a feckless foe.
"She robbed our coffers of the promised pence
after we plucked her first bloom at Wilton.
She broke the solemn vow she swore at Wareham,
murdering young men whose names you know.

27

She shirked on the indemnity agreed
for our restraint in sparing Exeter.
But faithlessness is not her foulest trait.
For we have seen, in battle and in parley,
the slut indulge her ignominious tricks.
She shakes her robe, and heroes grow confused.
She rubs her eye, and weapons lose their edge."

The pirates' laughter snapped, a crackling fire
kindled to clear a copse of trash and scrub.
They hooted the repugnant hag who soon
would sip the liquor of their searching swords,   *suiarþ (OEN)
and as they hooted, purged their souls of pity.

Again their captain lifted axe and sword.
"Tonight the Saxons offer gifts," he said,
"to mollify their baby deity.
Despite Queen Alfred's meanness, I have brought
two kingly gifts, my servants, Hugh and Perry.
This awl was Offa's token from King Karl,
who received it from the crushed Avar khan.
This wound-wolf, which I call my royal key,   *kunukslykil (OEN)
which wonderfully can open every chest,
this bone-beak Beorn carried at Seville,
at Luna, where Lord Haesten feigned his death—
we thought we'd conquered Rome, the queen of cities—
and Saracenic Alexandria.
The Saxon sow will grasp our argument
when we uncage the eagle in her back."

The oarsmen roared. Their leader lowered his arms
and touched his sword-tip to the oxhide map.
"Lord Froda's Ribe River men will ride   *Fruþa (OEN)
the Roman road to virgin Glastonbury.
Siward, Smala's son, and Earl Wiga,   *Sikurþr, *Uiki (OEN)
your crews will sweep southeast on Ermine Street.

I and Lord Halga and these heroes here   *Helki, *halir (OEN)
will follow Froda's force, then peel east.
Our envoy, Attila, has gone ahead
to spy a spot to spade—our lady's low."   *hauk (OEN)

The pirates paused, then howled with hostile mirth.
"Cousins, fathers, sons," said Godfred's offspring,   *Godrum*
"my boy, you know, was named for my good father,   *faþur (OEN)
who ruled the Jutlanders with royal Harald.   *Haraltr (OEN)
And as they galloped out with Godfred's earls
to thrash the allies of almighty Karli—
no hard feelings, friends, that was long ago—
Harald hacked the backstraps of the Saxons
in every fight we fought in this fat land."
Here murdered Godfred's grandson gulped to quell   *Godrum*
his grief as other oarsmen dabbed their eyes—
so mutable are desperate men's emotions—
then cried, "When Harald joined our hostages,   *Godrum's s.*
he wished to learn the art of governing
the God-fearing West Saxon folk.
But when the Saxons broke the blood-sworn truce,
the sow herself opened our pledges' throats.   *siur (OEN)
Poor Harald perished in that shameful carnage,
the purple current staining his white chest
as when, in prayer, a cleric paints the pale
vellum with his slaughtered Savior's blood."

The chieftain peered intently at his men.
Beneath their weathered cheeks and welling grief
he saw the cost of the hard game they played,
staking their lives for acres and a hoard.
The greater number now had lost that wager.
He seemed to glimpse the dead thronged with the living,
as when half-elfin Scyld conjured a force
of corpses to depose her royal brother,   *K. Hrolf Kraki 6th c.;*
or when, at Zulpich, where Frank butchered Frank   *Zulpich 612*

.

as Brunhild's grandsons' legions hacked each other,
so dense was the press, the dead stood unfallen.
He glanced at Hrothulf studying his nails.

"I wish to send a message to my son,"   *makur (OEN)
said Gorm, "who now carouses with Lord Grim.
Will any man step up, or any woman?"
A chuckle burbled through the crowded square.
Two Hwiccans, bruised and bound, were brought
                             before him.
"These ladies will," he said, waving his pommel.   *froiur (OEN)
They stared as rags of mist spilled from their lips.
The grizzled sailor scanned the tent of cloud   Godrum / Gormr
and waited for the words to fill his throat.
"All-Father, called by fifty names," he cried,   *Alfaþur (OEN)
"who shaped the earth and planted souls in men;
red Thor, the giants' unwelcome guest;   *Þur, *iatnar,
and you, three-headed Emperor, who threw   *Kæsari (OEN)
the runes of war and granted us this isle,
whose rumpled downs will pasture our plump sheep;
whose fields, now slumbering under snow,
come summer will repay the laboring plowman;
whose gnarled apple trees will foam with blooms—
tonight we brave the weapon-storm to claim
this new earth Harald earned with his death.
O give us heart," he prayed, "thrice royal lords,
and give us honor of enameled iron!"

Then steadying a Hwiccan's upraised crest,
he drew the whetted edge across his neck,
from which the spouting crimson pigment sprang.
He watched the spirit quit the victim's eyes
and turned to slit the second Hwiccan neck.
A second jet shot out, and drops congealed
and scattered on the steps like fleeing beads.
The freezing gore collected, pale and dull,
in shallow hollows many shoes had worn.

"Feast well," old Gormr heard his voice enjoin.
"This moonless night we'll rule the Saxon realm!"
Like man and wife, the spies lay side by side.
As the Dane bent to wipe his cutlery
on a drained traitor's soaked homespun shirt,
a qualm of loathing for his too-long life
strained against its shell with wrinkled wings.

⚬∞⚬

That night in Alfred's hall at Chippenham   *Jan. 6, 878*
the Saxons feasted the Epiphany
of our dear Lord, the Father's only Son,
whom officers commissioned to Judea
from newly reconciled Parthian lands
adored in the low cave where he was born.
Enrobed in smoke, the blackened rafters hummed
as gleemen chanted, struck the harp and tabor,
and blew their winsome flutes and quacking reeds.
The favored guests, displayed on Alfred's dais,
their gems and chains dispensing borrowed fire,
repelled the seeping chill of After-Yule
with breastworks of weasel, mink, and hare.
The flames of lamps and tallow candles shone
on beakers, bottles, bowls, and chalices
imbued with his creation's subtle hues
and trimmed with ribs and gouts and sober tears,
which Ealhswith and her companions filled
from Rhenish pitchers cradled in their arms.

To Alfred's left sat Abbot Herefrith,
the master of Britannic Glastonbury,
where Artorius sleeps, the Welshmen say;
next, the revered abbot and abbess of Frome,
a house founded by Aldhelm, Ini's cousin,   *K. Ini acc. 688; St.*

31

whom Ini called to the new see of Sherborne;   *Aldhelm d. 709*
then Aldhelm's eighth successor to that see,
Lord Athelheah, whom we saw hew the intruder;
then Alfstan, Dorset's *dux*; then Athelnoth.
To Alfred's right sat Tunbert, the incumbent
of Bishop Wini's chair at Winchester;   *Bp. Wini cons. 662*
beside him sat the abbess of twin Wimborne,
where Alfred buried Athelred, his brother;   *K. Athelred d. 871*
then Wulfhere, Wiltshire's prince, and his young son;
then silver-whiskered Cyma, crinkled Mildred,
and pale Ealhstan, three Wiltshire thanes
who'd fought with Athulf and his sons, five kings.

But Wulfhere's brother, Alfred's man in Hampshire,   *Wulfheard*
kept the Redeemer's feast in his own hall,
as did the prefect, duke, or count of Berkshire,   *Eadwulf*
while Devon's dread *patricius* watched his shores.   *Odda*
No alderman or prelate braved the roads
that shambled from the eastern underkingdoms,
Sussex, Surrey, vulnerable Essex,
or holy, rudely handled, Jutish Kent.

Approaching at a beck, a Wiltshire gate-guard
bent his ear to Alfred's moistened lips.
"Have we heard nothing from our spies?" he asked.
"I feel like blind Isaac, tethered here,   *Gen. 27:23*
a-groping for a goat-hair-shirted limb."

⚬∞⚬

When Alfred rose, the pleasant uproar ebbed.
His guests had gorged themselves on the king's beef;
on antlered stags stung by the bishop's bow;
on partridge, pigeon, heron, goose, and swan,
sweet-glazed and baked throughout the neighborhood;
on plump oysters prized from their western beds,

and pork and mutton seethed in copper kettles.
Unstintingly, the king had tipped his mead,
such goodness much diminishing the guests'
terror at the mariner's incursion.

What did they need to hear, he asked himself,
gazing across the glinting gulf of smoke,
what, to buck his nobles, could he tell them
they hadn't told themselves a hundred times?
"Aldermen, clerics, thanes," the king began,
"three thousand, less two hundred, less five times,
since God the Father summoned forth this world
had his resplendent deputy, the sun,
revisited his twelve celestial halls,
and dipped, and raised, and dipped his flight again
over the southern haunch of our great mother,   *A.M. 2795, Bede,*
when Greek and Thracian sailors and their kings,   Reckoning of Time, *ch.*
egged on by squabbling heathen deities,   *66*
obliterated Priam's citadel.   *Orosius bk. I*

"Another twice two hundred fifteen times
the orb that liberates the streams in springtime
had run his race before the fugitives
upreared the walls, which I have walked, of Rome.
The seven hundred fifty-second year   *A.M. 3224; Orosius bk.*
of Romulus' metropolis divulged   *vi*
a scene of peace throughout the Roman world:
the brazen doors of Janus' temple shut
and our Lord born, a citizen of Rome,
at Bethlehem in Roman-ruled Judea.

"Tonight, my friends, we celebrate the night
the mages from the often hostile east
acknowledged him as King of all the earth.
And as their gifts of myrrh and frankincense
and gold, of course, were numbered in his Word,

so yours of honey, grain, and silver coin—
a flood of pennies, minted in our image—
shall be forever tallied in our ledger."
A scattering of clerics laughed aloud,
but thanes and loftier churchmen frowned, aware
of the deep-dredged assessments they had paid.

"Our thanks for your benevolence," said Alfred.
"Our thanks, as well, to the Lord God of Hosts,
who led the Danes to Gloucester from our soil.
One year ago, he wrecked the Cimbrian fleet,   *877*
breaking the backs of six score pagan dragons
(a hundred in the old tolfrædic reckoning),
and feeding heathen seamen to the sharks.
And as salt pork adds relish to your ale,
his triumph was the sweeter for our sorrows."

All clapped their hands and cried, "Amen! Amen!"
"But do not think," the seed of Ingeld warned,   *Alfred*
"the fiends' retreat has made us safe for now.
The ancient enemy exults when we,
in giddy gladness, cease to whet our blades.
Then vices clothe themselves in virtue's robes,
our laxity as magnanimity,
our greed as charity, our fear as hope."
The optimates peered darkly from the platform.
A swordsman rolled an eye at his companion.

"The Danes will strike in mid-spring at the latest,"
said Alfred. "We observe their every move.
But our friends failed to forewarn your *frea*   *lord* (OE)
of the leech Godrum sent to let his blood."
Woden's offspring ducked under the table,
then raised the pagan giant's head up high,
the eyes of which, half-screened by raven tresses
on which gold firelight and lamplight played,

glared like Occhus Bocchus on the crowd.
The Saxons gasped, save Alfred's thane and bishop,
who frowned and glowered angrily at the prize,
so puny next to his the Geat hewed.   *Grendel; Beowulf*
Alfred set it down on a wooden platter
and drew a lock back from its bruised brow.
The smoky hall exploded in applause,
which, amplified by pounding palms and bones,
united Alfred's well-watered flock.
The seed of Ingeld let the throe recede,
then spoke in words that shook the narrow vault.

"This rower was a mighty man of war,
well named for warlike Attila, the Hun,
who kept a hundred kings, who mastered Rome,
but died knifed by his Burgundian bride.
He came disguised as an exiled Anglian thane,
but tried to emulate Ehud the judge,   *Jud. 3:15-26*
who skewered royal Eglon on his stool.
He breached the king's peace. He had to pay.
But maybe his big head will prophesy."

A silence, then a hound barked in the shadows—
a cachinnation shook the anxious throng.
The king went on, "You followed my three brothers.
I am the stubborn runt of Osburh's brood.
Therefore, I charge you, abbots, counts, and thanes,
to meet here on the Feast of the Conversion.   *Jan. 25*
So don the mail of light, like dirty ice,
and the dinged helmet of our Father's mercy,
and pay your farm in full to feed my sheep.

"For now, let us honor him with our revels,
for Gregory ordained the sacrifice   *Gregory I 590–604*
of cattle to the Lord God, our Father.
But do not overload your hearts, my friends,

with temporal, and temporary, joys.
To counteract the heatless season's phlegm,
eat mustard and hot pepper, leeches say,
don't soak your whole head when you wash,
and don't skimp on amorous refreshment."
King Alfred seized the beaker of clear glass
that Attila had brought from Edmund's hoard.

"Saint Edmund's cup!" he cried, lifting it up.
The mead disbursed red sunlight from the dais
as feasters scrambled to their fluid feet.
"*Wes hal!*" the king exclaimed and drained the vessel.   *be well* (OE)

"*Wes hal!*" the celebrants replied, upturning
their various horns, cans, goblets, pots, and bowls.
After six- or seventeen more toasts,
the gleemen launched a catch, some thanes uncased
their spotted dice, old friends rehearsed old tales,
and buoyant brothers brandished bovine bones.
The king asked Beorhthelm to fetch his harp
of willow, maple, ivory, and horn
and picked a commentary on the glee.
But as he touched the singing horsehair strings
a faint, discordant clamor grazed his brain,
a sleeping child's cry, heard in a dream.
When Beornstan, a hall-guard, hurried in
and cried, "*La,* king! The fiends! A host of fiends!"
the Saxon set his instrument aside.
Again he stood to rouse his countrymen.

"The King of Kings has sent an early spring.
So let us plant a crop of faithless Danes
in the dark, iron-hard West Saxon soil!"   *eard* (OE)
The servants ferried weapons from the storerooms
as eager thanes retrieved their helms and swords.

Alfred signaled Ealhswith and Addi,
remembering the time his senior hall-guard
questioned him respecting the married state.

"Get out," he said to Ealhswith, "get going.
A heinous sin it was to bring you here.
Follow her, friend, to Frome. We'll fight this fray."
They stared at him, transmuted into statues.
The monarch raised his forehead to the roof,
where gilded serpents licked the blackened thatch.
"Your plan," said Ealhswith, "your plan for Frome.
That's no longer a prudent course, good husband."

He turned and led his subjects down the hall,
not one of whom, no monk or nun, cried out,
their throats closed by faith in the Lord, or fear.

"Arm," he bellowed, "arm, shield and sword!
Lord Cyma!" he exclaimed in thrilling tones
over the heads of scurrying personnel,
"Lord Cyma, you have met these fiends before!"
For Cyma and his brother thanes had fought
with Athelwulf and Athelbald at Oakley;   *851*
with Athelred at Reading, Ashdown, Basing,   *871*
and Merton, where that *cyning* met his death;   *871*
and with young Alfred at disastrous Wilton.   *871*
Now Athelwulf's companions once again   *Alfred's f.*
pulled hammered helmets down on meager manes.

"Dear chief," said Cyma gravely to his king,
"the rowers yet owe us for Athred's blood."   *K. Athelred d. 871*
Behind their backs, beneath the worm that writhed
on Ecgbert's blackened standard overhead,   *K. Ecgbert d. 839*
the giant's relic grimaced from its dish.

III.

Three Kings

∝∞∂

Alfred and his thanes fight their way to the stables. Ealhswith prepares to take the children to Frome. The surviving guests flee across the Avon, but Alfred turns back to confirm Ealhswith's escape. He and a small band hurry to Frome.

King Alfred wrestled on his coat of mail
and joined the Somersetan in the doorway.   *Athelnoth*
Pale smoke blanketed the yard,
transpierced by flames gleaming in blades and helms
like fallen stars buried in deep water.
Amid the murk, the Athulfing discerned
a straggling palisade of Wiltshire spearmen
anchored on his mailed household guards.
The crash of arms and cries of pain and hatred,
perhaps because the darkness shrank the scene,
conjured in Alfred's mind the Roman folk
drunk on the liquor spilled in the arena.

"My God," he said. But now was not the time
to ask what sin, what vicious satisfaction,
had blinded him and his to an obvious peril.   *boar's head formation*
"*Caput porcinum!*" the monarch cried.   (L)

"*Caput porcinum,*" his thane repeated,
"for our Lord's feast! Arm, you novice miners!
We'll drive a bloody shaft to the king's stables!"

39

"Not so, Lord," a countermanding word
rumbled below the shouts and clanking iron.
Old Cyma spoke, King Athulf's Wiltshire thane,   *K. Athelwulf d. 858*
seconded by Ealhstan and Mildred.
"We claim the precedence," asserted Cyma.
Into the smoking flood the gray thanes plunged,
then Athelnoth and two of Addi's guardsmen,
succeeded by young Alfred and his bishop.   *Athelheah 9th bp. of*
The other guests, who dreaded lest their *dryhten*   *Sherborne; lord* (OE)
should die alone, now exited the hall,
while overhead the flame-cheeked billows shrouded
the moonless tomb of the Lord's festal night.

"For Athelwulf and Christ!" Lord Cyma called,
a wisp of mist dissolving at his lips.
A hundred Saxon throats threw back the slogan,
but twenty score invaders bellowed, "Har!"
another name for Grim, the hooded one.
Thrusting himself among the thronging Danes,
beating his feet against the frozen floor,
the elder penetrated several steps   *Cyma*
before the devils landed one good hit.
Shoving with his shield, the Wiltshireman   *Cyma*
parted a pirate's windpipe with his tip
and nimbly blocked and hacked at arms and limbs
deployed to check or hinder his attack,
till, staggered by an axe-blow to the helm
and a bold stroke that unhinged his jaw,
the warrior forgot to ward the oar
a steersman swung straight at his naked neck

His arms hung from his hands, his lean legs failed,
but Mildred rushed his shield against the sailor,
bore the man down, and drove through several more,
as Ealhstan and Athelnoth, his flankers,

bustled to blunt the blades the thane thrust past.
The thread of Wiltshiremen and royal guards,
now blown and bloody, cautiously backed in
to point and push the boar's rooting snout,
the cleft between their folding wings now filled
with clerks and ladies gripping glinting flames.
Marshaled by Mildred's banging boss and brand,
the band of Saxons bit into the body
more like an auger gnawing round its nib
than the keen edge of a maul-walloped wedge.
A slipping sailor stabbed his outstretched sword
through Mildred's foot, fixing him where he flailed.

The thane gave back a lacerated loin,   *Mildred*
but mangled mail clung to searching steel,
the veteran could not retract his blade,
and the burst brigand, buckling as he bowed,
drew the *guþrinc* over his nailed shoe.   *war-man* (OE)
A sudden sidestroke sundered hand from wrist,
and the gore poured as Mildred, in a muddle,
brusquely covered the cursing northerner.

Ealhstan flung forward, but his fury
could not fend off the flash that freed his friend's
illustrious headpiece from his prostrate trunk.
The last of Athulf's Wiltshire ministers
piloted his point at eyes and ears
and twiddled teeth and noses with his shield
before a foreign oarsman speared his side.

Down he drooped and doused the iron ground,
but Athelnoth and Alfred understood,
hustling to advance the Saxon sally,
the aged thanes had carved the corridor
that Athelnoth designed full half the way

to Alfred's burning barn, from which, they hoped,
their coursers might spirit them from this hell.
The king had grunted "Lord" at every blow
he dealt and every buffet he endured.
A miracle it was to have come so far.
"We need another miracle," he muttered.

As Godrum saw from where he sat, his stallion
stalled in the stogged, vociferating mob,
his mass of warriors could not get at
an enemy thus crushed among their friends.
Contented that the newborn moon had set
as forecast, scurrying abaft the sun,
he glimpsed only a string of bobbing helms
slithering through the chop of smoke and steel.
Meanwhile, monks and women hurled themselves
into the gallery that gaped before them,
stumbling on unseen, unstiffened corpses,
sluicing their shoes in uncongealed grume,
one hand gripping a neighbor's fur-clad elbow,
the other brandishing a one-edged blade.
Inimical to law and love and form,
it seemed a feast or liturgy of nothing,
the next-to-nothing out of which our Father
concocted all good things in earth and heaven.

The last to leave the hall, old Bishop Tunbert,   *Tunbert 19th bp. of*
whose lifting hairs flared with the rooftop's fire,   *Winchester*
lingered to sing a hymn to Christ the King,
who'd parted this flood of fiends with his arm
as once he spread the waves to rescue Moses.
"The Lord," he intoned, "is a man of war—"   *Ex. 15:3*
Wigred and Wulfred, thanes Wulfheard had charged   *ald. of Hampshire*
to bring the bishop safely home to Hampshire,
grappled his gaunt bones and bore him onward.

Behind their backs, a Wiltshire soldier toppled.
From where he lay in pain, the *beorn* saw   *hero* (OE)
a bear-cloaked lord, framed by the hall's dark doorway,
clasping a black, shapeless mass to his chest.

⸎

In town, the royal offspring sat on horseback,
each curtained by a guardsman's mailed arms.
Oppressed, the king's lady, Ealhswith,
raised her rushlight to examine Edward,
then beamed assurance into the dazed eyes
of Athelgeofu and little Elfthryth   *her youngest daughters*
and hardness into the eyes of their young warders.
She peered with fear at steadfast Athelflaed,
her eldest, and the eldest of her girls.
Hearing a shout go up beyond the houses,
which instantly a roaring answer whelmed,
she turned to see a raft of ugly smoke
sprawling and bulging over Athulf's lodge,   *K. Athelwulf d. 858*
its nether parts inflamed by glaring thatch.

"Let's go," said Addi, tapped to head this band,   *Alfred's hoard-guard*
"at this point we can only save ourselves."
The lady held her dim wand to his chin.
Hand in hand, they'd scrambled from the hall,
evaded Godrum's gathering heathen horde,
and roused the cubs and Hilda at the inn.
Her other hand rose to her breast and touched
the chain from which her silver sieve had fallen.

"Shall I abandon Alfred?" she replied.
"For all I know, the Danes have slain my kinfolk,
and he and these poor lambs are all my flesh."

The bearded hoard-guard said, "I too, dear lady,   *hlæfdige* (OE)
would rather fight and fall by my lord's side.
It shames a *scealc* to be sent away."   *soldier* (OE)
He cast a glance that compassed her five children.

"I've never seen him fight," said Ealhswith.
"The next time we embrace, we shall be changed."   *1 Cor. 15:51*

∽∞∾

The bishop and a guardsman, Beornstan,   *Bp. Athelheah*
whose faces fires broiled from above,
were fetching frightened equines from their furnace
when they encountered Halga's godlike son.   *Hrothulf s. of Halga s.*
His shoes were scarlet goat hide, scarlet leggings   *of Harald s. of K.*
molded his calves, and flames of fire flicked   *Hemming d. 812*
like twin worms in the steep curves of his helmet.

"Surrender, you who stain the sacrifice,"   **kuþablot* (OEN)
demanded Hemming's seed, "of blood and pain   *Hrothulf*
the sons of Dan tender to Father Grim!"   **Krim* (OEN)

Sending two asses scrambling for the door,
the Saxons moved to spit that apparition.
Beornstan went in with spearhead blazing,
but Halga's scion turned his thrust aside   *Hrothulf*
and laid him out with one bat of his axe.
Closing, clerk and captain poked and parried
as miserable horses shrieked and kicked.
The dung-smoke rankled the prelate's eyes.
He blinked. Something streaked between his feet.

"Is the monk nicked?" the fresh devil laughed,   **mokr* (OEN)
as Athelheah fell back and fell to coughing.

"May I despise the man that hates my Lord," *Ps. 139:21*
he gasped, and flicked a dirk, which Hrothulf blocked.
"Your Lord is weak, O saint," the Dane declared,
but like a thunderbolt, a burning rafter
crashed in a swarm of sparks before his eyes.
The startled fiend recoiled, dropped his ward,
and slapped at embers clinging to his lap.
Hauling the hurt hall-guard by his corselet,
and muttering impassioned thanks to Aldhelm, *Aldhelm 1st bp.*
the prelate labored into the dire air. *Sherborne acc. 705*

Between the sheds, the mailed chief of fiends *Godrum / Gormr*
found Alfred and knew Attila had failed.
"To me!" he cried, dismounting in the mud.
"Men, the enemy's mean, murdering queen!"
As sailors surged against the scrum of shields,
Utta pushed his way to Alfred's side,
where Osric fought, then lunged to stick the devil,
but Nyklot interdicted him, a brace
of Abotrites bashed him with both bosses,
and Utta flopped bodily into the snarl.
Relinquishing his shield, he wriggled rearwards,
clenching his worm-flecked weapon in his fist.
He raised his eyes to thank his heavenly shepherd,
but fathomed only flushing flanks of smoke.

Alfred had last seen the shipless steersman *Godrum / Gormr*
a-jogging up the Fosse Way towards Thames head.
He loathed his pledges, breached as soon as broached,
and his repulsive lust to foster slaughter.
Osric reached in close, alike athirst
to compensate the king-killer's crimes,
but murdered Godfred's offspring wheeled free. *Godrum / Gormr*

"The prancing pagan," scoffed the Saxon prince, *Alfred*
but Harald's father flashed his Hunnish staff, *Charles the Great's gift*
slashing Halmund's hamstring near the knee. *to K. Offa of Mercia*
He crumpled in the muck, where heathens hewed him.

"The sinking Saxon," sneered the oarsmen's lord. *Godrum / Gormr*
Though weariness burned in his limbs, the king *Alfred*
begged to buy his butchered boardmate's blood.
He growled at Godrum, "Devil out of hell,
where fire never fades nor dragon dims!" *Mark 9:44*
His teeth gleaming, Godfred's grandson backed *Godrum / Gormr*
into a barn, where smothered cattle cured.

"Devil in hell, with you, you mean," said Gormr
as Alfred flogged his blade, and when he flagged
the Dane withdrew further into the shade,
and thus slammed the slogging, gasping king: *Alfred*
 division of realm;
 K. Athelbald's
How holy he who humbly halved his home; *marriage to f.'s*
lavish the lord who left his lamb his love. *wid.; *haim,*
 *liuf (OEN)
"Devil!" Alfred yelped and wildly swung
as oxidized ox-hair galled his craw.

"Onward, bird," the priest of Woden taunted. *Godrum / Gormr*
The pirate pounced with unexpected power,
as when a gust of autumn winds, exploding
from the blue abyss of the far-northern heaven,
tumbles a struggling flock across the heights.
Into the night retreated Ingeld's seed, *Alfred*
half-blind, his hilt-hand slick, his flesh on fire,
bruises burgeoning under ruptured rings.
The mariner attacked with rapid taps *Godrum / Gormr*
and voiced a further verse to vex his victim:

*The *suinahirþir sobs.   Who serves his sow?*   swineheld (OEN)
                                                                                      siur (OEN)

But Alfred struck another vein of strength.
Again the pagan prudently recoiled   *Godrum/Gormr*
when through the clang the Saxon captain, hacking,   *Alfred*
picked up a supplication, "Lord, Lord!"
Athelnoth galloped in with Smoke in tow,
the king's hunter, a tall gray, uncut.
Shoving the sailors' skipper in the slush,
the Saxon caught the saddle, leapt, and fled   *Alfred*
according to the Frankish exercise
his brother's men had taught him as a youth.
Behind them followed mounted Athelheah
with Halga hotly hectoring him on foot.

"The other cheek, bishop!" taunted Halga.   *biskub* (OEN)
He halted next to Harald's haunted father,
who squatted, puffing noisily, in the muck.   *Godrum/Gormr*
Together they watched Alfred disappear
beyond the guttering glamour of the flames.
Old Godrum called, "I've got your glory, boy!"

They thundered unhindered over the bridge,
held only by a pair of prone Saxons,
and pulled up on the bank, where three roads split.

"Lords and ladies," Alfred said, his stallion
ramping under his hams, "this is no raid.
Wulfhere! He must be winging down to Wilton.
We'll meet your musters there in seven days.
Athelnoth, get word to watchful Odda.   *ald. of Devon*
Osric and you others, come with me."

The thanes said nothing. Not-far hoofbeats rattled,
their warning fretting the ash-freighted air,

but no star or planet pierced the murk
to prove a purer sphere endured from which
a purer mind might know our earthly toil.

"The heir is in God's hands," the bishop said.   *Athelheah*
"Send me. Send Utta." Athulf's son replied,   *Alfred*
"I need you to collect the men of Sherborne."
A briefer quiet followed, cruelly torn
by a blood-clotting cry across the river,
accruing judgment on the Saxon captains.

"We await your word," said Athelnoth, resigned.
"God keep our king," the other leaders murmured.
They turned their horses west and south and east.

The king surveyed the body that remained,
each man equipped with a notched sword and shield.
Silently they circled back to the inn,
unwittingly retracing Addi's track
and mocked, unwittingly, by wakeful birds.
The shop exhaled a stench of blood and ale.
A child's body curled beside the hearth,
the lad who manned the kettle, fork in hand.
Utta found the host, his spear beside him.
A maid lay on a table, her throat cut.
The Athulfing said nothing, stunned by woe,   *Alfred*
but Osric read his thoughts and growled, "Foul devils." *deoflas* (OE)

They climbed the steep ladder to the loft.
A man and woman lolled side by side,
his fleshy hand enveloping her small one.
Three perforated children sprawled where devils
flung them, in their fury, on the flooring.
The monarch crossed himself, as did his men.

"The Lord has spared us," Alfred muttered numbly.
Utta eyed the anointed one with dread,
but Osric, nodding, grimly pursed his lips.
Young Edward's end, repeated through the shires,
would smother the heart's heat in every chest.

Outside they met a squad of mailed shadows,
whose breath flicked like gold flame in the glare.
"A princely cap you've snatched," said one marauder
to Alfred, who stuck him through the throat.
The Saxons shipped those sailors out to Sheol,
though Cynewulf and Bald defrayed their freight.

Recovering their steeds, the shaken *frecan*   *warriors* (OE)
now flew along the black, unmoving flood,
the black, misshapen willow trees and elms
uprising horribly against the ceiling,
not halting till they crossed Lacock in flames.
"Dominus vobiscum!" Alfred cried.

On they galloped, gulping the curving trail,
now frozen mud, now broken ice and pools,
evading or dispersing clumps of shapes.
They passed through mild islands in the air,
which burned and burning barns and houses warmed,
where clouds of ashes blew like ghostly snow.
Melksham burned, and Holt, but on they rode,
and now a sanguine aura blushed to westward,
reflected like a dawdling midnight sun
by heaven's prisoning tent. Bradford burned,
where King Cenwalh mauled a British host.   *K. Cenwalh acc. 643;*
The glow gleamed on a swatch of old iron   *Bradford 652*
where Alfred knelt and recognized a friend.
"They travel quick as spirits," murmured Osric.

Beyond the town, beyond the flames and cries,
a luster glistened dimly on the crust
along the blackness where free water flowed.
They rinsed their faces, let the horses drink;
the current numbed their cuts and cooled their eyes.
Then on they came, through country ruled by wolves,
ascending into untouched Somerset,
or so they hoped, in their unhopeful souls.

But soon a new effulgence drew them on.
Dismounting, they approached behind the street
from where they saw a troop of fiends on horseback.   *Frome*
A woman clutched a devil's bright blue shoe—
his tool hewed through her entreating limbs.
Utta started up, but Osric stopped him.
Nearby, a wavering shriek cut through the smoke
and raised the filaments along their napes.
A fiend hoisted a baby on his spear,
the piteous creature, dyed red in the light,
the standard standard of the gods of war.
A pebble struck the devil's flaming helm
and the tall stalk and ruby burden toppled.
The foreign *feond*'s fellows laughed aloud.   *devil* (OE)

"Ceadwalla's Christian Britons frolicked so,"   *Heathfield 633*
the seed of Ingeld noted to his men,
"to signalize their triumph over Edwin."

They reached the abbey gate, which hovels flanked.   *Frome abbey est. ca.*
From there, across the firelit yard, they saw   *685*
a fiend with copper locks mocking the monks
that cowered under John the Baptist's church.
When his companion thrust a cross in a clerk's
face, young Alfred's heart sank in his stomach.
He knew the foes liked forcing folk to pick

twixt bodily and spiritual damage,
but in his years of struggling with their armies,
he hadn't seen such malice in the flesh.

"In Aldhelm's ancient house," King Alfred gasped.
"Shall we go after Athelnoth?" asked Utta.
"I must be sure," young Edward's father said.
They crept discreetly to the women's yard,
where pirates pawed the sisterhood for loot.
Poor Ealhswith was not among their prey,
but Octa made to rush against the rowers.

"Can I behold such wickedness?" he murmured
as Athelred's successor gripped his wrist.   *K. Athelred d. 871;*
"You can behold," said Alfred, "and you will.   *æftergenga* (OE)
Our times are worse than those Orosius knew.
When Alaric the Goth broke into Rome,   *410*
he robbed and hewed the Romans in their thousands,   *Orosius bk. vii*
yet he protected Paul's and Peter's churches
as sanctuaries for our Savior's sheep.
The Most High, it seems, has other plans
for Father Cerdic's posterity.   *Cerdic k. of W. Saxons*
Yet this is not the worst of what has been.   *acc. 519*
The desperate Cantabrians, besieged
by Roman troops on Mount Medullius,   *Orosius bk. vi*
destroyed themselves by poison, fire, and iron.
When Drusus whipped the Suebi and Cherusci,   *Orosius bk. vi*
their women, walled behind the towering wains,
to spare their lambs the pangs of servitude,
brained them and bowled their corpses at the invaders.

"Far worse if we were butchering our own,   *Orosius bk. v; Brunhild*
as Roman Marius and Sulla did   *w. of K Sigebert I d.*
in civil wars too terrible to tell,   *575, m. of K. Childebert*
or as the fabled Frankish fighters did   *II d. 596, gdm. of K.*

when furious Brunhild spurred the eastern kings,
her husband, son, her grandsons and great-grandson,
to visit her sister's death on western lands;
when Charles the Hammer smashed the western host
in three God-given victories that sealed
his lordship over all the Frankish realms;
when Louis's Bavarians licked Lothar's
host at fratricidal Fontenoy
and young Charles, later our Judith's father,
scattered Pippin's fractious Aquitanians;
and when, at Andernach, not long ago,
tricking out his men-at-arms as phantoms,
the younger Louis crushed his uncle Charles—
a drubbing Charles paid the Danes to avenge.

Theudebert II d. 612 &
K. Theuderich II d. 613,
gt.-gdm. of K. Sigebert
II d. 613; Galswintha
da. of Athanagild k. of
Visigoths d. 567; Duke
Charles d. 741;
Fontenoy 841

Andernach 876; K.
Louis the Saxon d. 882;
Emp. Charles
the Bald d. 877

"Thank God, we Saxons never stooped so low,
for when my brother filched our father's crown,
Saint Swithun urged them to disjoin the kingdoms
rather than loose a flood of Saxon blood—
whence Athulf kicked his heels in Canterbury
while Athelbald kinged it at Winchester,
until our father's death permitted him
to reweld the wheel his sin had split."

K. Athelbald d. 860; K.
Athelwulf d. 858

Young Octa made no answer but obeyed.
The Saxons stole away like careful voles,
but sailors saw them sneaking through the gate.
Astraddle their exhausted mounts they fled,
pelting towards the shelter of the woods
with Toca's Himmerlanders in pursuit.
A whirling weapon whooshed past Alfred's ear,
and Utta, close ahead of him, was struck
and swung in one motion down from his saddle.
On they labored, steaming horses wheezing,

when Alfred, turning, seemed to glimpse a black
spike suddenly sprouting from Osric's chest.

"God save you, friend," he muttered, "from the devils,
if not in this engagement, then the next."
They cranked again and traced a narrow track,
but Octa's courser tripped and pitched his master
hard against an oak. The guardsman rose,
but instantly, as if whipped up from nothing,
the mariners surrounded him, their arms
invisible in the dense, starless darkness.
Swerving, the seed of Athelwulf returned   *K. Athelwulf d. 858*
to bolster the beloved boy where hoofbeats
thumped the earth and steel scraped and crashed.

"Ride, *cyning!*" the *cniht* cried from the depths.   *attendant* (OE)
The king perceived a fiend light from his mount
and called to Octa somewhere down below,
"Fight and live, friend, for your tough grandfather,   *Athelwulf ald.*
the victor over Weland by the Itchen!"   *Berkshire d. 871; 860*

The Saxon felt a weapon scratch his back.   *Alfred*
He swung and struck, but a fiend's axe plunged
its whetted bill into his gushing thigh.
The stallion reared, and Alfred, shooting upwards,
with cheek and brow discovered flying iron.
Descending, he conceived a body sprawling
headless and faceless on the forest floor.
Lord, he thought, the Saxon realm is lost,
and fleeing from the misery that gripped him
like a sinewy wrestler out of hell,
alone the Saxon spurred into the brush
where switches whipped his bleeding face and hands.
"Where is God?" cried anguished Odovacar   *K. Odovacar d. 493*
when the Ostrogoth's sword clove through his trunk.   *K. Theodoric d. 526*

King Alfred thought of Mithridates, fleeing
Pompey, his forty thousand killed or caught,   *Orosius bk. vi*
despairing of his doubtful deities
and starting at the stirring things of night.

Our Father Grim, the Athulfing recalled,
escaping from the shipwreck of that fight,
embarked on his far-northern odyssey
to seek a homeland for his beaten folk.
But where could his defeated Saxons run?
The pirates held the whole bulk of Britain,
save a few British kingdoms north and west.

Young Alfred's blood congealed on his cheek.
His soul, it seemed, would shortly float to heaven,
there to rejoin old Osric, Halmund, Octa,
Utta, who was kin to Jaruman,
Mildred and Cyma, Cynewulf and Bald,
and all the Christian Saxons who had perished
this midnight of the Lord's Epiphany.   *Jan. 6, 878*
"O see, O blameless Savior," he exclaimed,
raising his eyes from the smooth azure pavers,
"see how I've led your faithful people here,
your people, who have died to show your glory!"
The angels would enroll him in a school,
there to wait out the dregs of the Sixth Age   *Sixth Age: from*
delighting in the Word with saints and kings.   *Incarnation to*
He let the reins drop and drooped in his saddle,   *Return*
hearing the hymn of David, son of Ruth.

And may I dwell   in the Lord's on þinum huse   *Ps. 22; in thy house*
swiþe lange tiid   oð lange ylde.   *forever* (OE)

Snorting, Smoke slowed to a halt where the sharp
fume of swine suffused the air and sleeping
suidae bellyached in their pens.

The seed of Cerdic harkened to their grumblings.
My mother bore me in her womb, he reasoned—
from where, and how, I came there, who can say?
At once, three darkling figures fronted him,
three iron spearheads thrusting in his face.
"Forgive me, Father, I have sinned," he murmured.   *Luke 15:21*
He heard a careful check expressed in Welsh.

IV.

In Selwood Forest

Guthrum feasts with his earls in Alfred's hall. Alfred has found shelter with Denewulf and Beornwulf, two brothers who herd swine in the Selwood. When Alfred recovers from his wounds, he sets out after Ealhswith and the bishop.

The heathen king presided on the dais
over his clutch of sanguine heathen earls.
Behind them on the blackened daub, where once
the blackened Saxon dragon hung, the sunlight,
the winter sunlight, pouring from a sky
as blue as any looming over Thule,
deterged and purified the raven flag
partitioned by the rafters' slanting shadows.
An ox had been prepared for Tyr and Grim,   *Tyr, god of law*
for Radagast, the Abotritan god,
and Alfred's threefold Roman mystery,
and meaty steam was wafting from the kettle
when Gormr recognized the Ringsted man.

"Wulfheard has submitted," Wiga said.   *ald. of Hampshire*
"Winchester unbarred without a blow.
The Hampshire nobles seek their Saxon kinsmen   *★frentur* (OEN)
in Bodiocassium across the sea."   *Bayeux*

"Which Hrolf the Giant rules, who married Poppa," *f. of William*
said Godfred's grandson with a pondering gaze,   *Longsword*
"having killed Count Berengar, her father."

"Let the fr-frightened foemen fly to Frankland,"   *★Fraklat* (OEN)
said Hrothulf from his hutch of vulpine furs,   *Hrothulf s. of Halga*
"the St-Stutterer has troubles of his own."   *K. Louis s. of Emp.*

The earls chuckled. Louis, Charles's son,   *Charles the Bald d. 877*
impoverished by his father's family feuding,
had little chance of freeing that sweet land.

"Dorset is mostly ours," reported Wan.
"Join us at Alfstan's hall in Dorchester   *ald. of Dorset*
to ship our fellow Attila to Grim."   *★filak* (OEN)

"Wulfhere has yielded Wilton," Halga said.   *ald. of Wiltshire*
"That magnate is King Alfred's relative.   *★kimsmantr* (OEN)
We plan for him to treat for the whole kingdom."

"The Saxons need a Saxon king," said Wiga,
speaking for his principals in Zealand.   *K. Sigfred &*
Unseasonably Theodric, the Saxon,   *K. Halfdan*
darted a glance at Godrum, but forthwith
he knew he'd slipped, for now the earls would think
that he himself hankered for Alfred's throne.

The seed of Godfred welcomed the diversion.   *Godrum / Gormr*
Dodging his Nordalbingian ally's eye,   *Theodric*
he turned to questions of good government.
"It's too early yet to hand out lands,"
he said, "as Halga's valiant son has done.   *Hrothulf*
If we get fat, we'll falter like the locals,
which we can ill afford, so many friends—
the Ribe men, the men of holy Viborg—
so many having swallowed Swanage ale.   *★aul* (OEN); *destruction*
Our ablest enemies remain at large.   *of fleet 877*
We do not own this country yet, my lords."
The lords concurred, though Hrothulf flushed
                                        and glared.

"Above all else," continued Godfred's grandson,   *Godrum / Gormr*
"we must unearth the learned murderer,
King Athulf's fingerling, the last free king.   *Alfred*
I fought him when we fired him from this hall—   *★hal* (OEN)

58

I recognized his prattle and his stroke.
Men spotted him at Wodensburg and Frome
or maybe saw his fetch, walking abroad.
If Athulf's seed is dead, we thank All-Father.   *Alfaþur (OEN)
But maybe he escaped across the sea.
His sister, Burgred's widow, lives in Rome   Athelswith d. 888
and his stepmother, Judith, collared Baldwin,
the gallant count of Gessoriacum.   Boulogne
I met the lovers at your uncle's court,"   Eric ct. of Dorestad
the chief remarked to Halga with a grin,
"where Lothar Lothar's son acknowledged them
to spite his uncle, Charles the Bald, her father.   K. Charles acc. 843
Karli had rashly nixed the match—her third—
but Lothar got the pope to give his blessing.   Nicholas I 858–867
All this to say, we might yet see the Saxon
splash ashore with a thousand mailed Franks."

He tasted, and pursued his meditation.
"He may have joined with Anglian Eadwald.   br. of K. Edmund d.
Or his God may have hidden him in a cave.   870; 1 Sam. 22:1-2
He may have flown, bird-like, into the woods.
We must assume that any wolf or bear   *ulfr, *biarn (OEN)
or any badger, otter, fox, or squirrel
might be the man who slaughtered my poor son.
Maybe he hears us now, here in this hall.
The pope declared him consul as a boy
and christened him his spiritual child.   *ontalikr (OEN)
Maybe he granted him spiritual power
over all the elves and devils in this island."

Confused, the foreign earls lowered their eyes.
"The elf-taught Athulfing," their captain mused.   Alfred
"At Merton, the imp stormed like Grim in fury.   *Krim (OEN)
I dickered with him, newly smeared, at Wilton.   871
The youngster would have made an able chief,
had he not been"—Gorm searched for words—
                                    "so trusting."

59

With shining eyes, he raised Saint Edmund's cup.
"And this was Alfred's, for an hour," he added.
The heathen earls snickered in their beards.

⚮

Denewulf and Beornwulf, two brothers,
kept herds of swine among the trunks of Selwood.
As tenants of the abbey, they had served
at Merton with King Athred and at Wilton   *K. Athelred d. 871*
and advantageous Exeter with Alfred;
but now the latter captain, Ingeld's seed,
lay groaning on a pallet in their hall.
He hadn't found a refuge overseas,
as Godrum speculated with his earls;
he hadn't donned the fur of wolf or bear;
nor had he quit this realm of bone and blood,
though many nights and days he roamed the town
that holy men returned from there describe
as a strait place of blackness, smoke, and hail.

"Behold," said Alfred's bishop by his side.   *Athelheah*
Across the mere of pain that heaved around
his wounded eye, the devils worked their blades,
butchering unresisting monks and nuns.

"Behold," said Godfred's seed, who gripped his arm.   *Godrum / Gormr*
A buzzing, blubbering chorus filled his ears,
but Alfred sensed it did not emanate
from them the fallen flayed, but from a flock
of captured girls and boys, crammed in a pen.
A squad of devils mocked his impotence
to shield even the weakest of his people.

"Behold," the devils cried through broken lips,
"behold the unanointed of the Lord!"

One called to Alfred, leaning on his spade:
"Now whither will you fly, O seed of Cerdic,   *K. Cerdic d. 534*
now that our prince will own your throne forever?"

Throughout these scenes, the Saxon's absent mate,   *Ealhswith*
her upward-growing form cloaked more obscurely
than the dread night on which the fiends attacked,
loomed motionless before a smoking door.
Each time he felt her there, he turned away.

Three dark and wiry figures caught his eye,
one of whom sprang close and challenged him,
naked, armless, its hideous face one scar,
or many scars, its mouth a lipless fissure.
The mask of hatred, pierced by twin red stars,
bent near, and nearer Alfred, and he feared,
deep in his heart of hearts and ever after,
not what the thing might do, or what it was,
but that his sin had made him one of them.

His head yet racked with seven shades of pain,
one day he raised the lid of his good eye
to the soot-plastered thatch of someone's roof,
from which soot-crusted hunks of flesh were hung
to frighten famine from a churl's board.
"He lives," said Denewulf, "he has returned
like Furseus, whose feast we keep today,   *Jan. 16; Bede,*
to this sublunary sphere of snow and fire!   Ecclesiastical History
Our loaf-ward, bred of Cerdic, has returned,   *bk. iii*
after many days, across the fetid Styx!"
(For Denewulf had studied with the monks
before his father's death had fetched him home.)

The Athulfing said nothing, shut his eye,   *Alfred*
and drifted on the tide of misery,
his nostrils sniffing swine instead of ocean.

A recollection of the fatal feast,
his guardsmen, nobles, clerics, churls slaughtered,
lurked just beneath his spirit's swamping hull.
But soon the king began to count the dead
including, probably, his family,
and knew damnation was his sealed fate.

Three times he'd purchased peace from Godfred's
                    grandson   *Godrum / Gormr*
instead of driving to eradicate him,
like Saul when he neglected killing Agag.   *1 Sam. 15:9*
Had cowardice unmanned both king and kingdom?
Had pride enticed him to accept the crown
instead of serving Athred's sons as regent,   *K. Athelred d. 871*
as the famed Jutish thane had served his nephew   *Beowulf; K.*
when Theodbert the Frank slew Hygelac?   *Hygelac d. 515; K.*
Or was it his campaign of ceaseless lust,   *Theodbert acc. 533*
beginning with his father's Frankish bride   *da. of K. Charles*
(whom Hincmar consecrated *regina*),   *the Bald; Abp.*
the glorious, gorgeous, archangelic Judith,   *Reims 845–882*
his mother, sister, preceptress, and friend,
whom he'd adored, most sorely, as a boy?
Which soreness he'd compounded in his youth
with every maid and matron he could charm.
Thus day and night he lay, chained to his sins,
afraid to sleep and meet his leering keepers.

Slumped on a chair, his blade bared on his knees,
the stripped branch of Cerdic watched the flames   *K. Cerdic acc. 519*
again engulf the roofs of Chippenham.
Again he fled from Toca's force at Frome
and Octa's fallen trunk among the trees—
so little had the waybread and the yarrow
administered by learned Denewulf
dispelled the hurt to the king's inward eye.

Fingering the steel's nicks and dints
and the plain legend Charles had had engraved,
et gladius meus non salvabit me,   *Ps. 43:7*
"and my salvation lies not in my sword,"
he thought of Saul, who leapt on his own weapon, *1 Sam. 31:4; end of*
his armor-bearer fearing to dispatch him; *Third Age*
of morbid, mean Ermanaric, who self-slew *d. 370*
when the Huns overran his Gothic empire;
of Mithridates, under filial siege,   *d. 63 B.C.*
who poisoned daughters, concubines, and wives,
but could not breach the wall of antidotes
in which for forty years he'd soaked his guts;
of Nero, Agrippina's son, who sinned   *d. 68; Orosius bk. vii*
with her, his sister, and an altered boy,
who sang the rape of Troy to flaming piles,
and quashed the Lord's apostles, Paul and Peter—
even the worst wretch that burdened Rome
cut his own throat when shouted from the palace.

While Alfred wallowed in these dismal studies,
his good eye watched the girl about her work, *Denehild da. of*
fetching eggs and water, sweeping the hearth, *Denewulf*
her motions shedding grace, her girlish face
a miracle of budding leaves in springtime
or a sickle moon lighting a waterish haze.

The swineherd's wife appeared and cried, *"La, cyning!*
The cakes I kneaded for Saint Anthony,
the patron saint of *porculatio*
whose feast we keep today, you've let them burn! *Jan. 17*
Has sorrow so dimmed your remaining light?
Do not lie down among the dead, my lord,
yearning to leave your misery behind.
Rejoice, instead, with us who joy to live,
for whom a glimpse of dove or firecrest
redeems this brief eternity of grief.

Four children we have buried in our yard—
but one remains, as you have but one peephole—
and yet I bless the Lord with every breath.
And when I see a fly caught in the web
a mother spider spun to feed her brood
I do not dwell on how my end will come,
but praise the ways the King of Kings conceived."
Raising Ecgbert's sword by hilt and blade,
Alfred pressed the metal to his forehead.

⚮

His wounds had knitted into ruby scars,
even the one that cut across his eyeball—
whose putrefaction Denewulf had foiled
by packing it with nettles crushed in salt—
when Alfred, king of all the southern folk,
crawled unassisted from his sodden bed,
breakfasted on rashers, bread, and beer,
and limped across the yard at Denulf's heels.
Beornwulf and Denewulf's young daughter,
Denehild, together with their herders,
armed with spears, were leading out the bands
of grumphing porkers eager for their feed—
for beasts did not desert the beaten Saxons
as once they fled when Latins threatened Rome—   *91 B.C.; Orosius*
and though the twilight, stealing through dark heaven   *bk. v*
to seize a forward bridgehead for the sun,
distinguished the unbarbered quadrupeds
from herdsmen dressed in heterogeneous skins,
it lit alike the docked plumes of breath
that flapped alike from snout of man and swine.

As Alfred hobbled after switching trotters,
he heard the birds dispute the porcine clamor
(for treading time, the urgent time, drew near)

as if to celebrate one man's return
to the Lord's realm from the dull rounds of men.
A woodwall let loose its rattling patter
and rested as the stock doves cooed and fed
on acorns left by hurried foragers.
A nuthatch launched a trill, to which a chaffinch,
a robin, and a brambling joined their songs,
then floating outwards from a beech tree's summit,
a mistle-thrush's flute diffused pure prayer.

Soon Paulus, one of Denewulf's Welsh hands,
erupted in a bellicose lament
that Athulf's gleeman formerly had sung,   *K. Athelwulf d. 858*
a hymn of blood to brace an ousted chieftain
who'd lost companions battling with the Danes.   *gebeoras* (OE)
When speaking, Paulus pinched his syllables
in sparing, parsimonious English,
but when he wrapped his breath in British music,
so grand a gift the Lord had granted him,
the glinting tide inspired every hearer
to live as nobly as his fable flowed.

They halted by a brooklet, laced with ice,
whose surface suids shivered with their hooves.
The seed of Ingeld turned to Denewulf.   *Alfred*
"Our Savior spared me from the bed of crime
but not our eldest brother, Athelbald,   *K. Athelbald d. 860*
who went into our father's widow, thus,
like Reuben, Jacob's fluid eldest son,   *Gen. 49:4*
uncovering our father's nakedness.
Before that deed, he filched our father's crown.   *855*
Do we bear these disasters for his sins?
Though years before, when our good father reigned,   *K. Athelwulf acc.*
a cleric prophesied of God's intent,   *839*
delivered by an angel in a dream,
to scourge our folk. Crops failed. Cattle died.

Was that because young Athelwulf and Wulfheard   *ald. of Surrey*
had chased the king of Kent across the Thames?   *K. Baldred exp. 825*
Or because our father's father, famous Ecgbert,   *K. Ecgbert acc. 802*
fixed his yoke on all the island's kings?   *d. 839*

"Bitter British wizards long foretold
the Saxon chiefs would reign three hundred years.
That time has run. Our godlike ancestor   *K. Cerdic acc. 519*
took office when Theodoric ruled Rome—
Rome, to which Ceadwalla fled from power   *688*
and bested Burgred crept in state post-Repton.   *874*
Perhaps the King of Kings now summons me
to Leo's Saracen-built citadel   *Leo IV 847–855*
to yield the sword he belted to my shoulder."

The swineherd knelt and pulled the king down with him.
"Dear Father, you were wroth with your anointed.
His iron rod you hurled in the dust,
his bones you turned to wax, his heart to water.
Bend his neck to your yoke, yet let him not
glory in having overmastered glory."

"Amen," the king replied, crossing his chest.
He struggled upright, clinging to his spear.
"According to the learned African,"   *St. Augustine of Hippo*
he said, "our life is pain, our death unknown.   *d. 430*
I've read that Greek philosophers," he added,
"discovered sacred doctrine unassisted.
Pythagoras commanded, 'Follow God,'
and Plato claimed a wise man might exhume   *Boethius bk. iii*
the truth implanted in him from his birth."

"I wouldn't swear to that," said Denewulf,
rising to face the king, his breath a cloud.
"The Holy Spirit is a mystery.
Someday, perhaps, it may reveal its ways.

See that goldcrest, the kinglet of this wood,
creaking on the twig there up above?
A fretful thing, the stature of a hatchling,
yet he constructs the most exquisite nest
of all the feathered builders in this temple
and his industrious head is capped with flame."

∽∞∾

The dawn was past and Denulf's hall was empty   *Denewulf*
when Alfred woke, his soul cumbered with gloom.
He padded the hard ground out to the woodshed,
where pecking wrens and titmice fled his step,
hefted Denewulf's cold wedge on his palm,
and tapped it through the bark of an oak log.
Heaving the maul and grimacing at twinges
that swarmed him like the Roman guardsman's arrows,   *St. Sebastian d. 288*
he muttered "Athelwulf" and swung the sledge.   *Alfred's f. d. 858*
The log cracked, uncovering its core,
while the shock jarred the marrow of his bones.
He set the wedge, acknowledged "Ecgbert," swung.   *Alfred's gdf. d. 839*
"Ealhmund—Eafa—Eoppa," he said,   *Alfred's gt.-gdf., gt.-gt.-*
for each name landing a ringing blow.   *gdf., gt.-gt.-gt.-gdf.*
Dropping his torn cloak, he wiped his forehead.

Another eight concussions drove his count   *Ingeld, Cenred,*
to Cerdic, who, like Brutus come from Rome   *Ceolwald, Cutha,*
or like Anchises' scion out of Troy   *Cuthwine, Ceawlin,*
or like the son of Nun escaping Egypt,   *Cynric, Cerdic*
arrived, grappled, and planted a new people.
"Elesa—Esla—Gewis, whose name we bore."
Five more reports brought Alfred's reckoning   *Wig, Freawine,*
to Baldaeg's father, son of Frealaf,   *Frithugar, Brond,*
the all-discerning, king-begetting chieftain.   *Baldaeg, Woden*

Here Alfred leaned the helve against the shed.
A chillness wafted from that parent's barrow.
The fiends cared not a whit for kindred blood
when offering West Saxon souls to Grim.

Fourteen more thunderstrokes rewound the cord   *Frealaf, Finn, Godwulf,*
to Noah, who survived the earth's demise   *Geat, Taetwa, Beaw,*
and took the law of slaughter from the Father.   *Scyldwa, Heremod,*
Nine more good hits and Alfred, drenched with sweat,   *Itermon, Hrathra,*
affirmed the name of our enduring sire,   *Hwala, Bedwig, Sceaf,*
progenitor of Saxon, Jute, and Dane,   *Noah, etc.*
the outlawed king whose seed has never failed,
whose name contains the quarters of the earth—   *Bede,* On Genesis *bk. ii*
for the east Anatole, the west Disis,
Arctos the north, the south Mesembria—
whose father was none other than our God.

His scion stacked the clean splits on the pile
and hugged a load to heap beside the hearth.
His gashes smarting, weeping for relief,
he fueled the fire and furled himself in his cloak.
Exhausted, Alfred heard the Baptist's words
admonish him, "The Lord can raise up children   *Matt. 3:9*
to Father Cerdic even from these sticks."

⧉

As Beornwulf set pickets in the trees
to ward off wolves and bears, as well as boars
who yet in rut in the midwinter season
might yet get wild piglets on his sows,
the king employed himself in setting snares,
then built a blaze to warm the men at dinner.
Their oatcakes, cheese, and ale brought to mind
the happy days before men hewed their foes   *Boethius bk. ii*
and plowed the waves to harvest gold and slaves.

The meal done, he found a kicking hare
suspended from the gallows of a shrub
and ran back to the grove to show his prize
to Denewulf's young daughter, Denehild,
who, seeing the king's face alive with glee,
his eye bright, his scars flushed in the chill,
ingenuously mirrored his emotion
and lighted on the turf as in a dream.
A squirrel objected sharply from a branch,
and the girl's charges gruntled where they grazed,
but after several kisses and caresses
the Athulfing pushed Denehild away.   *Alfred*
Their twisted clothing binding them like gyves,
they spouted clots of vapor at the clouds
and felt the stony soil goad their cloaks.

"Forgive me," said the son of Jutish Osburh,   *Alfred*
watching two gilts tussle over the hare.
"It is a sin for us to couple thus.
When I was weak, I took food from your hand.
Recalling Baldhild, whom we feast today,   *Jan. 30; w. of K. Clovis*
I stumbled into the pit that spoiled my youth,   *II d. 656*
and though I long ago disowned those vices,
my cursed whims still hiss as I pass
or tug my sleeve and murmur, 'Here I am.'"
They stood and shook crumbs of leaves from their wraps.

"But vile as it is to sin in sleep,"
the Athulfing went on, "enticed by dreams   *Alfred*
of those we know or those we wish to know,
as foolish as it is to fornicate
in a cavern mouth lit by Juno's lightning,
how baser still to stray in open daylight.
Your beauty charmed me; I became a beast,
but like Ulysses' luckless rowers, whom   *Boethius bk. iv*
the false sun god's daughter turned to swine,

by the Lord's grace, my soul remained unchanged.
'If eye offend,' they tell us, 'pluck it out.'   *Matt. 18:9*
You can see that mine's been plucked out already.
Besides," the king concluded with a smile,
"I'd owe your father, under my own law,
ten dozen *solidi* in minted coin   *shillings* (L)
(a hundred in the old tolfrædic reckoning),
which I don't have just now."

                              The girl replied,
"My lord is a wise, frugal husbandman."
"Unlike the Roman law," the king continued,
"ours would impose no penalty on you.
Popilia, Minucia, and Sextilia   *Orosius bks. ii, iii, iv*
were three polluted virgins they interred."

The swineherd's daughter said, "Your humble maid
begs leave, lord king, to plead in her defense.
A gilt in season traipses past her suitor,
draws none too near, but tarries none too far.
She shuns his eye, but in good time she stands.
My lord has tracked his handmaid with that eye,
that eye as blue as a shadow cast on snow,
from dark to dark as her ripe hour simmered.
Please overlook your lowly thrall's default,
bred by the lowly mores of the herders.
We butcher hogs that balk at breeding sows."

The chieftain beamed. "My *piga* is no piglet.   *maid* (OE)
But Alfred Athulfing is half an ass."   *s. of K. Athelwulf*

As day declined, they gathered in the herd
and ambled home along the hardening path.
A din of discord drifted from the steading,
so Beornwulf and Alfred ran ahead

to find herdsmen hammering Denulf's door.
Beornwulf, scuffing a whitestone trough
across the yard, smashed the planks from their hinges
and plunged, bellowing, into belowground gloom.

The boars' lord bear-hugged the beefy brigand
that buffeted his brother. Baldaeg's boy   *broþor* (OE)
(*viz.,* Alfred) faced the other fiend, whose features
the master's mate had marred. The massive man,   *Beornwulf*
fetching the felon's flayer, led the edge
along the curved equator of his paunch.
The pigman then pivoted where his partner   *Beornwulf*
held the other harrier at bay,
a haft of horn in one hand, one hand un-
gloved by Alfred's *gar.* The grim *gumfrea*   *spear, king (man-lord)*
treenailed the intruder to a stud,   (OE)
at which the tall one took his tool and with it   *Beornwulf*
notched the navigator's neck, good night.
Blowing noisily, they stretched the sailors,
side by side like two devoted friends.

Denulf said, "At the hand of each man's brother
will I require the life of man. Amen."   *Gen. 9:5*
"I'm off tomorrow," Athulf's lad decreed.   *Alfred*
"When Valens, after the fight at Hadrianople,   *acc. 364; Aug. 9, 378*
fled and hid himself in a lone farmhouse,
the Goths sniffed him out and burned it down.
I must find Athelheah to take the tiller,   *bp. of Sherborne*
should our Redeemer summon me to Rome.
And if the Lord," he said, crossing his chest,
"has spared our little ones, they'll be with him."

Said Denewulf, "I won't detain my chief.
But give us time to raise a following
to undertake a sharp strike at the fiends.

As all West Saxons know, or ought to know,
a swineherd slew the usurper Sigebert,   *d. 757*
rightly requiting his ring-giver's killer."

To which the last of Ecgbert's grandsons answered,   *Alfred*
"I'll just take Beornwulf, if you don't mind.
We'll fare on foot to filter past the devils."

"On foot is fitting," Denewulf reflected.
"But here's another stratagem to put
the uncouth crewmen off your scent."

One rower they arrayed in Alfred's shirt
and mail coat; then the hands haled his corpse
across the yard, ahead of Denchild
who bore, with more than noble dignity,
the monarch's helmet, folded cloak, and sword.
Behind her, Denewulf advised the king,
"If someone else spots stricken Smoke, we'll say
we buried you—and claim King Godrum's bounty."

"Five pounds in gold," the seed of Ingeld said.   *Alfred*
"How cruelly prices rise in troubled times.
The priests paid only thirty pence for our Lord."   *Matt. 26:15*

They rolled the rower's relics in the cloak
and wedged him in the trench the hinds had hacked.
Young Denehild, kneeling down at the lip,
with two hands laid the scabbard on his breast
while the sun, now submerged behind the trees,
daubed their wattled twigs with copper fire.

Tossing a clod that thumped the devil's helm,
the seed of Ingeld felt a purl of fear,   *Alfred*
as if to swindle death required him
again to lose his children, wife, and hall

and see his best-loved friends drowned in their blood.
Indeed, two ravens, peering from a limb,
seemed unconcerned by Denewulf's deceit
and calmly took in all they saw and heard
to bring the news to all-knowing Woden.

Returning from the sham-Saxon's howe,
they passed a pen where barrows shrieked and shoved,
watched by Welshmen leaning on the rail.
"What of the other rower?" asked the king.
Denewulf flung a long thumb at the swine.

V.

This Captive Land

⁂

Alfred and Beornwulf arrive in Sherborne, where the episcopal palace serves as Toca's headquarters. They continue to Dorchester, where Hrothulf rules. A morning on the downs after a snowstorm convinces Alfred to make his way to Rome.

Under a leaden breastwork of cloud,
a pair of herdsmen hobbled into Sherborne,
the one bearing a carcass on his shoulders,
the other leaning on an antique spear.
A gang of sailors, drunk with the new wine
of easy triumph, loitered by a doorway,
attracted like a pack of peevish hounds
by any hint of feebleness or fear.
Their rancor towards the Saxons had deep roots.
The early Danish kings, including Offa,
the ancestor of Mercia's royal house,   *Saxo bks. i–iv, vi*
fought frequent feral frays with Saxon neighbors
and won and lost Saxon and Jutish lands
long years before King Pippin's son, great Charles,   *Saxon wars 772–804*
annexed the Saxons to his "Roman" empire.

An icy snowball struck one herder's ear.
"Easy," his fellow urged, "they'd love to pick
a fight, but that won't help us find the bishop.
Remember how our Lord endured men's blows.
Take this one and ponder it in your heart."   *Luke 2:19*

A sweating devil stepped astride their path.
"Halt, boys," he said, "and pay your penny.   **penikr* (OEN)

75

Ugh, did hunger make you slaughter your daughter?
She has her mother's pretty pointed teeth."
The mariners guffawed. King Alfred paid.
"I see she turned to rend you," said the devil.
The *lidmenn* laughed again, for they had lived   *sailors* (OE)
long years in Christian lands and knew the Scriptures.

The seed of Ingeld grinned and shook his head.   *Alfred*
He becked at Beornwulf's frost-stiffened burden
and stammered they were headed for the palace,
at which the brigand briskly waved them on.
"But give me this," he said, gripping the weapon.
"You Saxons may no longer carry spears."   *⋆Saksar, ⋆keirar*
    (OEN)

The travelers approached the bishop's hall
adjoining the cathedral Ini built   *K. Ini acc. 688*
in the old Roman style he'd revived,
of quarried limestone blocks, with leaded windows
and limestone roofing sealed with lead flashing—
a high-walled grotto open to God's light.
Within, the king's two eldest brothers slept,   *K. Athelbald d. 860; K.*
though Athelred rested his bones at Wimborne—   *Athelbert d. 865; K.*
the abbey built by Cuthburh, Ini's sister—   *Athelred d. 871*
where Leoba, Saint Wynfrith's cousin, trained   *Abp. Boniface*
before she joined his mission to the heathens.

Fearing to find His Stoutness bound in fetters,   *Bp. Athelheah*
Alfred pounded the door with frozen fist.
"Your Grace," he cried, "Your Grace, we've brought
                  your supper!"
A black-bristled cook unlatched the door
whom Ingeld's injured scion recognized,   *Alfred*
though Gyrth (the cook) saw only grizzled churls,
for Denewulf had mowed the pilgrims' crowns
and Denehild, with blushing cheeks, had raked
ground chalk into their locks and whiskers.

Noting the dressed barrow Beornwulf bore,
Gyrth said, "Come in, come in, and thaw your trotters."
Alfred, wincing, lowered his rump to the hearth,
a scullion drew two wooden cups of ale
(in which the king discerned the fragrant Yeo),   *R. Yeo*
and the cook proffered Beornwulf a penny.
"I dare no more," he said. "Our Savior keep
this vanished, yet, we pray, unvanquished head."
The herdsmen frowned, but Gyrth threw one white thumb
behind him towards the fiend-infested hall.

King Alfred curbed his tongue and took the token,
which showed him in the headdress of a Caesar
goggling at the world with one good eye—
a coin indeed four times more valuable
than anything his brothers ever minted
as struck on unadulterated silver.
He'd based it on King Offa's Mercian penny,   *K. Offa d. 796*
modeled on Charles the Great's denarius,   *Emp. Charles d. 814;*
which Charles, in fact, had copied from his father—   *K. Pippin d. 768*
a triumph of administration like
the *solidus* of Constantine the Great.   *shilling* (L)
Some even trace the West Saxon *pening*   *penny* (OE)
to Alexander's stater of pure gold—
an oddity of our Lord's providence
perhaps to be unraveled in reverse,
for little did the Christian Athulfing,   *Alfred*
who claimed our common parent for his sire
and labored to preserve his Christian flock,
resemble that well-educated butcher
who undertook to conquer all the world
and dubbed himself son of the Most High God—
though maybe it attests the Spirit's force
in leading men to light from heathen darkness,
for Saxon folk, says Widukind the monk,

derived from that same Alexander's host,
a shaving of which sailed north at his death—
where, by the Father's grace and Charles's ardor,
they made their names as soldiers, kings, and saints.

"The earl thanks you, sir," said Gyrth, relieved,
"as I do, for considering my hide."
"May we salute the bishop?" Alfred asked.
"We're lay brothers up from Muchelney."
"Old Burghelm is our bishop now," said Gyrth.
"The mermen mitered the meek monk in jest."
"The other was a sturdy lad," said Alfred,
turning aside to contemplate the fire.
"I saw him hunting over Blackmoor way.
Does he yet live? Did he escape our friends?"

"Who, Lord Athelheah?" the cook replied.   *9th bp. of Sherborne*
A fiend exploded through the inner door   *cons. 871*
and glared disgustedly at Gyrth's two guests,
two staff-churls crawling from door to door.   *stafkarlar* (OEN)
"I only tell you what we tell the northmen,"
Gyrth said. "Our *guma*'s gone. To Gaul, I guess." *man* (OE)
His bulging back withdrew.

                    The scullion spoke.
"Good thing for you the jarl governs here.
When Hrothulf brought his crew from Dorchester,
he sacrificed a traveler to Grim."

Uncertainly, the strangers sipped their ale.
Alfred didn't distrust Gyrth or the scullion
but feared his scars might mark him, to the fiends,
as one who herded fiercer beasts than swine.
He quaffed the cup and struggled to his stumps
and, grunting an old grudge against his bladder,
he dribbled out the door. His fellow followed.

Three ruddy heathens tippled at the counter,
absorbed in quiet banter re: their lands.
The king and Beornwulf hunched at a table,
sipping at pots of honey-tinctured ale
with two Dorsetan couples wrapped in woolens.
Worn from wandering all night and a day,
they hadn't caught a whiff of the blithe bishop.

The Dorset folk surpassed the two in years
if not the haggard wranglers they portrayed.
The monarch recognized them from his circuit,   *Alfred*
though never having numbered them as tenants
or led the men as soldiers in his wars,   *drengas* (OE)
he had no ready notion of their worth.
His neighbor on the mead-bench, whose beard
encroached the tawny clearing of his cheeks,
arranged his whiskers with a sharp-crooked wrist.
"You're better off in Hampshire," he declared.

His balding, blazing neighbor fixed his grip
on the glazed crock before him, frowned, and said,
"At least King Hrothulf won't devour you there."   *s. of Halga*

"Or Earl Wan, his watchdog," said the other.
"They keep their heathen feast in Alfstan's hall—   *ald. of Dorset*
where he's their prisoner, if he yet lives."

"The kid claims half the herds," the bald one charged.
"And every maid in town," alleged his wife,
whose creased hide shone like wax in the lamplight,
"as if he were King Solomon of the Jews."

After a pause to taste, her husband said,
"They burned one of their great ones yesterday.
Gorged and guzzled a fortnight beforehand,
pegging the poor maids in a sailcloth tent.
Then cut their throats and cooked them with the corpse."

The seed of Ingeld sickened at the word.   *Alfred*
He waited for the outraged Dorsetans
to lengthen out the count of Hrothulf's sins,
but they just sipped their clover-honey brew.

"It makes a man abashed," said Beornwulf,
eyeing his interlocutors in turn,
"to hear such deeds and know our king has failed
both to prevent such crimes against the weak
and to avenge our loving Father's laws."
He looked at Alfred. "Think of those young girls
who died of terror at the gates of hell."

The monarch flushed so darkly that his scars   *Alfred*
drowned in the vinous flood that swept his face.
To Denehild's bold uncle he unclosed,   *Beornwulf*
"High heaven heaps these horrors on our heads,
whether to test or teach or torture us
we do not know, we shall not know till doomsday.
In every age, he bids us fight like men,
not against flesh alone but fallen powers,
the ranks commanded by our enemy.
Thus some must face the fiends with heartfelt prayer,
while others hack them on the battlefield.
We're lay brothers up from Muchelney,"
he ended, facing each of the Dorsetans,
"willing to serve wherever we are called."

Bending over his beverage, Alfred asked,
"Have you heard hide or hair of Athelheah?
They say he and his men escort the queen."   *cwen* (OE)

The elders traded looks but uttered nothing.
"Is Hrothulf holding them?" the stranger pressed.

"We don't know you, friend," the dark one answered.
"There's hungry Welshmen," his companion added,

"would sell a Saxon servant for a shilling,   *scealc, scilling,*
say nothing of a king for seven pound."   *pund* (OE)

"If he yet lives," the gleaming matron added,
touching her brow, her belly, and her breast.
The others crossed themselves, and Beornwulf
and Alfred did the same. The latter felt
a qualm of fear, as though the feigned interment
somehow gnawed at the chilled root of his soul.
"And hasn't died of shame," the bald one said.

The king sat back and squared his shoulders towards
this loose-tongued, ignorant accuser.
"What shame?" he said. "A lord who saw him swore
he fought like fourteen fiends at Chippenham."

The Saxons stared at him like wooden saints.
"We mean no disrespect," said Hedda gravely,
"but Alfred left these devils on our hands,
which his three kingly brothers never did,
nor Athelwulf, his faithful, fruitful father."

"I tell you," said the dame with shining skin,
"I never said one word against the boy,
but this time Godrum snuffed him like a candle."
She leaned across the planks and blew a puff
of honey-scented breath in Alfred's face.

❧

The pair of pilgrims paced the wintry downs,
still chasing Sherborne's lord and Alfred's lady.
No butterflies adorned the air, no blues
or coppers that patrol the turf in summer;
no grasses yielded, glinting, to the breeze,
revealing nests where bustards fed their young;
no wheatears whitened vacant rabbit holes;   *hwitearsas* (OE)

no partridges scrabbled at dry anthills;
and no dull larks, ascending by gradations,
descanted on the excellence of heaven.
Instead, the tent of lead enclosed a plain
emptied of living things, though raised above
the snow-filled dells that cupped the naked elms.
The wind had fanned the plots of snow like sand,
raking them into corrugated rows
or sculpting frigid haunches, hips, and flanks
whose northward hollows harbored bowls of shadow.
But all around the boundaries of this desert,
beneath the pall of mist and drifting forms,
a band of color curtained the horizon,
paler than peach or apricot, yet mild,
as if midwinter's menacing arena
were guarded by angelic sentinels.

The fellows' features roughened and grew lean
from short days in icy airs and gales
and long-drawn nights endured in herdsmen's huts,
but mainly from uninterrupted hunger.
They'd brought bread alone from Dorchester
nor had they bow or spear to take a deer.
A gray morning found them atop a ridge
peering down on the ditched Roman road,
on three British barrows built nearby,
and farther off, the ruined Badbury fastness,
from which the Virgin's champion, Artorius,   *ca. 516*
dispersed the overweening Saxon host.

The seed of Cerdic said to Beornwulf,   *Alfred*
"How hard it is to keep a people's love!
The emperor who mastered all of Britain   *Claudius*
without shedding a drop of Roman blood,
when famine struck, was pelted in the forum
by Romans chunking loaves of moldy bread.

When fat Vitellius was deposed, the Romans   *d. 69*
flung filth in his face, bored him with brooches,
and dragged his stripped carcass through the streets.
I myself was present as a child
when the mob mutilated Benedict,   *Benedict III 855–858*
the newly elected vicar of our Lord.
Three times I purchased peace, sparing our people.   *Wilton, Wareham,*
Unthroned, I'm the cynosure of scorn."   *Exeter*

After a time the swineherd asked the king,
"And has the Holy Ghost advised my lord
whether to fly to Rome like Mercian Burgred   *after Repton 874*
or lie in wait like David in his cave?"

The king said nothing. He could hardly cry,
Retro me, Satana, to a churl   *Mark 8:33*
for urging him to fight the foreign killers.
They watched a gliding merlin scan the plain,
quartering the lower heights for grouse
or waterfowl blown inland by the storms.
A shepherd of the downs would have the skill,
thought Alfred, with one deftly darted stone
to knock a flapping blackcock to the ground.

As shadows lengthened (later every day,
according to our Father's providence),
a sharp dampness nettled Alfred's nostrils.
They stopped. A merlin stooped on a lone stonechat,
riding the birdling earthward, pierced and stunned.
Beornwulf ran to meet them where they fell
and snatched up both predator and prey.

They found a shepherd's shelter stocked with wood,
a spare spindle idle on the floor,
and as the seed of Ingeld laid the tinder   *Alfred*
the smothered sun slipped underneath the cloud

and set the ruckled countryside on fire.
The travelers eyed the gold streaks of snow,
the burning turf, and the far flaming hills,
and Alfred said a prayer to praise the Lord's
mercy in serving up a Shrovetide feast.   *Feb. 4, 878*
They crossed themselves and plucked and dressed
                                        the fowls
and roasted them attentively on sticks.
That night they fell asleep, not satisfied,
but on the upward slope from desolation.
Like the Greek giant who regained his strength
from the earth's breast, the king sucked his from heaven.

All night he sensed the fullness of the air
until the dawn revealed a pregnant dream.
He stood atop a saddleback amidst
thick snowflakes swirling in faint light.
Congealed in the twinkling of an eye,
he saw Athelnoth knotting his helmet,
Athelheah touching the edge of his sword,
his guardsmen (some of whom he knew were dead)
gazing ahead, adjusting layered shields
or breaking icy scales from their eyebrows.
The West Saxon levies stood behind them
unmoving under the biting, blinding flaws
like the crushed Latin bands a blizzard caught
fleeing the consul's wrath into the mountains
after the ugly fight at Asculum—   *89* B.C.*; Orosius*
men rigidly at rest on stumps or stones   *bk. v*
or leaning on their spears, eyes wide with fear.

When Alfred woke, the dream fresh in his mind,
he knew he'd lost all that was precious to him,
his lady, children, servants, friends, and crown,
this last the emblem of God-given service.   *cumbol* (OE)
He didn't know how he could bear such sorrow,
though by his will, it was our common fate.

For all flesh perished. Only spirit lived.
He heard the morning's muffled soundlessness
and blinked at the low doorway filled with light—
or rather at the cloudless azure castle
presiding over an exploding field
of pure, plump, unblemished virgin snow.
Like heaven on earth it was, an earth of light,
the glory of the Lord made manifest.
He crossed himself and blessed the Thunderer;
he blessed the Word through whom he made each day
and blessed the Holy Ghost, by whom his power
was rendered knowable to mortal minds.

The Lord, he saw, had sent the sign he sought,
a heading for their march from that day forward.
How many kings the King of Kings had summoned
to quiet lives of scholarship and prayer:
West Saxon Ini, Centwine, Ceadwalla;
Mercian Athred and his nephew, Cenred;
East Saxon Offa; Ceolwulf of Northumbria,
to whom Bede dedicated his *historia*,
and Eadbert, the master of Strathclyde;
and East Anglian Sigebert, a saint
who rode to war armed with only a wand.
All had exchanged their crowns for shaven polls,
their royal robes for rough monastic gowns.
Now Alfred, too, would make his pilgrimage
to end his days, the Most High permitting,
praising him from the foot of Peter's tomb.

K. Centwine abd. 685;
K. Ceadwalla abd. 688;
K. Ini abd. 726; K.
Athelred abd. 704; K.
Cenred abd. 709; K.
Offa abd. 709; K.
Ceolwulf abd. 737; K.
Eadbert abd. 758; K.
Sigebert d. 634

"To Rome," he said to bleary Beornwulf,
emerging from beneath his salted cloak.
He exited the hut to gather wood,
wading down the slope to a buried grove,
for none who found that hut should die of chill
because the king had used up all the kindling.

Toiling eastwards into the sun, they trudged
between blue-shadowed domes of shrubs and anthills,
the rebounding light basting them from all sides.
They turned south and followed a thawing rill
down where snowdrifts shrank and the stream broadened
reflectively, observed by stands of alders
and flocks of snowdrops blotless as young nuns
and birches whose integuments were scarred
with ink-black, impenetrable spells.

⌁

The port caught fleeing families like a weir:
defeated people loitered will-lessly,
exhausted, hungry, guilty, hurt, bereft.
Some camped in blackened hulks that once were houses,
while others went about their rounds, bowed down
by the stout yoke the Lord had laid on them,
dismay stamped indelibly on their brows
in place of the day's cinerary stain.   *Ash Wednesday, Feb. 5,*
Such plentiful distress he'd never witnessed,   *878*
the seed of Ingeld, Athulf's youngest son,   *Alfred*
even when reoccupying Reading,
or Wareham, or Dumnonian Exeter,
or Nottingham, when Burgred purchased peace   *868*
and Alfred won his lovesome Mercian bride.

The monarch crossed himself. "And Jesus wept,"   *John 11:35*
he said to Beornwulf, who made the cross.
They asked for Athelheah and Ealhswith
at inns and churches and at noble doors,
but none would say they'd seen or heard of them.
Careful of children underfoot, the two
joined the solemn progress towards the quay
(even the dogs were quiet, out of respect)

and slid, their eyes downcast, along the flags
where Frisians, Franks, and Arabs handled freight.

The trade in thread and cloth somehow survived,
inspected and assessed by Wulfheard's reeves,   *ald. of Hampshire*
and casks of salt beef and cured pork
and columns of big cheeses cased in wax
embarked to make their way to distant tables
as wooden crates of clayware out of Frankland
or Anglian towns now governed by the fiends
in blackware, buffware, orange-, green-, or grayware,
wheel-thrown, incised, and glazed (as Alfred
once longed to manufacture in his realm),
were disinterred from belowdecks and stacked
on the slick, mobbed wharf for further haulage.

Thus men continued at their worldly chores,
which stupefied the roadworn travelers
as if the sun still drove his daily circuit,
as if the Lord still ruled in highest heaven,
as if the Saxon nation had not fallen,
dismembered, pierced, and flayed by sailors' blades.
A people does not perish when it yields,
Alfred mused, thinking of his past truces,
but when it spreads its spent limbs on the soil
and calls to wolves and ravens, "Come and feed."

Beornwulf and Alfred passed, appalled,
where heathen strangers hawked their haunted captives
to masters who would float them overseas
to Persia, Egypt, Syria, and Spain.
Seals thrust their heads up from the water
and disappeared on business of their own,
while pairs of mallards paddled past the ships
and seagulls loitered hungrily on piles.

Leading bewildered Beornwulf aboard,
the seed of Ingeld found a willing skipper   *Alfred*
preparing to make sail on the ebb,
paid the inflated fare to Frankish Cantwic
(first founded as a Saxon settlement),
and joined the refugees that jammed the rail,
keeping his distance from two hard-faced lords
as heedful of his humble herdsman's garb.   *hrægl* (OE)
Both had inherited lands near Winchester
and so owed threefold duties to the king,
road-work, wall-work, and war-work, meaning men.   *wigmenn* (OE)
One was meager Wulfric, Wulflaf's son,
whose cloak was lined with squirrel. The other, flushed,
was Boda Bolla's son, to cushion whom
from cold a sept of stoats had shed their coats.

"God keep My Loftinesses," Alfred said,
"and may he keep your relatives and friends.
Does a vile churl err in premising
my *frean* freight their families to Frankland?"   *lords* (OE)

"We do," the son of Wulflaf answered quickly,
dispensing with the chilliness of rank.
"The Danes have ousted us from house and home,
compounding with our puissant alderman."

"The jarl is the law in Hampshire now,"   *Earl Wiga*
said Bolla's son. "Old Wulfheard keeps to his bed."

Keeps to his bed. The seed of Ingeld swallowed   *Alfred*
as Beornwulf considered all three speakers.
"Have we no hope," the monarch asked, "in Alfred,
the son of Athelwulf?" The nobles glared.

"In him who fled at the first whiff of fiend?"
asked Wulflaf's son.

"Who vanished into Mercia,"
cried Boda, "thus disowning his own folk?"

"Why into Mercia?" Athred's heir inquired,
his ruffled blood surging under the grime,
but Boda had his reasons near at hand.

K. Athelred d. 871

"First," he explained, extending a pink finger,
"he lives, or else the avaricious Danes
would hardly offer ten pounds for his head."
He peered into the churl's one good eye,
glancing reluctantly at its dull twin
and doubtfully at frowning Beornwulf.
"To Mercia," adding in the middle digit,
"for Alfred was last seen in Chippenham,
not far from Mercian land." The king said nothing,
but thought he saw a skulking shade of shame
dive for cover deep in the exile's eyes.
"Item," said Boda, proffering three clean nails,
"his lady was of Mercian royal blood,
her father one of the top Mercian nobs.
And fourth, his sister, Lady Athelswith,
was married to the marrowless Mercian king."

Athelred Mucel ald.
of Gaini
m. K. Burgred 853

Alfred refrained from seizing Boda's "reasons"
and snapping them off backwards at the knuckles.
"Then surely Athulf's youngest son," he said,
"will reappear from Mercia with an army."

"For what," retorted Wulfric, grimacing,
"to gather gavel for our foreign feasters?"
"To feed their swine, more likely," Boda said.
"Old Gorm's a gutsy, galloping, godlike *guþfrea*.
Our Alfred was a cockerel beside him."
"A calf."
                    "A kid."

warlord (OE)

        "A field mouse."

                "A vole."

"The runt of a depleted, blighted litter."

"Who snatched the crown from Athred's little sons."   *after Merton 871*

"A theft for which we thole a thousandfold."

Sensing the swineherd stiffen at his side,

the prince placed a palm on his potent forearm,

dissembling, as he did so, like our Lord,

whom scholars, scribes, and scoundrels scurrilized,

the black storm that boiled in his breast.

"I see you suffer keenly," he replied.

"What, I suffer?" blustered Wulflaf's offspring.   *bearn* (OE)

"How *flitlice* I flee my forebears' fields   *eagerly* (OE)

with nothing but my father's cloak on my back!"   *bratt* (OE)

"*Gee*, truly," Boda blubbered, "what a blessing   *yea* (OE); *bletsung*

to beg a barren bone-house abroad!"   (OE)

The seed of Ingeld eyed the filthy flood   *Alfred*

that rose and fell along the vessel's side.

He turned from Beornwulf to streaming Boda

to Wulflaf's lad and cautiously inquired,

"But what if God has called our king to spend

his days in prayer, prone at Peter's bier?"

Bolla's offspring spluttered wrathfully,

"What God would call a king to leave his people

when they most long for their anointed lord?

By Thunder, if the runt were here," he cried,

his features bulging hideously with grief,

"I'd claim the Danes' twenty pounds in a twinkling!"

He rubbed his tears away and sniffed and swallowed.

"Forgive me, sirs," he said. "You're bound for Rome?

A worthy offering for evil times.

King Athulf traveled there, with little Alfred,   *ca. 855*
and Athelswith, his daughter, lives there still."

"Our ancient kings repose in Rome," said Wulfric.   *K. Ceadwalla d.*
"The pope himself christened Ceadwalla Peter."   *689*

The pope himself, thought Ingeld's scion grimly.
The graceless meddler, Gregory the Fourth,   *827–844*
induced the pious emperor's commanders   *Emp. Louis*
to shirk their oaths and join his rebel sons.
That was the Field of Lies, where honor died.   *833*
King Alfred would not hammer brass in Rome   *Orosius bk. iv*
like captured Alexander, Perseus' son,   *K. Perseus d. 166 B.C.*
nor, by God, would Ealhswith partake   *K. Beorhtric d. 802;*
of the fate of Beorhtric's vicious queen,   *Eadburh da. of K. Offa*
who died alone, a beggaress, in Pavia.
The Lord, it seemed, now granted him his Spirit,
his thirst for justice, hunger for revenge,
disgust at abject cowardice and treason,
and scorn for mere pain and bodily death.

"Not yet," the seed of Ingeld said, "not yet,   *Alfred*
much as we'd like to ride the whale-road
with two such patient, loyal, warlike thanes.
Hold, sailors!" Alfred shouted to the hands.
Just as the vessel parted from the quay,
he clambered on to the ship's rail and leapt,
and Beornwulf, elated, did the same.
Elated, ill, King Alfred watched the hull
wallow like a stunned ox on the tide.

VI.

Among Devils

⌒∞⌒

Alfred and a band of gleemen arrive in Chippenham. Alfred gains an
audience with Guthrum, but instead of killing him, he becomes his counselor.

Abundant-bellied Ymme, Halga's handmaid,
whom Earl Hrut had brought from Cirencester   *"Siziter"*
when the drubbed Saxon captains downed their swords,
hugged a pitcher of sweet mead to her breast
and by her bigness blazoned to the Danes,
victorious, though worn by years of toil,
the fruit of Freya's bounty, soon to yield
the bounty of the newly conquered land.
Unknowingly, the lass prepared those pagans
to yield to what, to them, was yet unknown,
the knowledge and the blessing of our Lady,
the Holy Ghost's beloved, heaven's Queen—
though even those whom heaven's King had chosen
to come to him through her, and her tough glory,
had yet a stony, blood-soaked road to tread,
which she with tears beheld from heaven's mount.   *munt* (OE)

The men had drunk and feasted for a spell
when a guard bent his lips to Halga's ear,   *★trik* (OEN)
old Gormr being absent from the platform.
"Heroes!" he cried, hammering on the table,   *★halir* (OEN)
"a troupe of Jutish gleemen, circling home,
they say, from entertaining Frankish kings,   *★kunukar* (OEN)

93

has come to Chippenham. Well, let them come.
If they be spies, their glee will be their grave."   *kraf (OEN)

The hooting of a hawthorn flute was heard
from the thick bank of smoke that screened the door,
and four capering gleemen soon appeared.   gleowmenn (OE)
First, Abba dipped, stiff-limbed, along the fire,
breathing the notes, his cheeks flicked by the flames;
his helpmeet then hopped in, thumping her drum;
next Edith wheeled into view, their daughter;
and last, the slender forepost of a harp,
thrusting from the chest of a one-eyed elder,
sundered the smudge as a dragon's fanged prow
saws the fog that shrouds a sleeping shore.

Aghast at the display of weathered heads
he'd passed atop the fiends' fresh-cut stockade,
and grieved to see the jarls' raven banner
glowering from the thinly whitewashed wall,
the harper (Alfred) struck the instrument
as sick with hate, like Christ entering hell
among the elves, he bobbled past the tables
in easy reach of his exulting foes.
Too late, he saw that murdered Godfred's seed   Godrum / Gormr
was not among the worthies ranged on high.

"My glorious lord," cried Abba, bowing low,
"your hand-thanes have performed for counts and kings,
but never yet beneath the imperial eye
of Denmark, Frisia, and quiescent Britain."

"The emperor has just stepped out," said Halga,
at which the rowers and their steersmen chortled,
"but I'm his *subregulus pro tem*.

A song, my good Jutes, to amuse the Danes!"   *søkr (OEN)
"A song!" cried the sailors, beating the boards.

"Dread master," Alfred answered, bending so
low the wood of joy just touched the rushes,
"excuse us, but we dare not mock your monarch
by rendering unto other men, though noble,
our panegyric to His Caesarhood."

The seed of Hemming, Ymme's husband, brightened.   *bunta (OEN)
"Presumably, you're murderers and thieves,"
he said, "in pay of some pig-headed personage
who kicks against the judgments of your God—   *Kuþ (OEN)
but you may play as long as your songs please."

A stirring flourish heralded a run
on the taut harp, the Danes fell more or less quiet,
and Alfred, Ingeld's seed, boldly intoned:

Nor trumpet we the trials   of Cerdic king,   K. Cerdic d. 534
who wafted to the west   and whipped the Welsh;
nor boast of Brutus,   his own father's bane,   K. Ascanius
who, banned from Rome,   bred Romans in the
                                    island;
nor glorify   Theodoric, the Goth,   K. Theodoric d. 532
the Amaling who upstaged   Odovacar;   K. Odovacar d. 493
no, we sing the Cimbrian   seed of kings,
the grim, greedy, groaning   Gormr the Great!

The singer watched his fingers peck, then listened
as fiendish applause rattled Athulf's hall.
When the Danes' din died, he resumed his lay.

With shoals of heroes huge,   from heath and shore
Gormr, guided by God   to goad the folk,

floated to once-fruitful   fertile Britain,
where one realm remained   to rack and maim.

Again the sailors shouted for sheer pleasure,
but Alfred, hot brine rising in his eyes,
sang louder, outclamoring their clatter.
He lauded Alfred's downlands, meadows, fields,
then traced the Danes' campaigns to treacherous Wareham, *876*
followed Gorm's escape to Exeter,
and haled the host from Gloucester back to Wiltshire, *Jan. 878*
feasting the fiends on his own feigned demise.

The chief chivvied   the cheat through chilly vales,
shivered his shield   and spitted him at Wilton.
The Wylye, winter-wild,   whelmed his relics,   *R. Wylye*
bouncing his body   off its ice-bound bottom:
Swanage swallowed   Sceaf's sorry spawn.

So Alfred twined the tale he'd meditated
from Hamwic, where he'd taken up with Abba,
on past the hanging stones and Woden's dike.   *Stonehenge*
He'd known the gleeman at his father's court
in Canterbury, during Athulf's exile.   *K. Athelwulf d. 858*
The Jute had had a little son named Samson
who joined young Alfred when he roamed the meadows,
harrying hares with a soft, boy-sized bow.
Now Samson filled the Frisian fosse he'd found
upholding Edith's, and their father's, honor.
The count (a northman) granted Abba wergild   *Eric s. of K. Hemming*
and leave to sail from Dorestad unharmed,
whence he'd arrived in Hamwic, where the king
encountered him, despondent, in a tavern.
Abba fell in with Alfred's scheme. That night,
a frigid, moonless night in vanquished Hampshire,
they set out on their march to Chippenham—

which, when they boarded, Beornwulf took leave,
hurrying home to Denulf and their herds.

The rowers, ravished by the rascal's fate,
which none had known, rocked the roof with their cheers.
Satisfied, the Saxon broached the theme
he hoped would win an interview with Gorm.

> *The region's ravaged raches,   reft of rule,*   *ræccas* (OE)
> *implore the pirate   to appoint a peace.*
> *Does Gormr grab   the god-descended scepter?*
> *Hang hundreds   to console young Harald's ghost?*   *s. of Guthrum*
> *The king recalls   the kinship of two kindreds:*
> *he waits on word   from wide-ruling Woden*
> *on how to hew   a keel for a kingdom,*
> *for as the stem strays,   so swerves the stern.*
> *Thuswise Godrum   governs the Gewisse,*
> *dealing dire dooms   to doleful docgan.*   *dogs* (OE)

The oarsmen rose. They rang the planks and roared.
The earls on the dais clapped their hands,
content to hear, in terms their foes could follow,
the justice of their cause and Alfred's end.
But Ingeld's imp begged pardon of the Lord   *Alfred*
deep in his heart, for unlike Hilda's herdsman,   *Cædmon ca. 680*
whom an angel taught the art of plaiting hymns,
he hadn't praised earth's splendor, or the hand
that ransomed Moses, or our Savior's passion.
No, to serve his folk, he caressed their foes,
for unlike Willibald, or Boniface   *Bp. Willibald d.*
who felled the fiends' world-tree at Geismar,   *787; Abp. Boniface*
the Lord had charged him not to save the Danes,   *d. 754*
but by his grace to flush them from the kingdom.

The gleemen had unrolled their humble bedding
when Halga summoned Alfred to the study.
"He overheard you from the passageway,"
said Halga. "Hew to the truth, or hello hell."

The harper's blood was thudding in his head,
so quickly did his business rush to meet him.
Again he saw his dame turning away
and Octa cut down in the skirts of Selwood.
Mercifully, the Spirit of the Lord
relieved him of the pangs of memory.
Like Ehud, Eglon's bane, like Eomer,   *Jud. 3:16; 626*
he wore a two-edged thigh-knife on his hip.

"Here is your one-eyed spy," said Hemming's grandson   *Halga*
"Obviously, you didn't finish Alfred.
We saw the scoundrel scram on a swift gray."
He cast a parting glance at Ingeld's seed.   *Alfred*
A hunk of pork appeared before the harper,
who crossed himself and drew his whetted blade.

"Excuse a hero's rudeness," Gormr said,   *halr* (OEN)
watching the gleeman manhandle the joint.
"I stood him as a mother and a father,   *muþur, *faþur*
but failed to inculcate our courtlier ways."   (OEN)

"He loves you with a brother's love," said Alfred,   *broþor* (OEN)
affecting an old poet's gruff abruptness.
Six, seven times he'd met the heathen chieftain,
but never had he glimpsed a kinsman's heart
pittering under the grim mask of war.

"How marvelously harp and song," said Gormr,
tapping his breast with a scarred, bristled fist,
"both rouse and soothe the tumult in the soul!   *siol* (OEN)

I bet the earl a shilling you were Welsh.
But is it true, this figment of our triumph?
Is Alfred Athulfing distinctly dead?
You paint him as a prize ass, a weakling,
but it took seven years to bring him down."

The Saxon brushed a sleeve across his lips
to cover an involuntary grin.

"I wish him dead, of course," the northman said,
"but as a reigning king, I wish him peace.   *kunukr (OEN)
The Saxons will not pull a pagan's wagon,   *uakn (OEN)
nor will the jealous Zealanders endure
me as their king. Had we but captured Alfred,
we could have salvaged his, and Edward's, reign.
Did I twig it? You are a Welshman born?"

"*Gise,*" the seed of Athelwulf replied,   *yes* (OE)
"a Briton from Dumnonia I am.
They snatched me when they massacred my kin.   *mægþ* (OE)
Old Ecgbert son of Ealhmund was *cyning,*   K. Ecgbert d. 839
the dragon egg the Germans call 'the Great.'"

"You hate them, then," concluded Godfred's seed.
"So tell me what you know of Alfred's death."   *tauþi (OEN)

"We halted, sir, three nights ago in Wilton,"
said Alfred, "where the whipped whelp retired.
I saw him, sir, I saw him plain as daylight
topple like a felled oak from his mount,
with purple blood spurting from every pore.
He broke the ice and disappeared from sight."

The pagan sailor halted by the table
and fixed the harper's solitary eye.

"Then you have seen him but as I have seen him,"
he said, "in the sly jugglery of thought.
A hurt hero can drop from his horse and live."　　　　*halr, *hect (OEN)

"Gee, sir, he can," the Athulfing concurred,　　　　yea (OE)
"he can, if there's a dram of blood left in him.　　　blod (OE)
By now the hræw has reached the open sea."　　　　corpse (OE)

Gormr examined Alfred's glabrous scars
and watched his fingers roll the idle knife.
The Saxon felt he now might stick the devil,
but doubted it would benefit his folk
to sic a pack of wolfish jarls on them.　　　　*iarlar (OEN)

"What is your name, old man?" inquired Gormr.　　*nafn, *gamal (OEN)
"They called me Mervyn at my christening,"
said Alfred, "Mervyn ap, or son of, Myrddin."

The sailor turned away. "Are you a wizard?
Can you commune with *alfar, ghosts, and trolls　elves (OEN)
and mutter spells like Saxon cunning men?"

The seed of Ingeld scanned the brigand's back,　Alfred
in which he read old pride worn down with toil,
and answered he could pray as well as any.

"Then you shall prove your worth," the northman said, *uarþ (OEN)
"by tracking down the ousted Saxon king
wherever he may be in the nine worlds.
Do it, and I'll hand over ten gold pounds
and my exhausted folk will have a home."

He poured a sack of thrymsas on the desk
collected from the hoards of Frankish lords.
Their muted clatter, softer than pure silver's,

startled Alfred, who never touched such spoil.
They flickered under his eye like sun-soaked pebbles
bathing in the bed of a shallow stream.
It struck him that the stranger, Harald's father,   *Harald s. of Guthrum*
was tapping him to serve, as Joseph served   *Gen. 47:12*
Pharaoh and preserved his father's house.
He fidgeted. It seemed the Holy Ghost
said no to nicking Godrum's jugular.

The Dane inclined his head so near that Alfred
could feel his vinous breath caress his ear.
"Two widowed sisters live nearby," said Gormr,   **sustur* (OEN)
"One will bear me the son of my old age
who, backed by his ambitious Saxon kinsmen,
will split and mitigate the natives' hate.
Now, which of these two fruitful Saxonesses
to wed and bed is what I want to know.
The one is forward, fit to rule our board.
The other, overshadowed, even grave,
would nurse our newborn nation on her wisdom."

The seed of Ingeld flushed and swallowed hard.   *Alfred*
He knew the noble families nearby
and didn't relish heaping up their troubles.
He spied Ealhswith's silver sieve on the chest.
"*Gee,* sir," he said, "our spell must ease their fears.
May I inspect the sisters?"

                    "By no means,"
said Gorm, his grained and pouchy eye aglitter,
"you might fancy the **froia* meant for me."   *lady* (OEN)

"Then lend me a short bow," said Alfred, rising,
"to spit a hare, whose heart we'll grind to dust."

"There's one more thing," said Godrum, "keep your seat.
If Hrothulf takes the crown, he'll offer up   *Ruulf* (OEN)
the whole Saxon folk to Woden's glory.   *Oþen* (OEN)
He must be crushed, for your good and for ours.
You do these things for me, and you shall be
my father, son, and mother, three in one.
Then I'll uncork the best of my adventures
which, I promise, you will find worth singing."

The Saxon stumbled out under the stars,
which seemed a sharper, harder testament,
now that he was the devil's captive bard,   *feond* (OE)
than when, though menaced, he'd possessed his realm.
His head aswim, he ranged the palisade
where farers, lit by fires, warmed their hands.   *ferendas* (OE)
"Lord, take this vial from my lips," he prayed,   *Luke 22:42*
"this sickening leechcraft of sin."   *læce cræft* (OE)

❧

Alfred awoke with Godrum's hugeous head
blotting out the charred beams of the hall.
Had the fiend pierced his sham? Was this the end?
Blindly they trod the hard-rutted yard
to the limed stables, dim gray in the starlight,
where two young mermen held four drowsy mounts.

"Can Mervyn ride?" inquired Harald's father,
watching a gelding nuzzle the harper's chest.
"Aye, sir," said Alfred, scratching bony noses,
"in Kent I had the run of a dun nag."

The heavens shed successive robes of gloom
as Gormr, too familiar with the track
for Alfred's liking, led them through the trees.

Screeching, a jay alighted on a branch;
a woodpecker rattled its alarm.

"We need all kinds of herbs," cried Ingeld's seed.   *Alfred*
He slid down and kicked at a hump of snow.
"A doe hare's belly, dried, will propagate
their goodness, but you too must swig the brew."

He knelt beside the path, tying a snare.
"Can't you compel your elves," the fiend inquired
coolly, "to inflame their widowed loins?"

Twisting his head, the seed of Ingeld saw
the heathen's eyeballs shining like wet stones.
"We do not call upon such sprites," said Alfred,
"but only spirits that obey our *Frea*.   *Lord* (OE)
A litany, a credo, and twelve masses
should saturate the potion with his power."

They breakfasted astride a rotting oak,   *ac* (OE)
shortening a sausage with their steel.
"Your ladies," Alfred added as he chewed,   *hlæfdigan* (OE)
"as Saxon matrons, surely serve our Savior."
"Of course they do," the foreigner replied.
"I told you the whole purpose of this union."
"The Church," said Alfred, "judges disparate cults
a diriment impediment to marriage."
He paused and said, "My lord, you should convert."   *hlaford* (OE)

The pagan cut an ample chunk of flesh   *Godrum / Gormr*
and masticated it in pregnant silence.
Tearing a loaf of bread, the harper added,   *Alfred*
"King Athelbert of Kent acknowledged Christ   *K. Athelbert d. 616;*
after marrying a Frankish maid.   *mægþ* (OE); *Bertha da.*
Their daughter wed King Edwin of Deira   *of K. Charibert d. 567;*

on promise he would study heaven's law.　　　*K. Edwin d. 632;*
The pope urged her to sermonize her husband　*Boniface V 618–625*
and sent her robes, a mirror, and a comb.
Chlodovech, that lady's ancestor,　　　　　　*K. Clovis d. 511;*
received a Catholic girl from Burgundy,　　　*Clotilde da. of K.*
Clotilde, as she is known, or Chrotochildis.　*Chilperic II*
She led him to the font, assisted by
the Lord's miraculous victory at Zulpich,
where he dispersed the menacing Alamanni.　*496*
Thus three prepotent pagan kings converted
based on acquiring royal Christian brides."

The sailor took a long pull from the wineskin
then cautiously surveyed the nearby trees.
Observing him, the son of Athulf thought,　　*Alfred*
I could dispatch him now, here in this grove.　*graf* (OE)
Yet by God's grace, we gabble peacefully.
Sufficient unto the day the ills thereof.　　*Matt. 6:34*

Soon a junior devil reappeared,
a nest of tangled herbage in his arms.
The Saxon extracted a blackened leaf.
"Waybread it is," he said, "the warrior's friend,
for wounds, sores, and the bite of a mad dog."
Just then the wintry overcast disbanded
as heaven's artisans blew up the flames
that lit their tilework above the trees.
The seed of Ingeld saw the other youngster　*Alfred*
high in the black branches of an ash,
straining to reach a sprig of mistletoe.　　*misteltan* (OE)
The anxious Athulfing felt comforted　　　　*Alfred*
by the sausage, bread, and staunch Frankish wine—
his own, untasted through these wretched weeks—
and by the oddity of heaven's ways.

∽∞∾

King Eric's august killer occupied   *K. Eric I d. 854; *bani*
the former judgment seat of Saxon kings,   (OEN)
as Halga and suspicious Hrut perused
the clustered suitors, muttering in the smoke.
The seed of Ingeld, lurking in a corner,   *Alfred*
revolted at the sight of Saxon swordsmen   *secgas* (OE)
humbly soliciting the devil's dooms,
but such disgust was nothing to the shame
that whelmed him when he saw his alderman,
Lord Wulfhere, his late brother's widow's father,   *Wulfthryth wid. of K.*
posted among the earls flanking Gorm—   *Athelred d. 871*
like one of those putrescent senators
that ratified their Gothic master's rancor   *K. Theodoric d. 526;*
and sentenced the philosopher to death.   *Boethius d. 525*
Unsure whom he should hate the most, the fiend,
his *princeps,* or himself, he seemed to sway,
but as he swayed, good Halga cocked a finger
at two devils dragging a monk between them,   *deoflas* (OE)
a man whose stricken features Alfred knew.

"What is it, lads?" King Hemming's grandson asked.   *Halga*
"Did Freya cast her fascination on him?
Inveigle him to thieve some sluttish sow?"
The younger fiend replied, "He was hoarding grain."

"You know your country's law," the earl said.   *Halga*
"Thou shalt not steal."

                 "I charge the wretched monk,"   **mokr* (OEN)
said Hrut, "with pilfering our property.
Cut off his hands and hang him from Ygg's tree."

"Kind lords, the people faint," the brother said.   *munuc* (OE)
The Saxons glared, incensed at his neglect
of Godrum's laws and waste of Godrum's patience.

Contemptibly, Lord Wulfhere lowered his eyes.
King Alfred bent his lips to Godrum's ear.
"A holy monk," he murmured. *"La,* have mercy.
Who loves his heavenly Father feeds his sheep."

Godfred's grandson, twisting in his chair,
stared into Alfred's single blinking eye.
"Enough," he said, "or you shall wield the axe.   *øhs* (OEN)
I know your God doomed his own Son to death."   *Kuþ, *Sunr* (OEN)

"Then take me in his stead," the harper said.   *hearpere* (OE)
"Take me. I'll hang for the man's criminal love."
The heathen growled to Halga, "Let him go."

That afternoon, the northman ordered Alfred   *Godrum / Gormr*
to join him for a jaunt, allotting him
the mare on which Edward had learned to ride—
but first they watched the fiends drill in the yard.
Lord Halga, vapor dangling from his lips,
strode like a god among his worshippers,
explaining how to shed a heavy brunt
or swing a swifter, shrewder, deadlier tip.
"Observe the science of the Franks," said Godrum.

They passed the gateway, crowned with pecked-at heads,
and trotted down the high street, where the townsmen
had patched their roofs with reeds hacked from the ice.
On Godrum's undertaking, they'd restored
their market day, when folk sold hides and cheese.
"The Saxons have declined since former times,"
said Godrum, "though King Alfred's father thrashed us. *Aclea 851*
I'd hate to grow as feeble as these Christians."

They galloped for a mile below the meads,
then reined in to track a crusted brook,

and as they jogged, the agitated Saxon
assailed the Dane's ignorant reluctance.

"A Christian crushed the Welsh at Heavenfield   *K. Oswald d. 641;*
after rearing our Redeemer's rood.   *Heavenfield, 634; rod*
When Penda martyred him at Oswestry,   *(OE); K. Penda d. 654;*
his brother pegged the unrepentant pagan   *K. Oswy d. 670;*
and won the warlike Mercian tribe for Christ.   *mægburh (OE)*
Among the Franks, the Christian emperor,   *Emp. Charles d. 814*
roaring like a fire through dry timber,
in eight campaigns devoured our Saxon kinsmen."

At this, the heathen chief had had enough.
"My grandfather stopped him cold," said Gormr,   *★afi (OEN)*
"despite the elephant called Abul Abbas   *★fill (OEN); Haroun*
the caliph sent him to stampede our men."   *al-Rashid d. 809*

"He overcame the Avar horde," said Alfred,   *796*
"and baptized their high chagan 'Abraham.'"
"His pious son betrayed his Danish allies,"   *Emp. Louis d. 840;*
said Gormr. "Men he'd sponsored at the font."   *K. Harald Klak d. 852*

The pair proceeded southwest in silence.
Then Alfred touched his heels to the mare
and shot ahead, outpacing Godrum's stallion
(though slowing at the brook called Cocklemoor
for the frail shells that lingered from the Flood),
and veered, laboring up the oak-wood slope.
Gormr, flushed, caught up with him on the crest.
From there, they overlooked the stripped elms,
the gray-black river, and the captive town.

"His throne is vacant now," the harper said,   *Alfred*
extending a cupped, reddened palm to Gorm.
"Our warlike pontiff craves a warlike partner   *John VIII 872–882*

to shove the Saracens from Sicily.
A murderous usurper rules the Greeks."   *Emp. Basil acc. 867*
He clenched a ruddy fist. The farer frowned.

"King Pippin worshipped Woden," he replied,   *K. Pippin II d. ca. 864;*
referring to great Charles the Great's great-grandson. *★Oþen* (OEN)
"I sailed with a man who feasted with him."
"Grim jilted him," the harper answered sharply,
"to perish, raving, in his uncle's dungeon."   *K. Charles the Bald*

The sailor shrugged, for such was Woden's way.   *Godrum / Gormr*
He eyed the chilly country with a smile.
"I wonder why you subjugated Britons,"
he countered, "haven't profited from our toil."

"No noble *dux bellorum*," Alfred said,
"has led our people since Artorius' day.
They say he'll come again. You may be he."

Returning, they drew up beside the river.
The heavens were a faceless, depthless mass,
as if the Lord, at large among the clouds,
had crushed the sun under his booted heel.
Across the pitch-black flood, a pair of swans
stood motionlessly on a bank of ice,
apart and yet unquestionably united,
their black shanks tying their shining bodies
to the bright shoreline under their black feet.

"The earls will be here in two weeks' time,"
said Godrum, rolling backwards as his stallion
stretched head and neck to clear the silvery shelf.
"My plan is, at that gathering, to unveil
the spouse you were supposed to help me choose."   *★spusa* (OEN)

"I thought you meant allegorical ladies,"
said Alfred. "Is my high lord decided   *sinfrea* (OE)
not to fish for a royal Frankish damsel?"   *fæmne* (OE)

"To thrust me from the throne and wed my son,"   *★sun, ★stiubmoþur*
the Dane rejoined, "like Alfred's Frankish stepmother, (OEN); *Judith da. of K.*
now trebly wedded to the count of Flanders?   *Charles the Bald;*
I saw her in Count Eric's ale-hall—   *Baldwin I d. 879;*
Halga's uncle, in case you didn't know.   *★Helki* (OEN)
He gave them sanctuary when her father
and Archbishop Hincmar banished them.   *★Ærkibiskub* (OEN)
A willful and experienced young quean,   *★snot* (OEN)
superbly cased in yards of crimson stuff."

"I counseled so," the Saxon countered coldly,   *Alfred*
"that my dread *dryhten,* dunked and dripping chrism,   *lord* (OE)
might row to Rome and reap the diadem.
Our Lord himself was born a man of Rome—   *Orosius bk. vi*
though if you'd bathed, my *brego* of the Bright-Danes, *king* (OE)
you wouldn't have breached your sworn pact with Alfred."

A surge of anger blackened Godrum's brow
as Alfred darkened to his stubbled scalp.
"Besides," he said, "I never heard that Judith,
tutored by Pardulus and John the Scot,   *Pardulus bp. of Laon;*
ever indulged in her own flesh and blood.   *John Scotus Erigena*
In justice, then, she may not be compared   *Orosius bk. i; bearn*
to Semiramis, who debauched her son;   (OE); *Orosius id.*
or poor Jocasta, whose exuberant womb
bore four ill-fortuned siblings to their father;
or Philip, who defiled Alexander,   *Orosius bk. iii*
the brother of his Epirotic queen;   *Olympias*
or Ptolemy of Alexandria,   *Orosius bk. v*
who spoiled his sister, then, his daughter-niece;   *swyster* (OE)

or Gaius, who molested his three sisters; *Caligula; Orosius bk.*
or Agrippina's lad, who smirched his dam. *vi; Nero; Orosius id.*

"Unlike such signal evildoers, lord, *domne* (OE)
our Judith but infringed an ecclesial scheme
adopted to amalgamate the nations,
which purpose she'd already served by marrying
the widowed Saxon *cyning*, Alfred's father, *K. Athelwulf d. 858;*
instead of one of her gilt Frankish cousins." *fæder, magas* (OE)
Here Alfred took advantage of the pagan,
for Judith, when she married Alfred's brother, *K. Althelbald d.*
in truth fused with her spiritual son. *860; sunu* (OE)
"Moreover, sir," the seed of Athulf added, *Alfred*
"you have no son to blast your nuptial comfort
with the shamefast stigma you detest." *sceamfæst* (OE)

Across the way, the swans had moved downstream
to keep their territory free of mallards,
a flock of which had occupied the reach.
"You vex me, Mervyn," Godfred's seed replied.
"You said yourself King Alfred breached the peace
when he withheld the wergild owed the Danes,
not to mention murdering my boy. **makur* (OEN)
As to the spotlessness of Baldwin's bedmate,
conceded, though when last I saw the lady,
she looked well founded to support the load
of sin that men's malice laid at her feet.
But I will never brook a Frankish bride. *Teutberga w. of K.*
You know what Lothar's dame was saddled with— *Lothar II d. 869*
and look at Brunhild, who destroyed ten kings." *Brunhild d. 614*

The seed of Ingeld warily declared, *Alfred*
"She was a Gothic, not a Frankish, frow."

After a time, the heathen captain growled,
"Your God won't grudge a favor done a friend."

But Alfred saw no amiable glint
in Gormr's speckled eyes. *"La,* sir," he said,
"You long to dive beneath the Savior's wave.
Why wait until you sniff the pit of hell?"

"I know your water rite," the Dane replied,   *Godrum/Gormr*
"is more than just a change of loyalty.
On peril of your head," he remonstrated,   *★hofoþ* (OEN)
then turned his steed and spurred it to a run.   *★hist* (OEN)

VII.

One Body

❦

*Beornwulf delivers a corpse to Guthrum, who celebrates Alfred's death by
offering "Mervyn" a bride. Mervyn learns that Ealhswith and the children
are Guthrum's prisoners.*

The winter sun's heroic pyre, on which
the King of Heaven slathered lavish hues
of dragon, iron, gold, elm, whale, and plum
of depth and subtlety, and on a scale,
our earthly artisans can never equal—
by which he regularly illustrates
the coming recreation of the world,
as well as his departures and returns—
the sunset had been stowed when a stout guardsman,
a Frisian lad, fetched "Mervyn" to the stables.   *Alfred*

The harper found Gorm bent over a cart
with Halga by his side, holding a torch,
and next to Halga, able Beornwulf.
When Gormr turned, the earl's flickering flame,
by swelling and enlivening the bumps
and hollows of their faces, changed the men
into a panel of three voiceless devils
deliberating judgment on the dead:
for on the cart a prostrate body lay
rolled up in Alfred's soiled scarlet mantle,
with Alfred's chain-mail coat tied at its throat
and Alfred's sword and scabbard on its chest.
The rodent-bitten forehead wore the casque

that Osweard's shop had wrought for Athelbald: *K. Athelbald d. 860*
two rows of garnets, carved from Cerdic's   *K. Cerdic d. 534*
congealed blood and set along each rib
led upwards to a little golden boar,
whose round snout and semicircular tusks
solicited that spirit's cunning fury.
In many a near-run scrap, this gilded hat
had kept the youngest Athulfing in life   *lif* (OE)
when his three brothers had gone down to death.

But now the maker's dome surmounted not
the Saxon monarch's cogitating brow,
but flame-enkindled swatches of dead flesh
that gripped a dead skull's ridges, seams, and curves.
The Welsh harper's heart flumped in its cage
at sluggish maggots curling in dark sockets
and the black cavern of the chewed-off nose
as the sharp stench the chill could not suppress
bit into his unstoppered passageways.
The swineherd dropped his eyes when he perceived   *Beornwulf*
the false British bard, his one-eyed lord.   *Alfred*

"Liar," Halga said to Beornwulf.
"This half-thawed lich has been dead for weeks."   **lik* (OEN)

"Lord," the swineherd said, still looking down,   *domne* (OE)
"we feared you foreign earls. And your king."

"This business stinks of Saxonish deceit,"
good Halga said to Godrum, Eric's bane.   *K. Eric I d. 854*
Again he rated the subservient churl.
"I say it was Lord Athelnoth who sent you.
Or the fat axeman, Bishop Athelheah."

At this, the northern chieftain intervened,   *Godrum / Gormr*
the torchlight trembling in his humid pupils.

"Do you deny, my unbelieving friend,"   *uinr (OEN)
he said, "that this corrupting lump is Alfred?
Was he so great and godlike, in your eyes,
the man who massacred my noble son?   *Haraltr (OEN)
His folk have paid in full for that infraction.
Born of his death, our ransomed life begins."

"Then drink it in, my friend," said Halga, yielding.
"Some Saxon satrap flashed these fancy trappings."

Again old Godrum turned to face his poet.
"Propitious, potent Briton," he began,
his flaming features cut across with pleasure,
"I take no satisfaction, as a rule,
in gaping at a beaten foe's remains,
but no more ample answer could he give,
this God of yours, to your industrious prayers."   *Kuþ (OEN)

King Alfred tacked a quick cross to his chest.
"We ask his mercy on your enemy,"
he said, "if said enemy is truly dead."

"Do you too doubt?" the heathen king replied.
"These are his arms. You said you saw him fall."

"He was as tall as you," the harper said.   *Alfred*
The pagan sailor, suddenly inspired,   *Godrum / Gormr*
nimbly hopped on Beornwulf's creaking cart,
which Halga and the Frisian guardsman steadied,
and bedded down beside the joggled form.

"Then measure us, old Mervyn," Godrum said.
"Take his sword and lay it against our feet."   *suirþ (OEN)

The seed of Ingeld drew the braided blade,   *Alfred*
which Ecgbert, Athulf's father, had received,   *K. Ecgbert acc. 802*

a parting gift, from Charles the Great before
returning to campaign for Ini's throne.   *K. Ini d. 726; Ecgbert's*
He hefted its familiar, balanced weight   *gt.-gt.-gt.-gt.-gd.-uncle*
in his well-rested hand and eyed the edge
of gemlike steel, whetted by himself,
that the scabbard's fleece lining had preserved.
A stream of firelight poured along the fuller
and sparkled in the runes that graved its banks.
King Alfred felt the Holy Spirit stir
and glanced at Denewulf's clandestine brother.

The chieftain asked him, "Can you read the legend?   *Godrum / Gormr*
I know the characters, but not this speech."   *bokstafar* (OEN)

"It's Latin, from King David," Alfred answered.
"Et gladius meus non salvabit me—   *Ps. 44:6-7*
My salvation lies not *in minum sweorde."*
He held the burning blade to four worn shoesoles.

"Now judge between us, brother," ordered Gormr,   *bruþur* (OEN)
groping for the soldier's covered hand,
"now who do you say is the nobler king?"   *kunukr* (OEN)

"Let's take off this helmet," Halga said,   *hialmr* (OEN)
and loosening the laces, found the ivory
crucifix beneath the sleeper's neck.
"King Edmund's inauspicious cross," he noted.   *K. Edmund d. 870*

"That's further proof this rottenness is Alfred,"
Godrum said. "The Saxons robbed our Atli."
He gripped the rail and pulled himself upright.
"Three times young Alfred had me by the beard.
But here I am, and here he is, or was."
Remembering Beorn's feigned death at Luna—   *Saxo bk. ii*

"Give me that," he said, grabbing the sword,
and pressed its keen neck through the waxy gullet.   *kunælt, war-flame*
                                                       (OEN)

The Saxon swallowed hard and searched for words.
"The good Lord broke him down to crush his pride.
The Spirit led this churl to his berth
just as he led Saint Ambrose to the place   *St. Ambrose d. 397*
Protasius and Gervasius were buried—
though Alfred was no saint, as we can tell
comparing this unregenerate odor
with Cuthbert's ruddy cheeks, still fresh, they say,   *St. Cuthbert d. 687*
after a dozen summers in his coffin."

He stopped, impressed with Beornwulf's design
or Denewulf's, or Bishop Athelheah's.
They must have thought, if he yet lived, yet free,
the heathens' misbelief in his extinction
would veil his survival from their sight.

"Your first commission is complete," said Godrum.
He fixed his favorite earl with swimming eyes.   *Halga*
"It seems she'll have to yield and remit
the year-long moratorium she begged for."
(Poor Alfred thought he meant his local widow.)
"In any case, we'll quickly crown our princeling,"
continued Gorm, "before her hero's howe."
The earl eyed the corpse and pursed his lips.   *Halga*

"And you, my boy," young Harald's father added,   *Godrum / Gormr*
bathing Beornwulf in lordly warmth,
"from now on you're our chartered royal swineherd.
Come back in ten days' time with forty head.
I'll pay you then your bounty for this—bounty."

∞

The greater light had breached the eastern woods,
illuminating tiny spikes and leaves
that in their millions tinged the withered earth
and unappareled trees a milky green,
when Alfred, breathing in the biting air,
mounted the robbers' newly built stockade.
In little time, he counted ravens, doves,
a goldcrest and a merlin and a kite
that tumbled, cruised, or wheeled on the breeze
or fluttered in the scrub in search of breakfast.
He listened to their variegated calls,
each in its lingo crying, "Here I am."

How fresh the newborn earth and air appeared,
now Godrum planned to plant his lying clay!
In days the early plowing would begin,
when husbandmen would sow their summer crops
and soon would be available to fight—
unless he failed to thwart the oarsman's scheme,
dreamt up by Grim himself, or by the devil,
to crown a Saxon puppet and transform
a people's struggle into civil strife.   *leod* (OE)

He found the king in his scriptorium   *Godrum / Gormr*
(both "king" and "his" referring to the farer),   *ferend* (OE)
perusing the accounts of royal lands
the Athulfing's successor would enjoy
along with food rents, leases, tolls, and fines,
the proceeds of the mints, if he revived them,
and tribute from submissive British kings,
for Alfred had instructed royal Godrum
in how to con the Irish minuscule,
which as the currency of holy writ
might lead him to explore the Gospel hoard.
He'd handed him his enchiridion,
a manual of graspable quotations.

He'd even taught him Bede's arithmetic
and the odd dance of fingers, chest, and thighs
whereby the scholar calculated sums.

The seed of Ingeld hankered to repair   *Alfred*
the sundial the Danes had vandalized
and frame the fiend a Christian calendar
replete with feast-days for the saints, and fasts,
the kalends, ides, and nones, the lunar quarters,
the equinoxes and the solstices—
contrivances whereby the Father urges
men to cherish the hours they've been given.
The grizzled Jutlander, adept from youth
in Woden's scrivening, speedily had learned
to sound the signs in silence to himself
(as could Augustine's mystagogue, great Ambrose),   *St. Ambrose d. 397*
for he well knew a vellum scroll conveyed
more substance than a stone scratched with a spell.

"Good morning, son," indulgent Mervyn said.   *maga* (OE)
When murdered Godfred's grandson raised his face,   *Godrum / Gormr*
the Saxon saw a sparkle in his eye
and an unfeigned smile stir in his beard.

"I have a gift for you," the shipman said   *Godrum / Gormr*
and led him down the hallway towards the nursery.
The Saxon marveled at his merry mood,   *Alfred*
imagining the man might make his magus
the keeper of the cold king's regalia
or bearer of a cup formed from his skull,
like that from which the Lombard Alboin gulped   *K. Alboin d. 573*
to toast dead Cunimund, the Gepid king   *K. Cunimund d. 567*
(which he compelled his Gepid queen to quaff,
revengeful Rosamund, the Gepid's daughter),   *Q. Rosamund d. 573*
or that with which old Krum, the Bulgar khan,   *K. Krum d. 814*
commemorated Emperor Nicephorus,   *Emp. Nicephorus d. 811*

beheaded while retiring from Pliska
after butchering heaps of Bulgar folk.

"You're jovial," the joculator said.   *Alfred*
"Now that your stubborn enemy's defunct,
which Saxon *magister* will you call king?
Lord Wulfhere, is it, or his worthy son?
You've met with them in private, I believe."

"The spring comes early here," said Gormr, grinning,
unwilling to divulge his current view,
"in this benign, subseptentrional clime."

Good Halga, rising when the pair arrived,
the prosperous conqueror and the crop-haired bard,
took up his stance beside three native women,
among whom Ingeld's scion recognized,   *Alfred*
in morning brightness pouring from the smoke hole,
the scraggy countenance of Lady Hilda,
his wife's companion, whom he'd last addressed
in that same chamber following Atli's fall.
The widow glared irately at the Dane,
ignoring his ill-favored, one-eyed slave.

"Come forward, Mervyn," Godfred's grandson said.   *Godrum/Gormr*
"Let none say Godrum stints the men who serve him.
I know your Lord won't let you wed all three."

Trembling, the harper eyed a plumpish girl
whose raven pigtails framed her flaming cheeks.
"What is your name, my dear?" the Dane inquired.   **nafn* (OEN)

"Nest, my lord," she said, ineptly dipping.
"A Britoness, my *brego,* from old Lacock."   *king* (OE)

"Your countrywoman, Mervyn," noted Gormr.
While Harald's father chuckled, Hilda goggled
at what her soul, astonished, had perceived,
the ravaged apparition of her atheling.

"And what are you?" the Jutish ruler asked   *Godrum / Gormr*
a wan and lanky lass with pallid hair.
"Alfflaed, sir," she said, dropping her chin.
"A Saxoness." She sneaked a glance at Nest.
"My lord," the earl vigilantly prompted.   *Halga*

"What do you say, good Mervyn?" asked the fiend,   *Godrum / Gormr*
"a Saxon stean to seethe a British babe?"   *⋆barn* (OEN)

"I humbly thank my headman," Alfred said,   *heafodmann* (OE)
"but my old woman, back in old Dumnonia—"
"We'll bring her here," the beaming chief replied.
"I fear she took another husband, sir,"
the singer said, at which a surge of feeling
purpled Hilda's cheeks and quivering chin.

"I know your law allows you to remarry,"
the fiend declared, then turned his eye on Hilda.
"Say what you are," he barked, a ruthless master.
The lady blazed. Her narrow nostrils flared.   *freo* (OE)
"This is Lady Hilda," said the devil.
She spat, hitting the mat at Godrum's foot.

"I hate to choose," the harper temporized.
"When Paris judged among three goddesses,
he lit the lamp that gutted golden Troy."

"We know of Troy," said Gormr. "⋆*Miklagarþr*.   *Constantinople* (OEN);
Red Thor was Priam's son. This gal's no goddess."   *⋆Þur* (OEN)

121

Hilda spat again, dewing his shoe.
"And I am no Greek god," acknowledged Alfred.

With the dame's fingers burning on his hips,   *Hilda*
the seed of Ingeld jogged behind the pagan   *Alfred*
along the trail northward from the lodge.

"My men have improvised a nuptial bed,"
Gormr, riding ahead, threw over his shoulder.

"We bless our kingly master," Alfred called,
then added softly to his wizened bride,
"the Lord bless your fortitude, dear lady,   *siþwif* (OE)
in holding out against the foreign fiends."

"The Lord God bless you, my dearest hero,"   *hæleð* (OE)
she murmured, "you must stick that sinner now!"
They reached the dripping, dim, neglected croft,
still littered with the autumn's black remains.
A devil trotted from around a corner
chivvied by a troupe of soiled children.

Startled, Alfred recognized young Edward
and Athelgeofu and little Elfthryth.
His spirits swelled, as when the living wind
stoops suddenly, an *ælf* among the waves,   *elf* (OE)
and fills the slack sail, which, with a shock
like thunder cracking, bellies and balloons,
a dazzling woolen cloud, harboring shadow,
and mariners, till then becalmed, rejoice
as the straked vessel scuds across the swells,
but then the gale fades and vanishes
and the weft settles limp against the mast
and the craft loses way and slews about,
exposed to the rude shoulders of the main.

His children were the sailors' prisoners,
and he lacked men and means to set them free.

He scarcely felt Hilda slide from the saddle
or heard the heathen's flippant admonition
not to frighten the pups with his evil eye.
Shivering where he sat, the seed of Ingeld   *Alfred*
watched his children swarm and grapple Ulf,
who'd steered for Godrum lo these many years,
and lever him, guffawing, to the ground
then scatter, shouting, through the muddy pools
and halt among the gnarled apple trees.
He saw and wondered, like the famous father   *St. Augustine of Hippo*
who stopped beside a snowy field to watch
a hound chasing a high-tailing hare.

When Edward halted, staring up at him,
their half-hairless, one-eyed bitch by his side,
he wore the worried look of one who sounds
each face he sees for one he longs to see
but who, his hunger regularly baffled,
now disbelieves his too hopeful eyes.
He gave the ugly traveler a grin,
as if acknowledging a stranger's wish
to comfort an unhappy fellow stranger.

⁂

With mock solemnity and modest pride,
as if he were a monk exhibiting
an antique episcopal sepulcher,
the Frisian hoard-guard unbarred a storeroom
in which the men had decked a wedding bed.
"No one has had her yet," the lad declared,   *Hilda*
his copper whiskers curtaining his lips.
"Our chief commanded us to tell you so."

The harper set a candle on a chest.   *Alfred*
She'd told him how the fiends had captured them,
wending their wild way from Frome to Sherborne,
and how his young hall-guards fought and fell.
She'd told him how poor Ealhswith had prayed,
revolted by Gorm's courtship, for salvation,
but when none came, she'd schemed to save her son,
whom Wulfhere schemed to set aside, or worse,
in favor of his grandsons, Athred's heirs.   *K. Athelred d. 871*
Accordingly, on seeing Alfred's cloak
and helm embellishing his feigned remains,
Ealhswith had agreed to stand with Godrum
the day her Edward donned his father's crown.
And all this time, he'd dawdled in the hall?

"I didn't know, I swear," the Saxon said.   *Alfred*
"Besides, I have my duties to our people."

"The whole world knew but you," Hilda pursued,
"you, our studious Christian sage."

"The sailor trusts me now," said Athulf's son.   *Alfred*
He turned and watched the candle's brilliance writhe.

"Your potions sap your spouse's soul," said Hilda.
"But we shall see who wields the stronger art."
She drew a homely figure from her bundle.

"A graven image," murmured Ingeld's seed.   *Alfred*
The *freo* gazed at it, her face a mask.   *lady* (OE)
"We will remove the devil," Alfred said,
"but not by begging help from hellish elves.
Behind their chief stands royal Hemming's seed.   *Halga*
Behind him, Hrothulf, who consumes our folk.   *Halga's s.*

124

Behind him, Godrum's five efficient earls,
any of whom the heathens could name king."

Hrut, Wiga, Wan,
Froda, Toca

When he was done, the lady boiled over
and shoved him hard against the storeroom wall.
"Behind me," Hilda cried, "behind old Hild,"
her anger so astringing Alfred's scalp
that every stem of stubble stood accused,
"behind me stand a thousand Saxon women
stripped of every blessed rag of worth!"
Her damp features pressed so close to his eye
he saw each thread of down along her jaw,
then suddenly she crumpled to the floor
and lay uttering bleak, metallic moans
that echoed pitiably in the daub cell.
The king discerned a wretched human relic,
a knot of sticks wrapped in woven stuff,
and scooped her up and held her to his chest.

"It is my burden," muttered Edward's father.
"It is my charge to bear. I will. *Ic wille.*"
He lowered her, still moaning, to the bed
and tucked a sheepskin rug under her chin.

When Hilda's lamentation ebbed, she said,
"Lie here beside me, *cyning.* I feel cold.
Don't fret. I'm old enough to be your mother."

The seed of Ingeld wobbled onto the pallet
and edged beneath the weighty, stale fleeces.
He heard the lady's breathing near his ear.
"Forgive me, gracious *frea,*" Hilda said.
She felt for Alfred's hand under the rug.

Alfred
fliesu (OE)

lord (OE)

⁓⊗⁓

Lord Halga lay awake, with Ymme's belly
rising like a barrow from their bed.   *haukr (OEN)
A tallow candle propagated soot.
The Frankish girl shifted under her burden.

"My king is quiet," Ymme said. "No thoughts?"
"This island is alive with snakes," said Halga.
"Specifically, the Saxon and Welsh rabble
that feign willing obedience to our rule."

"You worry like a mother hen," said Ymme,   *Matt. 23:37*
"but your accomplished cousin has prevailed   *Godrum / Gormr*
behind his even greater cousin's shield."

"I'll tell you what disturbs me most," he said.
"Gormr's saddle galls my gallant get,   *niþr, son* (OEN)
yet I must nurse the greatness of them both."

"And nurse your own," said Ymme soberly,
stretching across her breast to stroke his cheek.
"I pray our Lord will ease your worries, dear one.   *liufr* (OEN)
He made the Danes and longs for them to know him,
just as he made the Saxons and the Franks."

But Halga said with sudden bitterness,
"Somewhere some troll, the imp of Athelwulf,   *Alfred*
is mustering a secret Saxon host.
If that unreal Mervyn the Physician
harms one whisker on our chief's chin,
he'll wish he'd never squirted from his mother."
He laughed, emitting a sharp, vulpine bark.
The seed of Hemming nuzzled his young maid,   *Halga*
but Ymme felt a shiver up her neck.

∽∞∾

Ten nights had passed since Beornwulf consigned
the pseudo-relics into Godrum's keeping
when Edward's father, desperately grateful,   *Alfred*
again breathed the chill dark at his side.
No moonlight whitewashed Athulf's lodge, for cloud
blanketed the upper and lower heavens,
though cheerful voices, mingling with the gleemen's
measures, filtered down from the unseen eaves.
Like devils who detest the joys of men,   *"atolum aglæcum,*
the swineherd and his secret chief conspired   *Caines cynne": dire*
and parted with religious valedictions,   *monsters, offspring of*
when suddenly two strangers seized the king.   *Cain*

"So Welsh Mervyn has a Saxon friend,"   **uin* (OEN)
said one as Alfred strained against their strength.
"You know they hate us, sir," the other twitted,
mimicking the churl's servile drawl.

The seed of Ingeld knew Lord Halga's son   *Alfred*
and guessed the other was the mollusc-eater,   *Wan*
chief of the clam-foraging Limfjord men.
Alfred thought of Wisdom's dear philosopher,   *Boethius*
whose letters to the emperor the Goths   *Emp. Justin I 518–527;*
under Theodoric had intercepted—   *K. Theodoric d. 526*
Theodoric, the father of us all.
The heretic confined his minister
and had him questioned—*id est,* clubbed to death—
but not before he filled five wondrous books
with literature on Wisdom and her Lord.

"The swineherd is a faithful servant, sirs,"
said Alfred, baiting his interrogators.
"Delivering the Saxon king's remains,
he brought our king security and joy."

"As you have done," the junior fiend replied. *Hrothulf*
"Your name is recognized throughout Saxonia
as that of Gorm's counselor, and his leech."

"And of Gorm's fetch," the other devil said. **fulkia* (OEN)
"But Gorm's royal kinsman needs your care." **fronti* (OEN)

"I suffer," Hrothulf said. "I sweat. I pine.
An evil **alfr* blocks me on my path: *elf* (OEN)
the wretched, murdered, prophesying wizard
the Saxons and the Welsh adore as Lord."

"He works through witching women," Wan pursued.
"The Frankish wench has feminized his father
and nurtures a usurper in her womb."

"While Gormr courts the Saxon queen," said Hrothulf, **trutnik* (OEN)
"and promises her son will rule the Danes."

"You shall repel this troll," the earl said, *Wan*
"by cursing Christian Ymme with your herbs."
"By cursing Alfred's widow," Hrothulf said, **ankia* (OEN)
"and Gorm, who means to reign in Edward's name."

"My Jutish chiefs mistake me," Alfred quailed.
"I am Godrum's loyal slave, and though
you mock the Savior, I too revere him."

"You think us fools?" demanded Halga's son. *Hrothulf*
"You think no druids dwell in Dorchester,"
the black berserker scoffed, "no cunning men?" *Wan*
"You'll help us," said the hero, "with your spells."
"And then," said Wan, "you shall install this prince **iufur* (OEN)
as overlord of all the British kingdoms." **rikir* (OEN)
"For we know who you are," said Hemming's scion. *Hrothulf*

"And we know what you are," said Jarl Wan,
"foresightful, potent, venerable *Merlin.*"

At last the gleeman grasped their argument.   *Alfred*
He shuddered as the lesser light, uncovered,   *tungolscin* (OE)
defined his foes and lit their tenuous breath.
"Wala, you have sniffed me out," said Alfred.
"Midnight tonight, I'll howl an elfish spell
to purge these elfish evils from your souls."

VIII.

Visit with a Witch

୶

*The earls arbitrate a dispute between Hrothulf and Wiga. In a private
meeting with Guthrum, Alfred summons his own departed spirit. Hrothulf
rebels. With Beornwulf's help, Alfred attempts to rescue his family.*

The raven flag, untouched by meager rays
escaping from the fragrant reek, their prison,
to sparkle on the fastenings that prinked
the earls' pelts and silks, hung high above
the one-eyed bard who stood in shadow next
to Godrum's trophy of his final triumph:
a wooden cross displaying Alfred's helm,
his Frankish sword, his chain-mail coat, his cloak,
and the piteous crucifix of tusk   *flotmenn* (OE); K.
the float-men had filched from Edmund's hoard.   *Edmund d. 870*

"Welcome to our refurbished hall," said Gormr,   ★*hal* (OEN)
"especially Lord Wiga and Lord Hrothulf,   ★*Uiki,* ★*Ruulf* (OEN)
who bring your controversy to this body
instead of craving comfort from the choosers.   ★*kyrriu* (OEN)
By way of thanks, you'll each lead home a calf   ★*kalfr* (OEN)
fatted on milk and mash in Alfred's barn."

Lord Wiga, with his pained, important mien,
aware of the distrust the rugged Jutes   ★*Iotar* (OEN)
cherished towards the royal *locum tenens,*
indeed towards all the haughty Zealand men,   ★*Siulunt* (OEN)
stood and scanned the faces round the table.

131

"High lords," the Ringsted nobleman began,
"as assignee of Cuthred's lands at Twinham—"

"Excuse me, rulers," Hrothulf interposed,
"but isn't it ridiculous, and strange,
that we should wrangle over a dead Saxon?
Our Haca was provoked," the hero urged,   *halr (OEN)
"for which the meddling monk was justly punished.
That said, let Hampshire's high steward speak,   *hofþiki (OEN)
but not before you satisfy our queries
pertaining to the nature of this meeting."

Wiga glanced at Godfred's grandson's face,
a sea whose skin no swimming serpent creased.   *snakr (OEN)
"Go on," said Gorm, aware beyond all doubt
the youngster meant to dent his dignity.
Wiga sat as Hrothulf moved behind
their chief and placed two paws on his broad shoulders.

"First," he said, "confirm our friend and cousin   *fronti (OEN)
presides here as a brother lord, a peer,
not as our king or as our *dux bellorum*.   *kunukr (OEN)
We've come to settle private grievances,
not seek direction from our martial council."

The warrior's presumption irked the earls,
who knew he gloried in his royal blood.   *bloþ (OEN)
"That's so," conceded murdered Godfred's scion,   *Godrum/Gormr*
"that's why no Saxons sit with us today
except, of course, our Nordalbingian friend,   *Theodric*
whom I don't even think of as a Saxon.
That cohort meets tomorrow. We expect
Lord Wulfhere, our co-regent, to attend.
Athelnoth has raised a force on the Thone."

Ingeld's seed, unmoving in the gloom,   *Alfred*
felt like a falcon's flapping, plunging prey
that dives into the shelter of an elm
only to tumble out the other side,
exposed to his pursuer's twitted fury.
So Athelnoth yet kept his men in arms—
yet Wulfhere's men would muster with the Danes!

"Second, heads," said Hrothulf, rounding on Alfred,
"must we deface the wisdom of the Danes
by suffering this Christian in our midst?
Doesn't he have hogs to slop or slaughter?"
He clutched a fistful of the harper's shirt
and scrutinized his eye, his hair, his scars.
"We hear he scorns our gods," the youth pursued.   *Hrothulf*
"We hear our cousin lends his ear to twaddle
on how the Roman god was born a slave
who let himself be nailed up and speared.
Don't let that wizard part us from our fathers
who fry, the Christians say, with Frey and Grim."

Said Wiga, "Don't balk at their so-called Savior.
Our rulers haven't banned the Christian shrines,   *hærar* (OEN)
which comfort traders up from Christian countries.
If Hrothulf grieves for our neglected gods,   *kuþ* (OEN)
let him address his briefly royal uncle,   *K. Harald Klak acc.*
who licensed Anskar's mission to repay   *812, 819, 825; abp.*
the emperor for backing him as king."   *of Hamburg; Emp. Louis*

"Enough," admonished Gormr. "Mervyn stays.
Respecting his religion, we may study
the customs of the foreigners we govern."

Now Alfred listened as the Ringsted lord
recounted killings by Lord Hrothulf's crews.

He watched as honest sailors climbed the dais   *æscmenn* (OE)
and told what they had seen and heard and done.
The Saxon nation-king detested hearing   *þeodcyning* (OE)
foreign lords expounding foreign laws
on Saxon soil, yet he recognized
that men adept in council, war, and trade
would make fit ministers for Saxon princes
if they would only bow to heaven's King.
Indeed, he marveled at our Father's mercy,
which grants even to fiend-ridden strangers—
men who'd never chewed on Lupus' digest   *Lupus abb. of Ferrières*
of Salic, Ripuarian, and Lombard codes,   *d. 862*
as well as Alamannic and Bavarian—
which grants even devilish invaders
the wherewithal to manacle their rancor
in bonds of law and nurture peace with judgment.
And yet, old Godrum and the seed of Hemming,   *Hrothulf*
this kingdom-builder and his junior scourge,
for all their deference to legal forms,
sought each to wield the harper's hidden arts
against his lawless, irritating rival.

Some hours later, in his counting room,
"Discourse, O leech," the weary heathen said,   *Godrum / Gormr*
"you saw how Halga's offspring mocked my office."   **afspriki* (OEN)

Old Mervyn paced the floor and wrung his hands.
The Dane had no more patience for delays,
but Alfred had a stratagem to sway him.
"Domne," he said, "when I learned Alfred's widow,   *lord* (OE)
as well as his remains, were in your hands,
I thanked the Thunderer, who'd heard my prayers.
But then he grudged me further signs and wonders,
so last night I lay down among the swine—
for dreams may come from devils or the Lord."   *fiend, Frea* (OE)

"And did you dream?" asked murdered Godfred's seed.   *Godrum / Gormr*
"I was back in Dumnonia as a boy,"
the harper said, "before King Ecgbert came,   *K. Ecgbert acc. 802*
the dragon egg the Germans call 'the Great.'
The sea was seething far beneath the cliffs,
as dark as lapis streaked with marble foam,
and gulls were lifting on the breeze like snowflakes.
Inside I found my mother at her altar."

From a cloth sack, the Saxon took a flask,
a beechwood bowl, and oak-plucked mistletoe.
"'Poor Mervyn,' said my mother," Alfred said,
"'you shall endure much grief before our Savior
reunites us in the Resurrection.
But you can always call on holy David   *6th c. bp. of Mynyw*
to disentangle your perplexities.
Burn mistletoe,' she said, 'the mystic sign   *misteltan* (OE)
that we survive our graves—'" Dead Ingeld's seed   *Alfred*
laid the plump spray on Godrum's brazier.
"'—then dab the sign of victory on your lips,'   *sigetacn* (OE)
she said, 'with water from last summer's hail.'"

"Another sign of deathless life," said Godrum.
"'But Mama,' I replied, 'your son is old now,'
for in the dream she saw me as a child.
She said no more, but stared at me with eyes
as vast and black as any painted saint's."

As Osburh's offspring blinked and wiped his cheek,   *Alfred*
the sailor stroked his silver-salted beard.   *Godrum / Gormr*
"Saint David," Alfred muttered seven times.
The seed of Godfred was about to speak
when the dull sprig broke into yellow flame.
The Saxon crumpled, widening his eyes.
"No!" he cried, "The smoke! The stink! The fiends!"

The pagan stared, his interest mixed with fear.
"What creeping thing defiles my prayers," said Alfred,
or the harsh ghost that occupied his throat,   *elf, demon* (OE),
"some ælf or orc, or the mongrel known as man?"   *monkyn* (OE)

Gorm's lips parted, but Alfred ducked and spun.
"So please your worship, Mervyn of Saint Merryn.
Is this the noted hermit, holy David?"

The harper turned to face himself and cried,   *Alfred*
"Saint David to the likes of you. Be gone!
But wait. A training angel hails me.
I see, sir. *Gise.* Yes. Thy will be done.
Son, a spirit needs to speak with you.   *sunu* (OE)
I must resume the arduous devotions
by which I scour the plaques that mar my soul."   *sawol* (OE)

Godrum clung unmoving to his perch,
gripping the seat with white-knuckled fists.
The harper rose, his clouded globe exposed,   *Alfred*
and rumbled at his interlocutor:

"Where is this epigone of Roman Brut,
slave to the Dane and traitor to the land
that fed him milk and honey all his days?"   *meolc, hunig* (OE)

The balding, one-eyed joculator quaked.   *Alfred*
"Down here I'm known as Mervyn the Musician—"

Straightening again, the Saxon roared,   *Alfred*
"As Mervyn the apostate renegade
shall you be cursed and damned forevermore
when heaven whips the heathens from this island!"   *hæðnas* (OE)

The farer frowned. The Athulfing looked down.   *ferend* (OE)
"I'm just a vile servant, holy lord.   *halig hlaford* (OE)

What can the likes of me—" "Silence!" he bellowed.
"You know that you're as free as any Caesar
to execute the King of King's commands.
The shield of righteousness, the sword of truth,   *scild, rihtwisnys, soþ*
the breastplate of faith, inlaid with stones   (OE)
spelling the names of the twelve reigning fathers,   *fæderas* (OE)
these things were given you in your blessed youth,
yet here you serve the devilish invader!
It is reported, worm, that you have conjured
ill spirits with your spells, unwholesome things,
who, but for your dear mother's wakeful prayers,
would speedily have drowned you in hell's mire."

Meek Mervyn bowed his head. "Have mercy, master,"
but angry Alfred brushed aside his plea.

"You have with you, have you not," he said,
his chest thrust forward like a dragon's prow,   *draca* (OE)
"the covetous, stubborn, lustful, wrathful chieftain,
the murderer the savage Danes call king?"

The pagan raised an unoffended hand.
"I'm here, I'm listening," said Godfred's seed,   *Godrum / Gormr*
"but why disparage us as savages?
The Saxons, who are murderers and worse,
currently occupy this lovely country,
which we want for our families and friends.
The Saxons' pastures, fields, orchards, woodlands—
their herds and flocks, their houses, folds, and byres—
we harvest what we need to live, no more,
which is our way as men. Of course we cow
the foreign folk, as any stranger must.
You call that savagery? We feed our sheep."

"*Weg la,* say you glut the jaws of wolves,"
the Saxon cried, "and make the fiend your god!   *Alfred*

You long to rehabilitate this kingdom?
The higher good, perverted, generates
the more devastating, venomous sin.
But know, you feller of your father's brother,   *K. Eric I d. 851*
that he who speaks, by the Almighty's grace,   *Ælmihtiga* (OE)
to steer your steps from their perilous path
is Alfred, progeny of Father Cerdic,
by grace, king of the West Saxon nation,   *leod* (OE)
of Surrey, Sussex, Essex, Wight, and Kent,
overlord of Cornwall, Gwent, and Dyfed,
whom the pope crowned consul of Britannia!"   *heretoga* (OE)

Relenting, Mervyn babbled to the Dane,   *Alfred*
"That nails it, chief. Your dead enemy's dead,
as dead as dirt, we say. His house has fallen,
folded into the filth from which it crawled."

"Keep your titles, ghost," said Godfred's grandson.   *Godrum / Gormr*
"Just tell me you have truly left this earth."

"You sot!" the son of Athulf cried. "You think   *sott* (OE)
departed spirits be strengthless beings?   *mægenleas* (OE)
Observe your Mervyn. We can cramp his bowels—"
"Ow!" he uttered, buckling—"Singe his footsoles—"
"Aye!" he cried, prancing on mashed reeds—
"Or choke his breath in his throat—" "Agh," he gurgled.
"We do not trouble you," the shade explained,
fixing the Jutlander with daunting eye,
"because we know the seed of godlike chieftains   *Godrum / Gormr*
disdains to yield his manhood to mere pain."

"You have my thanks," said Gormr, "Mervyn's too.
Now what about our other inquiries,
or do you charge a slug of blood to comment,
like our blade-ale-bibbing Danish elves?"

"Don't mock me, cousin," Alfred warned, "but hearken   *mæg* (OE)
to your last chance to duck the Father's wrath."

"What do you mean, 'cousin'?" Godrum asked,
"I know my blood relations all too well."

"We two descend," the seed of Sceaf said,   *Alfred*
"from Father Grim, the fruit of Frithuwald,
who led his nation north in hurried flight   *þeod* (OE)
when Pompey toppled Pontic Mithridates.   *Orosius bk. vi*
But what has old Woden to do with Christ?
You shall not die a heathen. *Na*, our Father
wields you as a rod to chide his children,   *cildru* (OE)
but he will judge the Danes, and they will pay
to the last faceless penny for their crimes."   *pening* (OE)

"He brings us here, then beats us for our trouble?
That's how we treat our slaves," the sailor said,
"but we don't claim their undying love."

"What foreign dog yaps at the Lord our God?"
cried Alfred. "Fiend, if you bow down to him,
release our fields, and restore our laws,
then you may triumph as the ninth *Bretwalda*   Britain-ruler (OE)
and leave a rich dominion to your heirs.
But woe if you refuse his clemency
and spit on his commiserating hand!"

"Of what heirs do you speak?" retorted Godrum.
"Will your long-suffering Christian widow bear—"

"Touch one blessed hair," the spirit cried,
"and you'll endure unceasing punishments,
punctures, fractures, burns, abrasions, maimings—"

"Compose yourself," said Gormr, unperturbed,
"for as you say, a Dane disdains mere pain.
You want your Edward to succeed—I'll crown him—
and drown the twins if Wulfhere interferes.
But what if Father Woden, who sees all,   *Open (OEN)
or the sole God the Saracens adore
or the Greeks' gold-panoplied Pantocrator
should override and thwart your prophecies?
The Danes will say I cheated god and man
just to salve my old-womanish conscience."

Impatiently, the Athulfing exclaimed,   *Alfred*
"Our father has submitted. He atones   *Orosius bk. vi*
for his unnumbered sins by continuous prayer."

"Not in your Christian hell," the northman answered,
"where Radbod said to Bishop Willibrord   *k. of Frisians d. 719; St.*
he'd rather roast forever with his forebears."   *Willibrord d. 739*
"Nearby," the Saxon said, "in shrieking distance.   *Alfred*
Where men and men upheld by men as gods,
whom evil angels have impersonated—"

"I've been there," Godfred's seed declared, "I've seen him.
At least he need not watch the honored dead
hack and gorge, gorge and hack till doomsday.
But may I speak with our wise ancestor?
Get his advice on shepherding these sheep?
I'd also like to chat with my poor Harald,"   *Godrum's s.*
he added with transparent carelessness.

"Nese," Alfred said. "We have business here.   *no* (OE)
You must admit the Lord God's sovereignty   *Dryhten, dryhtendom,*
now, or damn the Danes to endless death!"   *deaþ* (OE)
The pirate pondered, disinclined to bare   *Godrum / Gormr*
his soul to such an unindulgent judge.
"We think it best," the heathen captain said,

140

"not yet to brave the celebrated bath.
Your herdsmen aren't inured yet to our rule,
nor do the earls concur in governing
the shires as one realm. Thus many sins,
O brother king, remain to be incurred
before your God will hallow our new home.
The founders of your line were prudent men.
Old Cerdic and one, two, three, four successors
toiled long at mowing down the Welsh
before King Cynegils frisked in the flood."

K. Cerdic d. 534; K.
Cynric d. 560; K.
Ceawlin d. 593; K.
Ceol d. 597; K.
Ceolwulf d. 611
635

"You do not know the torment they endure,"
the seed of Ingeld answered solemnly,
"for spurning him they knew was hovering near—
nor what undying joy they might have won,
those kings and their imbrued *guþgesithas,*
had they revered our King instead of Grim."
Godfred's grandson offered no reply.
Alfred laid an oak split on the coals.

susl (OE)
Alfred

war-companions (OE)

Godrum/Gormr

"Then what if I accept the dip," said Godrum,
"espouse your mousy widow—ouch—and vow
not to enlarge our holdings save by gift,
devise, foreclosure, partnership, or purchase?"

"Thou shalt not palter with Almighty God!"
the harper cried. "Stiff-necked Cimmerian,
your hour is come: eternal bliss or torment!"

Alfred

"But am I not Artorius reborn,"
the sailor countered, slumping on his stool,
"avenger of the miserable Cymri?"

Godrum/Gormr

The Saxon started, stammered jaggedly,
then dropped, juddering, churning the trampled rushes.
The fearful heathen chieftain fell to his knees.

"Alfred son of Athulf, can you hear me?
I didn't refuse your offer. Let me speak
with my unjustly slaughtered son, my Harald."
A moment passed. "Whom call you, sir?" asked Mervyn,
rubbing his eyes as if to scatter sleep.

The seed of murdered Godfred helped him up.   *Godrum / Gormr*
"The Saxon king was here," he said, "young Alfred.
Your soul must have traveled to Christian hell."

"I know we summoned spirits," said the singer,   *Alfred*
"contrary to *Liffrea*'s living law."   *Life-Lord* (OE)

"Call for some honeyed wine," said Harald's father.   *Godrum / Gormr*
"And Alfred's willow harp, which you repaired.
We have a weighty matter to rehash
before the jarls gather at the trough."   *⋆iarlar* (OEN)

While they reposed, the alderman appeared,   *Wulfhere ald. of*
looking uncharacteristically concerned.   *Wiltshire*
"It's Hrothulf, *rector*. He has taken Wulfthryth   *wid. of K. Athelred;*
and her two sons, the athelings, my boys.   *Athelwold and*
It's mutiny. Wan fought and killed good Siward.   *Athelhelm*
Halga commands the gate. Lord Hrut is with him.
I swear I had no inkling of this treason."

The skipper scowled at Wulfhere's news and said,
"Tell them I'm coming. You keep out of sight.
Your presence is a sore spot with the earls."

Throughout this conversation, Alfred saw
Gorm's and Wulfhere's eyes shift to and fro,
both seeking, both evading, his dim orb
as though they recognized him, but conspired
to make believe he wasn't Wulfhere's *cyning*
and Gorm's hereditary enemy—

as though to give him time, if so God willed,
to cut their throats and repossess the throne.
For his part, Alfred loved his brother-sons   *broðorsuna* (OE)
as much as their grandfather Wulfhere did,   *ealdefæder* (OE)
but lacked the men and arms to ransom them
just as he lacked the means to free his family.
He felt like one submerged in evil dreams,
though truly every passage of his life,
the best, the worst, lit up by grace or sin,
both when he lived it, and in memory,
betrayed a like dreamlike, elvish sheen.

The alderman departing, Godrum said,
"She threw herself at Hrothulf. We have eyes—   *Wulfthryth*
some of us more than one—and we have ears.
I half-believe your devils are behind this,
scourging me for serving my own folk.   *folk* (OEN)
You take this blade," the Jutlander continued,   *Godrum/Gormr*
proffering a polished antler grip,
"and ride to where we hold the Saxon royals.
Take Edward and my lady and some guardsmen
to Cirencester and wait for my instructions.   *"Siziter"*

"The loss of Smala's son strikes at our heart,"
he said, "as though Lord Wan were now our god.
He'd fixed a date with Tunbert for his christening.   *bp. of Winchester*
Lord Wiga would have joined him in that plunge."   *⋆Uiki* (OEN)

The devil rose. "You disappoint me, Mervyn.
If not for you, I would have crooked the knee
to him who hammered out this hellish tale,
the lord low wretches tortured on the cross."

Gorm stepped into the corridor, then peered
at Grim's remote descendant through the doorway.   *Alfred*
"If the lad gives you grief, just cut his throat.   *Alfred's s.*
It's a meager, ambiguous revenge,

but Harald won't disown it, nor will I. *Godrum's. s.*
And your all-loving Savior will forgive
a Briton butchering a Saxon atheling."

Nearing the croft, King Alfred heard the noise
of fighting men and the ill clash of steel. *billgesliht* (OE)
He found the Selwood men pressing the cottage,
outnumbering Godrum's guards, who goaded them
with swords and swearwords in their northern tongue.
The singer slid to earth, the swamping sun *scop* (OE)
glazing his blade—he'd snatched it from the hall—
glazing his blade the gold of Weland's forge.

"Mervyn!" shouted Ulf, old Godrum's steersman,
"back to the beer-hall, now, and send some men!"
A Briton turned to spear the new arrival,
but Beornwulf exclaimed, "My cunning king!"
The pagan Danes, puzzled to see their harper, *Alfred*
old Hilda's one-eyed husband of a night,
advancing, weapon bared, through slanting beams,
now faltered, fearing a fraud wrought by Grim.
Beornwulf stuck one beneath the ribs,
who crumpled like a sail struck inshore,
as Alfred hewed another through the shoulder.
The sailor leaned left and pinned Ulf's elbow, *lid* (OE)
which Denewulf observing, swung his oar
at Gorm's steersman's *healsbeorhleas* neck. *hauberk-less* (OE)
The forehand effort floated forcelessly
but the Lord God's misericord allowed
dear Denewulf to deadhead able Ulf.

"Yield, fiends!" the Athulfing declaimed. *Alfred*
"Your Godrum, Gormr the Great, is in the dust!"

"Surrender Guttorm's queen?" a brigand answered.
"Better to bleed out while sticking Saxons!"

He thrust, and as the monarch made to parry
he glimpsed a glinting implement approach
the man's mailless back, trailing a wrist.
He wheeled and whipped a gleaming arc behind him
but hurled high at Hilda's hunching head,
his edge catching fast in the dwarfish doorjamb.
King Alfred stabbed his unprotected side   *ungescilded* (OE)
and hacked into the ridge right of his neck.

Like Cynewulf's last man, who scorned to serve   *K. Cynewulf d. 786;*
the killer of his king, the comer coiled   *killed by br. of*
then launched into the pack, slashing attackers,   *K. Sigebert d. 757*
until a swineherd seized his slippery arm,
another pried the hide grip from his fist,
and Beornwulf and both big British lads
wrestled the rough, still wriggling, to the ground.   *rinc* (OE)
Alfred saw him fade, just as he felt
the first taps of wet, then followed Hilda
under the cracked lintel of old oak.

The gloom within was dimmer than the twilight,
the embers lighting nothing but themselves,
and the void quiet after wild swordplay   *sweordplega* (OE)
opened a sudden gulf in Alfred's thought.
Drawn to the far corner, he discovered
a drift of tiny ghosts, their features lit
by a single soot-proliferating candle.
They gaped up at the shape, *spatha* in hand,   *sword* (L)
that loomed and blocked all escape from the cottage.

Pitying their fear, he sought his lady
and spied a shadow squatting on a footstool
beside which, on the sacking, Athelflaed
sat with baby Athelward in her arms.
His daughter's eyes, wary, juniper-gray,
looked roofward from the rampart of her brow,

the elf epitomizing Ealhswith
as always—not her gaiety and trust,
but her God-given righteousness and courage.   *rihtwisnys* (OE)

The candle lit the Mercian matron's shoulder;
a treasury of bracelets cuffed each wrist,
some known to Alfred, some unknown and foreign.
Shuddering as the sun of wedded love
commenced to melt the filth that clogged his heart,
the monarch knelt and held his helpmeet's shoe.

"Come, quean," the man commanded tenderly.   *cwen* (OE)
"We've relieved your Jutish guard, but Hrothulf's rowers,
berserkers who are murderers and worse,
will soon be here to press their ugly work."
Despite his fear, despite the nearing fiends,
joy sprouted in him like an acorn.

"I knew you'd come too late," the lady murmured.   *ides* (OE)
"I promised, to preserve these little ones—"

"We must abscond, my darling," Alfred answered.   *leof* (OE)
"He's broken every oath he ever swore.
This knife, which you may recognize, is both
his token to deliver you from Hrothulf
and my direction in re our lamb."

"Dogmatically, I claimed the mourning time,"
she said, "that our law grants abandoned wives,
but then he led me to a thawing carcass   *hræw, gefrætwe,*
fraught with the adornments of my lord.   *frea* (OE)

"I thought it was an artifice, a trick,"   *unwrenc* (OE)
she added. "Day and night I fed the hope
my husband would exterminate our jailers.
But no heavenly angel broke this prison,   *heahengel* (OE)

146

and then I learned my Alfred was nearby
and knew the merman's mind but martyred no one,
despite our wedding vows at Wigstan's tomb." *St. Wystan d. 850; K.*
For Wigstan, Wiglaf's grandson, was her cousin. *Wiglaf d. 840; K.*
King Beorhtwulf had murdered him for barring *Beorhtwulf acc. 840; K.*
the marriage of his mother, Ceolwulf's daughter, *Ceolwulf I acc. 821*
to Beorhtfrith, the king's ambitious son,
on grounds, now unexplained, of consanguinity.

Uncomprehendingly the children stared
save Elfthryth, whom the Spirit moved to laugh.
Poor Alfred's heart turned over in his chest.

"You take the *lytlingas,*" he said to Hilda, *little ones* (OE)
unable to absorb his consort's words.
He feared she might smash in the children's heads
as Gaulish mothers did, who then self-slew *Orosius bk. v*
when the southern sun melted their men at Aix.

"Don't try to breathe life in the dead, my friend," *freond* (OE)
said Ealhswith. "It cost my life, this change
of loyalty. I do not have another."

"A promise under threat of death," said Alfred
at random, "may with justice be withdrawn.
Like John the Apostle, we may sleep, yet live."
How changeable the poor thing's face, he thought,
aglow in former times with heaven's daylight,
now ugly and distorted as a devil's.

"I don't know how I earned your hate," she said, *Ealhswith*
"though hating me, you hate yourself, for we
are man and wife, one flesh, or so they say. *wer and wif, leof,*
You turned away, my love. Now listen, lord. *hlaford* (OE)
Before the fiends had even crossed the border
you had a plan to shut us up in Frome.

Although I had attended on my lord
since I departed from my home, and clove
to you—although I kept your bed alone
the lean years you toiled in the field—
although I crossed five times the deadly strait
of the birth bed to fetch your progeny—"

"Bone of my bone," King Athulf's offspring answered,   *ban of minum*
smearing the streaks on his blood-mudded cheeks.   *banum, bearn* (OE)
"I sent my guards. I thought it was a raid."

"You thought, you thought," she said, "and while
you thought—   *Ealhswith*
he's an old *guþfrea*, like my father—   *warlord* (OE)
I gather neither of you wants me now,
but this time I'm not going anywhere."

"Come," said Alfred, holding out his hand,
"only the Lord can see inside our hearts."

"Go," said Ealhswith, "and take your yield.
I wrong him, though, in giving you our son."   *sunu* (OE)

The king felt Hilda's shallow breath behind him.
"Come out of here, dear Athelflaed," she begged.

"I must attend my lady," she replied.   *hlæfdige* (OE)
"She won't survive alone among the fiends."
She spoke as freely as a wise confessor,
as boldly as a black-gorgeted sparrow
defending its abode from harrying crows.

"Come, sir," said Hilda. "You can only run."
Speechless, Alfred knelt before the girl,
encircling her slight stem in snaking limbs.

"Now go," said Ealhswith, dropping her eyelids.
Following Hilda, Alfred turned once more
and saw his spouse's face interred in shadow.
As Simeon said, the sword pierced his soul,   *Luke 2:35*
"suam animam pertransit gladius,"
or *"þæt sweord hine sawle þurhfor."*
He saw his daughter crush close to her dam,   *dohtor* (OE)
pillowing her head on layered gems,
as with one hand, her mother touched her cheek   *modor* (OE)
and with the other, pinched the beating flame.

IX.

The Flight into Athelney

෴

Alfred and company flee Chippenham. They bypass Bath, take refuge in a cave, and skirt the flooded moors, reaching Athelnoth's encampment on Easter morning.

Have mercy, Maker, on your chosen child	*Metod, cild* (OE)
and let your rainfall irrigate and thin	
the poisons coursing through his spirit-home.	*feorhbold* (OE)
Defend him as you shielded King Edwin	*K. Edwin d. 632*
from fever on his promise to convert	
when our Eomer needled him at Easter;	*626*
spare him as you spared Saint Benedict,	*St. Benedict d. 543*
whose envious brothers dosed the evening wine,	*broðor* (OE)
by shattering their pitcher as it passed;	*crocchwer* (OE)
and fortify him as you toughened John,	*St. John the Apostle*
for whom the pagans poured a poisoned pot	*attordrinca* (OE)
as once they served subversive Socrates.	
Don't let him perish like his predecessor,	
West Saxon Beorhtric, who bibbed the brew	*K. Beorhtric d. 802*
his *ides,* Eadburh, King Offa's daughter,	*lady* (OE)
prepared for Worr, her husband's favorite hoard-guard.	*hordweard* (OE)
She fled to Charles the Great, her father's friend,	
but spurning him in favor of his son	*sunu* (OE); *Charles s. of*
and irking him with her poor governance	*Charles*
of the now-unknown nunnery he gave her,	*nunnhired* (OE)
she died alone, in poverty, in Pavia—	
where Liutprand entombed Augustine's bones.	*d. 744; d. 431*

Veiled by falling rain and falling night,
the company emerged from sodden woods
and crossed a sodden field, yet unplowed.
They forded Avon just above the mill,
below the flooded claypits and the shops
where potters wound and welded snakes of clay
into bowls, beakers, pitchers, pots, and jars.
From there they headed west to Slaughterford,
from which they straggled, via greasy tracks,
up the hills that hedged West Saxon land.
The rain had lifted and the moon had sunk,   *Mar. 19, 878*
uncurtaining the darkness to the west,
when Beornwulf addressed young Athelgeofu,
poor Ealhswith's and Alfred's second daughter.

"Yonder Dyrham lies," the hero said,
"where Ceawlin and our pagan ancestors   *K. Ceawlin acc. 560;*
killed three Cymric kings and crushed their legions.   *577*
He planted Hwiccan folk from Bath to Gloucester."
He paused, but Ingeld's scion added nothing.   *Alfred*

"They were a Saxon clan," said Denewulf,   *mægþ* (OE)
"but Mercian kings cut them off from their root.
Now even their kings' names are lost to speech."

King Alfred turned his mare southwest and rode
the Roman road by which, victorious,
he'd trailed the sailors after Exeter.   *877*
He stopped at last beneath the ruined roof
of an old Roman horseman's tiled mansion,
since frequented by herdsmen and their flocks.   *hyrdeas, heorda*
The meager wing, including their worn steeds,   (OE)
crowded, a steaming mass, into a corner.

Next night, his flock refreshed—save Athelward,
who wouldn't take his pap from Hilda's finger—

the mood-sorrowing monarch marched his mare   *modcearig* (OE)
across the threshold into drenching gloom.
Shunning the town Minerva's waters warmed,   *Bath*
they swam their steeds across the swollen *Afen,*   *Avon* (OE); *Mar. 20,*
now shrouded by the downpour and the dark,   *878; St. Cuthbert*
i.e., the shadow cast by the western ocean.
The troubled suckling sobbed incessantly
as the beasts braved the gushing Mendip grade,
until familiar Hilda charged the king
to find a hiding place from heaven's weep.

The Selwood Britons knew a nearby cave
that could accommodate them, man and mammal,   *mearh, horse* (OE)
but which unquiet *ylfa* occupied,   *elves* (OE)
the souls of British folk who'd gone to ground
before Artorius swept Badon Hill.   *ca. 500*
Dismounting, they crept up the drowning slope,
and soon the soaked company was gathered
within the cavern's humid vestibule.
The herders raised a smoky blaze from sticks
their brother herders had collected there,
and when the spent band was bedded down,
Athulf's offspring plucked a burning brand   *Alfred*
and stepped into the black throat of the hollow.   *hol* (OE)

He knew he had dishonored Father Cerdic   *Cerdic d. 534*
by forfeiting his kingdom to the foe—   *feond* (OE)
indeed, he'd forfeited his very manhood.   *werhad* (OE)
Alone in this remote, low-ceilinged tomb
he might relieve his people of the taint
his sin would drizzle on their hearts forever.
He drew his knife, the kind once knapped from stone, *saxum* (L)
from which the hardy Saxons took their name
before Weland taught them to soften iron.
Freed from his foulness, Athelnoth and Odda   *Odda ald. of Devon*
would set up Edward atheling as their king.

The Saxon's footstep quickened; then he stopped.
Did he deserve to see his son succeed?
What if our high Deemer wanted him   *Demend* (OE)
to slaughter Edward and his other lambs
to quash the propagation of his shame?

The twig lit up a pillar not far off
the Lord had dyed with tinctures of the sky
and rusty swords drooped like thorns from the roof.
Another, straighter, column just ahead
was stained the verdigris of fir or pine
and at its base, abandoned, sat a skull.
The flame-light glistened on the king's keen edge
and on his living nails, and now he knew
our fathers' God, the Lord of Hosts, was near.
He spoke no word of judgment or command,
nor did he illustrate the curse of sin,
nor figure forth the fortunes of his folk,
yet Alfred, son of Athelwulf, was changed.
He felt as if he'd wakened from a dream.
"There is a God in Israel," he said,   *1 Sam. 17:46*
and then in book Latin said the same,   *boclæden* (OE)
"Hodie est Deus in Israel."

The moon had risen and the sun had sunk   *Good Friday, Mar. 21,*
when Alfred and his squadron halted where   *878; St. Benedict;*
the Roman road to Salisbury began.
"Men," he said to Denulf and his crew,   *Searburh, secgas* (OE)
"you've freed our family from our iron bonds.   *isenfetora* (OE)
Your wives and children yearn for your return.
This army road will take you home. Now go."   *herestræt* (OE)

"You misconstrue your troops," said Denewulf
without so much as glancing at the herdsmen.   *Luke 9:62; onward,*
"We've put our palms to the plow. *Porro, princeps.*"   *prince* (L)

154

Passing the last crest of the Mendip heights,
the company descried a glittering net
of icy stars thrown by the near-full moon
over the flooded Somersetan moorlands.
Heaven on earth lay spread below that vantage,
though Hilda said the imp was deathly ill.

Descending, they took shelter in a barn,
disquieting sheeted cattle where they slept,
and when they met the husbandman at daybreak
they breakfasted on saffron-colored cheese
and cider redolent of marrow bones.
The king declared they'd fled from Holt in Wiltshire
intent on joining up with Athelnoth
at Athelney, the hummock in the flood.

"An eager chief, for now our country's king,"   *eðelcyning* (OE)
the churl said, to Denewulf's dismay,
"and we may join you there if Eadric,
the king's thane at Wells, calls up his throng.   *þegn* (OE)
You'll need a pair of punts to float your ponies.
Best let them rest until this weather breaks."

Alfred set out at nightfall with the men   *Mar. 22, 878;*
and Edward, leaving Hilda and the babe   *ecclesiastical full*
and puzzled Athelgeofu and Elfthryth   *moon*
behind to quarter with the cattle-herders.   *cuhyrdeas* (OE)
They skirted Glastonbury's flooded shores,
a kindly shower wafting from the clouds
and screening even its outline from sight.
"I'd love," said Athulf's son to Denewulf,
"to see again the chapel where our Lord,
who traveled here in youth, prayed to the Father
and the mud hut from which he watched the ducks
and which he consecrated to his mother.   *modor* (OE)
I'd love to see again the flowering thorn   *St. Joseph of*

155

Joseph, his relation, planted here, *Arimathea; gesweor,*
when he returned to preach Christ to the Britons, *Bryttas* (OE)
and contemplate, again, Saint David's sapphire.
I'd love to ambulate the abbey grounds *K. Coenwalh acc. 643;*
that Coenwalh confirmed to Bregored, *abb. ca. 667*
to hear mass in Ini's Roman church, *K. Ini acc. 688*
and feel the perpetual choir's swell."

Only Denewulf heard Alfred's comments.
"I pray my king may soon enjoy these things,"
the swineherd said, "but now is not the time.
Tonight we recollect our Lord's descent
to hell and the victory he won there. *guþgewinn, battle* (OE)
Besides, the holy isle is thick with devils."

They splashed and swam across the sunken Brue
and turned south, then bent west with the Cary,
threading the poplars, elms, and ill-shaped willows
that cloaked the feet of the low Polden Hills.
Soon they forded, flailing physical moonlight,
and swashed across the moat that ringed Ham Hill.
Mounting the slant past ragged apple trees, *æppeltreow* (OE)
Alfred espied three tortured trunks up top
that loomed above the long-abandoned works.
He signaled Denewulf, who cried, "Redeemer!
You know our misery, for you were sold
and mocked and scourged and tried and crucified.
And on the day that thrust us in this darkness,
you cried your Father had forsaken you." *Fæder; Ps. 21:2*
Each traveler carved the King's cross on his chest.

They found another crumbling Roman home
whose tessellated pavement told the tale
of a tall spearman landing from abroad,
Aeneas, maybe, or his grandson Brutus.
It showed him marrying a naked dame

attended by two hovering naked striplings.
Flanked by twinned, sinuous, man-sized trees,
the couple pledged their heaven-sponsored love,
a scarlet, snake-like scarf or garment girdling
the sinuous trunk of the stout, lustrous bride.
"*Non sicut ego volo,*" Alfred murmured.   "*not as I will*"; *Matt.*
Decent Denulf, dumb with dread, looked down.   *26:39*

They searched the neighboring shore for fitting craft
in which to skim the inundated moor.
Watching a house, which they perceived the seamen   *sæmenn* (OE)
had seized to keep an eye on Athelney,
they found a pair of punts equipped with poles.
Then Sceaf's scion started up the trail   *Alfred*
to scrutinize the devils' bivouac.
"Brother," Beornwulf breathed and briskly followed, *broðor* (OE)
expecting him to wreak a swift revenge
as when our Lord plundered the ancient foe.   *ealdfeond* (OE)

The sinking moon disclosed no sentinels,
but unlike Nisus and his friend, who pricked   Aeneid *bk. ix*
scores of befuddled Latins where they slept;
unlike the Saxons under Hathagath,
who ran the Thuringians through in darkness,   *þeostru* (OE)
forestalling their unfaithful Frankish friends;   *Scheidungen 531*
and unlike that voracious spawn of Cain
who gobbled thirty guardsmen, numb with guzzling,
they fled the stead without a single kill,
for they intended, with Lord Athelnoth,
to drive the Danish devils from the realm,
not just to murder them as fate allowed—   *wyrd* (OE)
to hide themselves, like our cloud-buried *Beorn,*   *hero* (OE)
until they deemed the time was right to strike.

They rested all that day, and when the glorious,
the overplump, the post-paschal moon   *Easter Sunday,*

157

scaled the eastern sky, expounding triumph,   *Mar. 23, 878*
they pushed the punts around and shipped the steeds.   *stedan* (OE)
"Yesterday, the fifth day came to pass,"   *Gen. 1:21; fifta dæg*
said Denewulf, now poling off from shore,   (OE)
"when he first fashioned fishes, fowls, and whales."

"He formed the fish from water, densified,"
said Alfred, one hand trailing in the flow,
"the fowl from finer vapors up above.
Amphibians, like crocodiles and seals,
like hippopotami and walruses,   *nicras, horshwalas,*
the otters who scrubbed Cuthbert's feet with their fur, *oteras* (OE)
and like the *luligo,* who flocks aloft
six months a year, the other six afloat,
he must have made by mixing thick and thin."

"The day before, he lit the firmament,"   *Gen. 1:14-19*
said Denewulf, "with round refulgences
to warm the earth and turn the calendar.
He launched the other so-called wandering stars,
which we know by their pagan names, like Venus.
Et factum est," he added, "the fourth day."   *feorþa dæg* (OE)

"Bede claims he hoisted the full moon at sundown,"
said Alfred, "which depicts his lit-up church.
That time returns, Egyptian sages say,
when night and daylight gallop neck and neck
the twelfth calends of April every year.   *Mar. 21*
The Nicene bishops blessed that calculation   *325*
but now, in nature, equal day and night
come earlier, I think, by about a week,
while the natural full moon anticipates
the Church's by two circuits of that body.
Thus providentially, our *Frea*'s feast,   *Lord* (OE)
in this year of uncountable disasters,
follows a full moon that rose before,

not after, as the Prophet's law commands,   *Ex. 12:6*
the equinox the fathers ratified,
but doubly providentially it yet
will follow the one his handmaid displays.
In short, our tables are so wrong, they're right."

"You listen to your king," said Denewulf   *mentel* (OE)
to Edward, huddled under Alfred's mantle.   *Gen. 1:9-13; gærs,*
"The third day, he threw shores around the floods   *treow* (OE)*; morning*
and heaped up earth, which sprouted grass and trees.   *and evening* (L)*; se*
Mane et vespere were the third day."   *þridda dæg* (OE)

"We made landfall in a dead Briton's barrow,"
said Ingeld's seed, "then savored bread and cheer   *Alfred*
from the churl's herb and apple-bearing *treow.*   *appelbære* (OE)
Corporeal things," he added, squeezing Edward,
"unlike the angels, yield after their kind."

"The second day, he fixed his *firmamentum,"*   *Gen. 1:6-7; uprodor,*
Beornwulf declared, "and called it heaven.   *heofon* (OE)
He propped the upper waters on his tree."

"A deluge pounded us from on high,"
the Saxon monarch somberly recalled,   *Alfred*
"the Avon's swollen *frigidarium*   *cooling pool* (L)
the sole ablution granted us at Bath."

They heard the water slapping at the boards,
the hollow thump and slosh of shifting hooves,
and their low voices carrying in the dark.   *Gen. 1:3; geweorðe*
The elder swineherd ventured, *"Fiat lux—*   *leoht* (OE)*; and there*
let there be light, and *leoht wearþ geworht."*   *was light* (OE)

"A chill light it was," the people's king   *leoht, leodcyning* (OE)
said, "its beams piercing the vitreous deep.
We iterate that day the fifteenth calends,   *Mar. 18*

three days before he lit the heaven-candles."
The king fell silent as the wavelets lapped.

heofoncandele (OE)

"The Word brought forth all things, all men agree,"
the seed of Ingeld said, in easier mood,
"the Word the Ruler got before all worlds.
But we have heard the heaven and earth he founded
were mere inchoate realms of soul and matter,
the matter formless yet, a next-to-nothing
from which he bred the elements we know."

Alfred
Wealdend (OE)

A gliding bank of clouds snuffed out the moon.
"Tomorrow he returns from hell," said Denulf.

"Hwæt la, tonight," the Saxon chief replied.
"A day is sown at dusk and sprouts in darkness.
On the sixth day, he molded man from clay
and woman from his rib-bone as he slept.
That doze was our demise, says John the Scot.
We closed our eyes to him and cherished sin."

se sixta dæg (OE); *Gen.*
1:27, 2:21-22
John Scotus Erigena d.
877

"That teaching we reject," said Denewulf.
"The woman was a blessing, not a curse.
Thus 'male and female he created them.'
Eve's daughter brewed our Savior in her womb."

"werhades and
wifhades, he gesceop
hig" (OE)
Hælend (OE)

"He made us flesh and blood today," said Alfred,
catching a fleeting glimpse of reconcilement,
"the day we praise and feast his resurrection."

"His victory blessed the age," said Denewulf,
"the Sixth Age of the world." King Alfred drifted.
He woke to gentle rain. The punt had struck
a tussock or a stump, and Paulus sought
to calm the clattering colts. The other craft
came up as white light limned the hulks of hills.

sige (OE)

"Here flooded Parrett meets the flooded Tone,"
the son of Athulf said to Denewulf,
"that pimple off our bow is Athelney."   *blædre* (OE)

Three men like angels held the muddy verge,
a trampled landing place among the sallows.
"Halt," cried one, "declare your names and purpose!"

By providence or mere coincidence,
King Alfred recognized the voice of Bucca,
the son of Athelsige, Taunton's thane.
Young Aeffa, Theobald's son, he also knew,   *"Tibbald"*
and tall Tata, an Aller farmer's son.
His cloak black and overweight with rain,   *bratt* (OE)
the seed of Sceaf struggled to his feet.   *Alfred*

"We're friends of Athelnoth's," he cried, "no rowers!"
"You come ashore alone," young Bucca shouted.
"And hold your boats a little farther off.
Good. Now throw us your spears and swords."   *wæpengeþræc* (OE)

The rain had ceased when Bucca and the king—
his hands bound fast, as if he were a traitor—
stepped up the track among the budding willows.
The Athulfing rejoiced to tread free earth.   *Alfred*
Rounding to greet the risen sun, whose coming
the improvising thrushes magnified,
he asked whether the folk would keep the feast.   *folc* (OE)

"The Mercian monk who served the king," said Bucca,
"served mass last night. Today we'll roast a lamb."   *lamb* (OE)

Soon Alfred saw a makeshift hut, then others,
and Saxons hauling water and hewing wood.
No man or woman recognized the king,
though one young creature quickly crossed herself

when she caught sight of his ill-boding eye.
Stopping, the youth knocked on a sagging lintel.

"Sir," young Bucca called, "a Saxon chieftain.   *leof* (OE)
With half a dozen men and seven mounts."
The thane of Somerton emerged bareheaded.   *þegn* (OE)
He scanned the prisoner's scars and weathered cheeks *hæftling* (OE)
and groaning, fell heavily to his knees.

"Down, soldier," barked the thane to startled Bucca.   *scealc, þegn* (OE)
"On your knees, and cut these shameful bonds.
Pardon, Lord. The boy still mourns his father.
As do we all. Lord Athelsige's dead."

The youngster knelt and said, "I thought you might— *cnapa* (OE)
I thought you were—I don't know what I thought."

"Another gap in the shield-wall," said Alfred.
It seemed to him that Athelnoth was making
a rapid calculation in his head.
"Your brother was my brother," Alfred added.   *broðor* (OE)

Soon other Saxons gathered, kneeling down
and calling out, "The king is here! The king!"
The Athulfing turned slowly where he stood,   *s. of K. Athelwulf d. 858*
imbibing with his unbenighted eye
a lonely people's longing for their lord.   *leod* (OE)
He greeted several ministers and friends
including Werwulf, his unwarlike cleric,
and Wiglaf and his brother, who, with Alfred,
had felled a fearsome tusker on that spot.   *eofor* (OE)

Sobs and embraces, joy and shame exchanged,
the seed of Ingeld cried, "We praise the Father,   *Alfred*
for he has loosed our Savior from the tomb!   *Hælend* (OE)
And as he floated Noah through the flood

with newborn Sceafa, his son, our father,   *Sceaf*
and set him on a summit striped with vines;
so has he spared our lives and brought us to you   *Gen. 9:30*
under this kindly blue and these high trees.
And just as he hid David from mad Saul
in woodlands, hill-forts, caves, and palaces,   *1 Kings 22:1, 5; 23:14-*
so has he shielded me from heathen fiends.   *18; 27:3*

"*Pax vobiscum,* Saxons. When the Lord   *peace be with you* (L)
first fetched our fathers to this footing
to fight the Picts and Scots for the drubbed Britons,
he gave them no more room than this low hill,
this hip, this hump, this Athelney, this clay!
Rejoice, friends, and feast his resurrection!"

With sharp applause the gathering disbanded,
and folk set about readying the meal.
Lavishly they fueled the cooking fires
and simmered *næpas* (turnips) and dried peas,
cabbages and beets, parsnips and carrots.   *cawelas, betan,*
They broiled trout and eels in the flames,   *feldmoran,*
cracked lapwing eggs to scramble with new ramsons, *wealhmoran, ælas,*
and briskly parted the blessed lamb from his dam.   *hramsan* (OE)
Before the sun, swimming the upper sky,   *sunne* (OE)
had touched the furculum of her excursion,   *turning point* (L)
the Saxons had forgathered in the clearing
to munch and gulp and jest in memory
of our Redeemer's temporary death.   *Alysend* (OE)

The feast dispatched, a grappling match was held
in which a fleshy Welshman won the cup,
the last ration of Athelnoth's red mead,
by bloodying a boy from Somerton.
Young Bucca bore away the bowman's prize,
the wrinkled, blood-black apple that he bored,

while one of Athelnoth's proficient tenants
merited half a length of boiled pudding
for outpoling the other seven punts
by half a length from a far, flooded elm

When the seventeenth moon had heaved its paunch
over the shire's corrugated bourn,
King Alfred joined his thane and Eanfled,   *þegn* (OE)
his lady, in the darkness of their hut.   *freo* (OE)

"Our chief has seen and shared our poverty,"   *hæfenleast* (OE)
said Athelnoth. "Our feast today will whet
tomorrow's fast. A sack of grain remains.
If need be, we'll survive on elver pie."
He halted, then resumed, his somber voice
a candle in the night to Alfred's ear.

"I fear, *Frea*, our meagerness of spirit   *Lord* (OE)
more than the devils and our lean-limbed fare.   *fiend* (OE)
We have a dozen sword-carrying guardsmen,   *sweordboran* (OE)
ready on any day to stake their hides
on ousting the horrible oarsmen from our country.
Another dozen nobles and their cousins
are here to fight for cattle, friends, and fields.
The rest are untrained husbandmen, good churls   *yrþlingas* (OE)
who may have clashed with badgers, wolves, and bears
but never with these veteran invaders.

"The boldest would join Athelheah in Selwood,"
the thane of grassy Somerton went on,   *þegn* (OE)
"and kill our less-than-welcome guests piecemeal.   *cwellan, bitmælum,*
I pray it is no sin to let, post-Easter,   *Easter* (OE)
the blood of men that shed our brothers' blood.   *Gen. 9:5; blod* (OE)

"The fearful urge surrender on such terms,"
Lord Athelnoth, invisible, continued,

"as lowliness might coax from Godrum's scorn.
They point to the prosperity of Wulfhere
and other Saxon chiefs who serve the sailors.

"Some Saxons even hold the time has come
for us to flee the fields our forebears seized,
citing Cunedda's settlement of Gwynedd   *K. Cunedda I 5th c.*
with the men he led south to fight the Scots.
They say we should petition our Welsh allies
for plots of dirt to plant new building-timbers.   *boldgetimbru* (OE)
We've spent a wretched winter in this prison."

The *cyning* lay in blackness on the bed
that Eanfled had spread with musty fleeces.   *fliesu* (OE)
"There is a God in Israel," he said.
"*Hodie est Deus in Israel.*   *1 Sam. 17:46*
We must not disappoint our fighting men,
for they hope in the Lord, a man of war.   *Ex. 15:3*
Tomorrow sundown, Beornwulf and I,"
he said, "with seven of our hoard- and hall-guards,   *hordweardas,*
will strike out for the nearest Saxon steading.   *seleweardas* (OE)
Night after night, our men will cross the moors,
spreading a sweat of fear among the sailors   *ferendas* (OE)
and gathering grub for growling Saxon bellies.
To nourish our people's souls, we'll build a church
and sing the psalms at nightfall and sunrise.
And every *wer and wif,* each man and woman,
will undertake the exercise of arms."

As Athelnoth took in his chieftain's words,
he sensed a largeness in his voice, which filled
the hut as though it were a vaulted hall.
Resuming, Sceaf's studious scion said,
"As for abandoning our fathers' country—
when Rome lost forty thousand men at Cannae
and the foes collected three pecks of rings,

Metellus moved to yield Italy.   *Orosius bk. iv*
But Scipio, *agnomen Africanus,*
holding his drawn sword to the senator's throat,
forced the man to swear to hold the land."

The king fell silent. Lady Eanfled,
after a pause, spoke from her rustling couch.
"I pray for dearest Ealhswith and Wulfthryth.
May *Frea* keep them safe among the Danes."   *the Lord* (OE)

Her words cut deep. Within the cabin's shadow
a thicker darkness shrouded Alfred's heart.
The wound was still too fresh, despite the mercy
the Lord had poured on him, for him to join
the lady in her prayer. He lay awake   *siþwif* (OE)
until an angel brushed his lids with sleep.

At daybreak, Alfred unsheathed his sword,
great Ecgbert's gift, you know, from Charles the Great,
and, followed by the thane of Somerton
and crowding churls, servants, reeves, and thanes,
ripped in the mold the footprint of a church.   *feldcirice* (OE)
While some set stakes, ran line, and dug the ruts
that would hold fast the stripped and dressed
                                        foundations,
others toppled trees the moon would seal,
oak for the roofbeam, elm for upright posts,   *ac, elm* (OE)
alder for sills, and apple for the rood.   *alor, æppel* (OE)
Some squared and bored the timbers, some
                                        carved pegs,
while boys and girls cut withy-whips and reeds   *wiðigas, hreod* (OE)
to wall and roof the hopeful edifice.
The king designed a nave with no arcade,
no transept, apse, or diaconicon—
a wattled ark to waft his people homeward.

The thane remarked, "I doubt our ancestors   *þegn* (OE)
built shrines to Grim before they filled their guts."
His captain said, "I don't doubt they prayed."

Next day, the king and Athelnoth looked on
as untested churls, paired with guardsmen,
waggled wooden swords and woven shields.   *scildas* (OE)
"If they shrink so from our own men," said Alfred,
"what terror will the foreigners inspire?"
He called the mismatched files to attention.
"Listen, Saxons," Ingeld's scion cried.   *Alfred*
"You drill like men who love their wretchedness.
Through Adam's lapse, or by our Father's will,
unceasing warfare is the lot of men,
our place in life to seize and fight for land.
The Romans opened Janus' temple gates
to signify the city was at war.
In seven centuries before our Savior
assumed the flesh and vesture of a man
the brazen gates were shut for just one year.
And this is how Orosius describes   *Orosius bk. iv*
the Romans' second Carthaginian struggle,
when Hannibal invaded Italy:
'Hopeless, the Romans fought, and fighting, conquered.'"

He felt he'd said enough about the Romans.
"When the Lord God lent his strength to our arms,
we whipped the Danes at Hingston Down   *838*
                              and Oakley,   *851*
at Winchester, and ever-glorious Ashdown,   *860; 871*
a name that will endure a thousand years."
He stopped, choked by a hard lump in his throat.
"Our fathers and their fathers—they were men.
What they did, by his mercy, we can do.
Don't fear the fierce berserkers in their fury.
Madly, they invoke the souls of bears   *wodlic, beran* (OE)

but summon only hateful, treacherous devils,
while you, washed by his blood, watched by his angels,   *blod, englas* (OE)
who quick as thought receive intelligence
and strength and courage from the higher choirs,   *eafod and ellen* (OE)
you will prevail, for a faithful *guþbeorn*   *warrior* (OE)
is more cunning, more skilled, and bolder
than any ghost or prisoner of hell."   *gast, hellehæftling* (OE)

The churls listened quite religiously,
for every moment Alfred spoke was one
the guardsmen's onset didn't petrify them.
"I trusted my two eyes," the king continued.
"I now trust *Tirfruma* to light my way.   *Source-God* (OE)
Come, Athelnoth. Men, this is how we fight."

Equipped with ashen wands and willow shields,
they faced each other in the silent ring.
No sooner had their targes touched than Alfred
pushed the expectant minister's up high
and thrust, his thane at once both parrying   *þegn* (OE)
and hollowing like a sail catching air.
The bashful *buras* murmured their esteem   *farmers* (OE)
as Alfred thrust again and Athelnoth
parried and purled about and punched at him
with a long length of limb and peeled blade.
The churls cheered and cheered, for they soon saw   *ceorlas* (OE)
their captains were accomplished warriors,   *frecan* (OE)
and they could not imagine that the mermen
could field abler fighters than their *frean*.   *lords* (OE)

"Come," said Alfred, "like a wild beast!"   *wilde deor* (OE)
Rolling his eyes, the Somersetan growled
and champed the plaited margin of his play-shield,   *plegscild* (OE)
then roared and rushed the waiting Saxon chieftain.
Alfred son of Athulf was transformed   *K. Athelwulf d. 858;*
into a monster more than merely man,   *forsceapen, ælwiht* (OE)

tempting his friend by feints and frenzied jinks
to waste his fighting power on images.   *ellencræft* (OE)

The men forgot these bruisers were their *guþfruman*   *war-chiefs* (OE)
and cheered as though two village rivals fought
to vindicate the honor of their cousins.
The thane fell on his elf-instructed king,   *þegn, fengel* (OE)
pinning his prince's paw under his punnet.
"Yield, chief," he said, "unless you mean
to show us you won't just pour your blood-wine   *onblotan blodwin*
but will retake this God-forsaken land.   (OE)
Or sink and see me make peace with Gorm!"

The *frea* feared he'd faint before he freed   *lord* (OE)
his bone-house from the brunt of his bold *beorn*.   *hero* (OE)
"*Dryhten,*" he muttered deep in his dull spirit   *Lord* (OE)
and, swiftly twisting trunk and neck, he banged
his basket into the battler's whiskered chin,   *cempa* (OE)
then paddled free and pounced upon his provost   *prafost* (OE)
and shoved one elbow towards his shoulder blades.
A curt struggle, a strangled yelp of pain,
and the rough Somersetan reeve surrendered.
The people's king stood up to jubilation   *þeoden* (OE)
and like a well-loved village champion
was carried through the camp by cheering men.

The next night, after hours of rehearsals,
the seed of Cerdic launched his maiden raid.
They fetched a folk-cow and a freight of hay,   *folccu* (OE)
and a red buck Bucca took with his spear.   *buc* (OE)
Another night, three crews retrieved three oxen,   *þry, oxan* (OE)
whose owners Alfred promised to make whole.
The king and twenty men assessed Low Ham,
returning with four oxen and five cows,
six sacks of grain, eleven kegs of ale,
and eight herdsmen to enhance their host.

Arming the churls was the chief's next office,	*ceorlas* (OE)
so Alfred met with Athelnoth to craft	*cræftan* (OE)
a foray to resplendent Glastonbury.	*Glæstingaburh* (OE)
Some fifty men they picked for the attempt	*fiftig menn* (OE)
and borrowed boats from nearby villages.	
They even built an abbey out of sticks	
to illustrate the movements of each troop	*truma* (OE)
and practiced landing in the reeds by night.	

Those times, the Athulfing was given dreams.	*Alfred*
In one, he and Denewulf swam their horses,	*mearas* (OE)
whelmed by heaving swells, towards the high minster	*mynster* (OE)
that guarded Glastonbury's barns and halls,	
but as they neared the building it dissolved,	
as if its walls and beams were formed of mist.	
Choking, he heard the choir singing mass	
and woke with pounding heart before he drowned.	
Another night, he knelt before the abbot,	
his mother, Osburh, watching as a witness,	
just as he'd once knelt before Pope Leo,	*Leo IV 847–855*
who dubbed him consul of Britannia—	*heretoga* (OE)
but standing in for Herefrith, whose doom	*abbot of Glastonbury*
as Glastonbury's abbot was unknown,	
he thought he saw Saint Cuthbert or Saint Neot,	
Saint David's sapphire blazing on his brow,	
enjoining him to glorify the Life-Lord.	
These dreams, which Denewulf construed as signs	*Liffrea* (OE)
the Saxons would dislodge the dire invaders,	*scipfaran* (OE)
buoyed up the son of Athelwulf's resolve	
until, one night, he chanced on Ealhswith,	
who gestured at him from her fiery doorway.	
When Alfred woke, concupiscent yet stricken,	*lustgiernende* (OE)
he knew not whether his brave Mercian make	*maca* (OE)
was trapped in blistering Chippenham or hell.	*hell* (OE)

One day a churl and the churl's household   *ceorles hired* (OE)
appeared from Horsey under Polden Hill.
Levying local folk, including miners,
the Danes had ditched a strong redoubt at Down End.

"When our encircling sea," said Sceaf's seed,   *sæd* (OE)
"withdraws into its subterranean hollows,
this ark, like unclean carrion, will draw
Froda's Jutes from Somerton and Taunton.
Despite our efforts here, our Saxon farmers   *buras* (OE)
will not brook the foreigners' shield-wall.   *bordhaga* (OE)
A rapid relocation may be prudent,
as when the Prophet fetched the folk from Egypt."   *folc* (OE)

The western thane replied indignantly,   *þegn* (OE)
"Our Glory-King, *Þrymcyning,* cursed the cowards
who clamored to evacuate to Egypt
when Babylon invaded Israel.   *Jer. 42:15-22*
This country is our home, our cherished ground.   *ham, eardlufu* (OE)
God brought us from the Saxon swamps,
                    where Roman
swordsmen sawed our fathers' fathers' fathers.
A Roman highway rides the Polden ridge.   *herestræt, hrycg*
A swarm of Saxons pouring down that track   (OE)
would roll Godrum's host into the Parrett."

King Alfred stared with glassy eye beyond
his Somersetan satellite and said,   *dryhtgesith* (OE)
"Maybe the end of the Sixth Age has come.
There is a pregnant prophecy in Scripture:
'I saw a beast rising out of the sea—
vidi de mari bestiam ascendentem.'   *Rev. 13:1*
If John predicted Gorm's bloodthirsty horde,
our Lord wants us to challenge them, not run."

X.

The Burning Ridge

∽

*Guthrum and Halga contemplate the coming conflict. Toca feasts with Wan
in Dorchester. Alfred meets up with Athelheah and leads their army to the
Polden Hills.*

"The tinder has been laid," said Godfred's offspring,   *K. Godfred d. 810;*
"and now awaits a spark from him who hurls   *★afspriki* (OEN)
the thunderbolt, whoever he may be:
far-seeing Har, tough Thor, or Laufey's child;   *Woden; ★Þur, ★bærn*
or fate, or providence, the Christians' word   (OEN)
for all that is and everything that happens
by order of their threefold head, their *★Þrenik;*   *Trinity* (OEN)
or Satan, heaven's clever enemy,
who officers the powers of the air.
Who do you think will show himself, my friend?
Our father, who demands the foeman's blood?   *★faþur, ★bloþ* (OEN)
Or Mary's Son, who shares in all our sorrows?"   *★Mariu Sunr* (OEN)

So Gormr said to Halga, Ymme's man,   *★uir* (OEN)
whose meaty hands were cupped around the peaks
of freshly whittled pales of beech and elm   *★bok, ★almr* (OEN)
atop the sailors' new-built palisade.   *★borþuækr* (OEN)
As Halga sniffed the brine, blent with the damp
that wafted from the breastworks and the ditch,
the bulging sun unrolled a sheet of gold
on Parrett's flooded bed west of the ridge
and daubed a reddish fire on his forehead.

"Just look at us, as chatty as two Saxons,"
said Gormr, seeing Halga's features color.

"Such thoughts have dogged us since my heathen
                                                    kinsmen
contested Hedeby with your drenched uncle.
Enough. We're here to crush these cattle thieves,
not hire on our future kingdom's gods."

Staring, King Harald's great-nephew asked,
"Will Hrothulf join us here, my headstrong son?
That's what you're really wondering, it seems.
You did wisely, bringing the Mercian with you."

"We don't know whether Siward's men," said Godrum,
"aggrieved by his unpunished death, will show.
There's much we don't know, Halga, but I swear,
my crown, such as it is, and all I own
will pass to you as heir of him I served,
your uncle Eric, royal Hemming's son,
King Lothar's Christian count of Dorestad."
A gull flared overhead, then veered from sight.

"Alive to my disgrace, I thank my king,"
said Halga, almost envying a father
who'd never known the rancor of an heir.

"Then let us pray," said Gormr, "to our hero,
the elf or god or ghost who governs here—
though I for one would rather cast the runes
than launch our men on the mad froth of battle.
Sir, send us strength to shatter Saxon swords
and bring the unruly Danes and kingless natives
under the leafy heaven of one law.
But if you don't intend us to prevail,
then grant that we remain faithful to you
beyond whatever failure you decree,
so when you cull your picked men, your chosen,
we may dwell in your longstanding hall
together with our never-dying friends."

kimsmin (OEN)

K. Harald Klak acc.
812, 819, 825
rein, rulers (OEN)

Halga
Ruulf (OEN)

Sikurþr (OEN)

Helki (OEN)

Himik (OEN)
Kristn (OEN)

þekil (OEN)

halr (OEN)

runar (OEN)

suiarþ (OEN)

lakstaþin (OEN)
utauþlikr (OEN)

The Danish chieftains, with no further word,   *Tanskar trotni* (OEN)
descended from the twilit parapet
and, leaving behind the near-finished fortress,
entered the smoky, crowded Danish camp   *Tanskr* (OEN)
that huddled in a flock beneath the works.   *flokr* (OEN)
Small cooking fires blinked among the tents,   *tiald* (OEN)
and cooking tackle clacked with quiet cheer.

Toca, Toca's son, now reeve of Sherborne,   *Tóki* (OEN)
sat next to Wan, ex-follower of Ingwar's,
in Hrothulf's hall, where prudent Alfstan ruled   *hal* (OEN)
before the foreign floaters cut him down.   *flotnar* (OEN)
Turning his horn of beer, the bishop's brew,   *bior* (OEN)
a tun of which he'd trundled from his cellar,
the reeve revolved admonishments for Hrothulf,
which it appeared he must impart through Wan,
the youngster being absent from the high seat.

"To Dorchester," the Orbaek man began,
"we've marched, burdened with byrnies   *bryniur, *benlaksar
        and bright blades,   (wound-salmon),
with cattle, swine, and chickens in our train,   *naut, *suin, *sauþir
although we might have mustered at Down End."   (OEN)

The head berserker frowned disgustedly.
"With Athelheah's freebooters loose," he said,   *Bp. of Sherborne*
"I don't know why you'd rush to shore up Gorm.   *Kurmr* (OEN)
There's virgin earth to plow in Saxon Devon.
The Cornish lords, unraveling Tamar's braids,   *R. Tamar*
will thrust Odda back on our keen steel."

A twinge of fear flickered in Toca's innards
as though the one-eyed strategist drew near.
"Guttorm plans to pacify the land,"
he said, "and plant a kingdom for the Danes.   *Tanir* (OEN)

We didn't vote to plunder Hrothulf's father,   *faþurbruþur* (OEN);
whose father-brother Eric we all served."   *ct. of Dorestad*

Ingwar's messmate said to Toca's son,   *Wan*
"King Gorm intends to Saxonize the Danes
or Britonize us, urging us to cringe
before the perforated Christian image.
That's madness, mad, unmanly foreign fraud.
Name the English kings that boaster succored—
Edmund, Osbert, Aella, Athelred?   *d. 870; d. 867; d. 867;*
The latter's callow agnate, now interred?   *d. 871*
Grim enjoins us to destroy our foes   *Krimr* (OEN)
and string them up in tribute to his godhead.   *Eric s. of Hemming vs.*
Had we foreknown that backing Hemming's son   *Eric s. of Godfred;*
would later count as throwing over Thor,   *Oþen* (OEN)
we wouldn't have fought King Eric's Zealanders."

Candle fires swayed in his glazed eyes
as, leaning forward, Wan, confiding, said,
"I wouldn't bet on Gorm in this reshuffling.
Besides our swordsmen, we have well-placed allies:
the alderman of Wiltshire, who commands   *Wulfhere*
a Saxon swarm dispersed in Guttorm's rear,
as well as Gorm's disgusting British bard.   *braki* (OEN)
We have your Halga's would-be Frankish queen   *trutnik* (OEN)
and Wulfthryth, who still pines for Athred's throne.   *Dumgarth;* *kunuk*
At need, we have the embittered Cornish king."   (OEN)

Dissembling his dismay, the Himmerlander   *Toca*
inhaled the scent of Athelheah's ale
then sipped and gulped and looked away to where
a scald of Hrothulf's entertained the diners.   *skalt* (OEN)
A younger warrior from Walcheren,
he struck the anxious oarsman with the sheer
vivacity and polish of his song,   *søkr* (OEN)
although he prostituted Kvasir's cup   *kar* (OEN)

to counterfeiting mirth with shabby lies
instead of nursing courage in men's souls.
He offered up the portrait of a provost   *provastar (OEN)
who boasted of his feats in love and war,
which he adorned with references to gods
the circumstances made ridiculous.

Lord Toca understood, with growing anger,
that the blusterer was begging for his life,   *lif (OEN)
attempting to persuade some unknown foe
that slaying him would stain the slayer's name.
"One hidden dimple in my hide," he whimpered,
"a sparrow's droppings made impregnable—
elsewhere a man might slice me like a pie."
His treasures, too, would taint his conqueror.
"This bead found in the street, this stolen brooch,
this copper anklet from a lady's slave,
the earspoon men call Gram, and this black horse"—
fearing at first the fool was fliting Frey,
the earl realized that the base braggart
was none other than the sober Scanian,   *Sikurþr (OEN)
Smala's son, the much loved lord of Lund.   *sunr (OEN)

As Hrothulf's haughty satirist, whose name   *skapsmiþ, mind-smith,
the seed of Toca still could not recall,   *nafn (OEN)
approached the fatal stroke Lord Wan bestowed,   *banahak (OEN)
the captain turned and caught Wan's ugly grin.
Thus do the giants pass their nights in hell,
the lord of Orbaek mused, slandering Thor.   Toca
Thus they stoke their revolt against the world,   *uaralt (OEN)
which if they could, they'd burn to the last cinder.

⚬∞⚬

Fear of the fiends and fear of treason's steel
counseled a slow approach to Ecgbert's stone.

The Saxon and his Somersetan column   *Alfred*
waited, screened by apple trees in flower
(whose petals glowed with their own inward light
and whose unworldly scent perfumed the hollow),
for Aeffa, son of Theobald, to return,
for at the risk of bumping into devils,
he'd run ahead to scout the mustering place.

The king had issued summonses to men
who owed him service as his ministers,
recipients of privileges and lands,
but only if he deemed they'd pay their debt
and not report his purpose to the fiends.
He hadn't sent for Wulfhere, for example,   *Wulfhere ald. of*
but he'd dispatched Tata to fetch Lord Odda,   *Wiltshire; Odda ald. of*
quick Witbrord to petition Sherborne's ruler,   *Devon; Bp. Athelheah;*
and Acca to call Eadwulf of Berkshire,   *Eadwulf ald. of*
son of and successor to that Athulf   *Berkshire*
who fell at Reading, hacking Halfdan's henchmen.   *871*
Old Alfstan, Alfred's royal father's friend,   *ald. of Dorset,*
was dead, he'd heard, as was Saint Swithun's heir   *Tunbert bp. of*
who'd sung his psalm escaping Alfred's hall.   *Winchester*
How many Saxons died that night, the night   *Jan. 6, 878; High-Lord*
the learned Persians hailed the *Heahfrea!*   (OE)

All told, he'd launched a dozen messengers,
bread cast upon the flood, of whom yet six   *flod, six* (OE)
had not returned when his company set out
from Ham, having poled the protecting gulf.

All day they labored, wending along swift streams
whose banks the Lord had prinked with yellow flag
as he had primped the air with varied birdsong.
Without a fire they made camp and slept,   *fyr* (OE)
and rising when they spied the morning star,   *morgensteorra* (OE)

they trudged from lauds to vespers, meeting no one.
But now, among the branches, Alfred saw   *bogas* (OE)
young Aeffa, helmetless, his face aglow,
approaching with Witbrord, said royal envoy,   *boda* (OE)
and a *geoguþ* of Athelheah's household.   *youth* (OE)

Witbrord knelt before him. "Lord," he uttered,
"I roamed until the bishop's pickets found me.
He stood beneath an oak, whose newborn leaves   *leaf* (OE)
lay curled among their leathery predecessors.
The waterfall of iron rings that poured
from his wide shoulders to his trunk-like thighs
towered over my head, a frozen cliff.
I spoke your word: 'Hopeless, the Romans fought.'   *Orosius bk. iv*
The man of God replied, 'And fighting, conquered.'"

Now Ingeld's troubled scion rode apart.   *Alfred*
As if a flood of feeling broke its dam,
stubborn remorse assailed him, and shame
at having watched marauders maul his flock,
and constant terror of discovery
endured for deadly weeks in Gormr's court.
Advancing through the gloom to Ecgbert's stone,   *stan* (OE)
erected by that king in imitation   *K. Ecgbert d. 839*
of everlasting timbers reared at Avebury,
he apperceived Saint Aldhelm's eighth successor,   *Bp. Athelheah*
the *rector* of his *regnum*'s western see,
his cousin, captain, crammer, and companion,
on foot beneath the undressed monument.
Beside him Alfsige stood, who ran his chapter;
Regenbald the reeve; Esne the priest,
who'd stewarded the bishop's rich estates;
Athelwulf and Athelhelm, two brothers;
Leofheah, the bishop's sister-son;   *swistorsunu* (OE)
and Beorhtwulf, who sowed far-scattered fields.

Frea defends us from the enfeebling grief,   *the Lord* (OE)
the sad disease, the burial alive
we suffer separated from our friends.
Before that moment, neither priest nor king
had plumbed the pit of sorrow in his heart,
but now the bishop fell to his stout knees
and fondled, fervently, his *frea's folma*.   *palms* (OE)
He kissed them, weeping, as the holy twelve
must have kissed the hands of their dear Healer,   *Hælend* (OE)
returned from hell and death on Pilate's tree,
and no one mocked the son of Athulf's tears   *maga Æthulfs* (OE)
or the strong sobs that shook the bishop's bulk.

"I heard you lost an eye," the bishop said,
the salty channels gleaming on his cheeks,
"but I believe you live. I scorn to beg   *John 20:25-29*
leave to touch the smooth stone in its socket."

The seed of Ingeld hailed the Wiltshiremen   *Alfred*
who'd left behind their overwelcoming chief: *Wulfhere*
young Athelhelm, the shire's junior elder;
Sigewulf and Beornstan, stray guardsmen;
and, wonderfully, Wulfheard, Wulfhere's son,   *bearn* (OE)
by whom recruited, heaven only knew.

He turned to greet the Hampshiremen and found
that Cuthred, his young alderman, had come,
although he'd married Wulfthryth, Wulfhere's
                 daughter,
bringing his brothers, Tort- and Wulf- and Wigred.   *broþor* (OE)
Alfred hailed the wrinkled, studious Hunsige;
the brothers Beorhtmund and Beorhtnoth,
who'd served with each of Alfred's elder brothers,
as had tough Cynelaf and Athelred,
true Hampshire thanes defecting from the foes;   *fiend* (OE)
Dudig, Athelred, and Heremod,

three men who'd manned the works at Wareham   *þry menn* (OE)
                                   with him;
and dear Deormod, the latter's brother.

Depleted of his glee, the people's king   *leodcyning* (OE)
unhappily lacked Eadwulf and Odda,
his princes of the Berks and Devon men.   *Defnas* (OE)
He beckoned to his chiefs. "No fires tonight,"
he said, "and no carousing in the camp."

They made their way to Iley, where they lay   *weg* (OE)
at rest as Esne numbered all the men.   *secgas* (OE)
There Alfred led a party through the trees
until they found a freshly flowering maple   *mapultreow* (OE)
(the wood the woodwrights worked to frame their harps),   *wudu, wyrhtan* (OE)
which felled, they stripped and dressed in
                            two bright beams,
the living wood the tint of shining skin.   *scinn* (OE)
The seed of Ingeld crossed himself and said,   *Alfred*
"With these we'll build the Danes a Grecian steed."

At dusk, the Saxons' evening meal done,   *æfenmete* (OE)
the king addressed them from a fallen log.
Although no word, no men, had come from Devon
or Berkshire, it was time to launch the struggle.   *camp* (OE)
If they delayed, the Danes would slay them   *bitmælum* (OE)
                         piecemeal
and time and tide would fetch another fleet.

"*La, Seaxe,*" the seed of Sceaf cried,   *O Saxons* (OE)
"our fathers won this land by God's command.   *Godes willa* (OE)
And now the Danes are here—we don't know why—
to test us or requite our sinful deeds.   *firenweorc* (OE)
We've drunk such poisonous shame that by his grace
alone do we yet live. Yet by his grace
we live, we muster here, we rest, eat, march
armed with the filed iron of his Word.

The Lord made earth and heaven. Every day   *Liffrea* (OE)
he summons up the sun and wind and trees.
He molded us from soil and endowed
mankind with his spiritual image.   *monkyn, onlicness,*
Again, we don't know why he sent the sailors,   *scipmenn* (OE)
but next to such astounding miracles,
to see his Saxon folk, his loyal sons,   *suna* (OE)
recover their old homes is nothing to him.

"On Aphek's battleplain, King Ahab's levy   *oretfeld, fyrd* (OE)
slaughtered a hundred thousand Syrians   *1 Kings 20:29*
and proved *Tirfruma* rules both hill and vale.   *Source-God* (OE)
With but three thousand, Matathias' son,   *þry þusend, magu,*
bold Judas, called the Hammer of the Lord,   *bald* (OE)
dispersed an army many times as large   *1 Macc. 4.13*
of Syrians and Greeks outside Emmaus.
And when Northumbrian Oswy, nation's king,   *þeodcyning* (OE)
fought pagan Penda, godly Oswald's slayer,
his Mercian foes had thrice his complement,   *fa* (OE)
but *Frea* gave his son the victory
by Winwed's flood, and gave him Penda's head.   *Nov. 15, 655*
For battles aren't won by shield and sword,   *beadwa, bord, brond,*
or numbers, engines, silver, or full bellies,   *seolfur* (OE)
but by a soul devoted to the Lord.

"We are but three hundred eighteen men,   *þry hundeahtatyne*
as many as the bishops in Nicea   (OE)
who took our credo from the Holy Ghost.   *325; Heahgæst* (OE);
We have as many men as Abram brought   *Gen. 14:14; camp,*
to battle in the war of the nine kings   *nigon cyningas,*
to rescue captured Lot, his brother-son.   *broþorsunu* (OE)
Bede says that number signifies the tree,
the living timber of our Victory-Lord.   *Sigedryhten* (OE)
The crosslike *tau* in Greek denotes three hundred,
ten *I,* eight *H,* betokening his name.

We bear our *Frea*'s rood to bruise the fiends,　　*fiend* (OE)
as did fane-bearing Abram, figuring Christ.　　*segnberend* (OE)
Another type of Christ, Melchizedek
blessed his triumphant band with bread and wine.　　*hlaf and win* (OE)
Remember, when we march before the light,　　*uhtantid* (OE)
what Leonidas said to his six hundred　　*Orosius bk. ii*
before they met six hundred thousand Persians.
'Break your fast,' the Spartan urged his spearmen,
'as though tonight you feasted with the dead.'"

Oppressed with dread at wielding such slight force,
the seed of Ingeld, twenty-third successor　　*Alfred*
to Father Cerdic, rode with Athelheah　　*K. Cerdic d. 534*
and spoke to holy Aldhelm's eighth successor:　　*Bp. Aldhelm d. 709*
"If I go down today, I beg you, bishop,
to crown my Edward king and serve as regent.
I pray my lord will fortify our towns
as Bacchides walled nine Judean burgs.　　*2 Macc. 9:50-52; burga*
Build ships, my friend, to interdict invaders　　(OE)
and raze Danish ports with fire and sword.
We must have learned volumes in our tongue,
such as the great *De civitate dei*　　*St. Augustine of Hippo*
the great Numidian penned and great Charles studied.　　*d. 430; Emp. Charles d.*
I fear the fiends will seize the atheling,　　*814*
whom Parrett's ebbing waters will expose.　　*wætru, dun, feld,*
I fear they'll occupy each down and field,　　*hæfen, stream, mædwa,*
each harbor, river, meadow, brook, and grove,　　*broc, holt* (OE)
so long no man will know the Saxon name."

The timid light that skulked among the trunks
revealed the bishop's meditative frown.
"Sufficient unto the day the ills thereof,"　　*Matt. 6:34*
said Athelheah. *"Genoh on hys ymbhogan.*
Diei sufficit malitia sua.
I ask you, son, why did our *Dryhten* die?　　*Lord* (OE)

To spare his sheep the pains of death? Not so.
He died to spare us from the pangs of hell,
which, for our sins, we sons of Eve have earned
and which he too, despairing, has endured.
Despairing, he found souls chained to their torments
and evil fiends commissioned to mistreat them.   *yfel* (OE)
But *Frea,* unfathered, fought for his friends.
He gave the word to those who loved the Lord   *word* (OE)
(the *uuort* in Charles's Old Franconian tongue),
and at his signal, all in unison
abruptly seized the ugly devils' weapons,   *wæpen* (OE)
their mallets, flails, pruning hooks, and goads,
and, massing in a *caput porcinum,*   *boar's head formation*
rushed the arrogant gang that manned the gate.   (L)

"The fallen freed, our Lord returned to earth,
and since that time, his men have taught all mankind   *menn, moncynn* (OE)
how we may march together, fight for him,
and live with him, forever, after Judgment."

The Athulfing said nothing. He knew hell.   *Alfred*
He'd gladly stake his life, his fame, his fate
to save the *Seaxe* and free his *freo.*   *Saxons, lady* (OE)

                        ⌘

As red as pig-iron in the forge's jaws
the sun had blazed, then blinked and disappeared
behind the massive bastion of cloud,
when Gormr and his gang of tested captains
passed Cossington along the Roman highway.
King Eric's bane, apart from that ill dread   *bani* (OEN)
that frets each warrior before engaging,   *trek* (OEN)
was certain that his mailed men-at-arms
would quickly cut to shreds the slender cohort

his pickets had reported from afar,
apparently the Saxons' last attempt,
the most abundant bevy they could muster,
to knock the northmen's collar from their necks.   *halsar* (OEN)
Anticipating easy victory,
King Godfred's grandson yet was gratified   Godrum / Gormr
to think the stormclouds heaping the dark welkin,
beginning now to weep fat, limpid drops,
would curtain from their risen Savior's eye
the massacre of his miserable folk.

With no preliminary boasts or slurs,
the foemen met along a narrow front,
hurrying to their deaths as to their beds.
As quickening raindrops tapped both Dane and Saxon,
men thrust at throats, men swung at necks and flanks,
and grunts of pain and hatred graced the din
of iron and steel beating blade and shield.
Like wolves the Saxons fought, each warding strokes
directed at his neighbor as himself,
and bore appalling wounds until they stumbled,
languishing, as if drugged, from loss of blood.
The outnumbered natives held their ground
despite the rising ire of the Danes,
as Godfred's seed and Harald's son observed.   *sap, *barn* (OEN)

"Grim!" cried Gormr, and his swordsmen echoed,   *Krimr, *kumnar*
"Grim!" and separated right and left,   (OEN)
for it was Grim who'd counseled Sigurd Ring
on how to counter Harald War-tooth's wedge.

"The swine!" cried Athelnoth, who swung his wings   *swin* (OE)
back to withstand the fiends' envelopment,
trusting in his Somersetan troop,   *truma* (OE)
the nobles and the freemen of the shire,

porcarii and foresters and sailors
and monks drawn from Blagdon Hythe and Banwell,
to execute in calculated steps,
not bolt in terror at the rowers' rage.

But sheer numbers surging on both flanks
threatened to overwhelm his weakening band.   *werod* (OE)
Instead of calling on his hard-pressed van
to split the tide of fiends and roll their right
over the cliff-like rim, he bawled aloud
for Somersetan churls to withdraw.

One half the little thicket disengaged   *þiccet* (OE)
and ran for their lives back up the Roman road.
The other half attacked ferociously,
resolved to halt the heathens at all costs
and give their fellows half a chance to flee.
Athelnoth and Garulf poured on blows,
despite the rain the wind whipped in their faces,   *ren, wind* (OE)
hacking at Gorm's and Earl Halga's helms
and drawing younger *drengas* to their aid.   *soldiers* (OE)
Bellowing out the Frealafing's **nafn,*   *Woden; name* (OEN)
Gormr urged a vigilant pursuit,
refusing to buy back the feigned retreat
the Saxons swallowed, gullibly, at Wilton.   *871*

He saw the thane of Somerton break off,   **þekn* (OEN)
leap down the slope, and gallop, slide, and roll.
He let the landsman go, lest tumbling rowers
lose the odds on ruggeder terrain.
Instead the sailors strode with steady step
along the road to the black-tented east,
exulting as they went to see their prey
fleeing like frightened sheep. They feared the foes
might scatter in the woods of Socombe Hill,

but soon the rump of Athelnoth's command
reformed, thinly, along the line of trees.

Meanwhile, Alfred, hidden in that same timber,
had stepped away, alone, to pray for strength,
though the black ashes rubbed into his visage   *andsyn* (OE)
felt hot, as if foretokening hellfire.
His heart ached in its cage, his innards churned
as if to purge his poisoned flesh of sin   *flæsc, firen* (OE)
until, his weasand sucking spit, he choked
and choked as if to drown in the sopping air.
Is this the dragon's last attack? he asked,   *draca* (OE)
desperately drawing breath between the spasms.
Spare me, *Frea,* to do your work, he begged,   *Lord* (OE)
and spare your servant the indignity   *servus* (L)
of smothering in his own surging filth.   *fylþ* (OE)
But the filth climbed convulsively, a bitter
worm of mire birthed in his throat with woe.   *wyrm* (OE)
"And can you drain the cup," the Savior asked,   *fæt, Hælend* (OE); *Matt.*
"prepared for me, the sin of the whole world?"   *20:22*
He heaved, he hacked, he spat, he spat again—
an unseen angel chased away the fiend.   *engel, feond* (OE)

King Athulf's son, secure in his reliance,   *K. Athelwulf d. 858*
body and soul, life and limb, on him,   *lic and sawel* (OE)
remounted to regain his waiting place.
He scarcely heard the progress of the fight
over the rain's *tæp tæp* on leaf and helm,
but in a pause he heard a mistle-thrush
hidden in the summit of an oak,
rejoicing in the gusting, drumming rain
as Saxon sailors sang in squalls at sea—   *bp. of Auvergne d. 489;*
or so Sidonius wrote, a count of Gaul,   *Emp. Avitus 455–456;*
a bishop, and an emperor's son-in-law.   *aþum* (OE)

A drenching gale whipped the rowers' backs
and drove them up the rise as towards a shore,
when suddenly the Thunderer unloosed
a blinding bolt that lit the open ground
in a strange, fitful burst of purplish light,
in which Jarl Gormr, murdered Godfred's grandson,   *sunarsunr* (OEN)
half-dazzled, with a tingling in his scalp,
could see the features of his enemies.   *sakutulkar* (OEN)
Were they a cohort ordered up from hell
to castigate the sailors for their crimes?
Or living men, who like the Harii,   *Tacitus,* Germania *ch.*
to unnerve enemies, had dyed their hides?   *43*
When the glare dissolved, an unearthly crash
and an earth-shattering racket smashed the air.

A war whoop rolled along the Saxon line,   *hærob* (OEN)
an "Alleluia!" sounding through the gloom,
and then another elf-shining stroke
lightened the green field and green hill.   *grøn,* *ualr,* *fial*
Godfred's seed, with shuddering heart, perceived   (OEN)
his foes had grown in numbers three-, fourfold,
and when the rattling peal rolled away
their alleluias likewise multiplied,
as once the Welshmen generaled by Germanus—   *St. Germanus bp. of*
Armorica's ex-*dux bellorum,* then   *Auxerre d. 448; war*
antistes (bishop) of Antissiodorum—   *leader*
as once the Welshmen bellowed "Alleluia!"   *429*
so loudly that they stunned the massing Saxons,
who threw away their weaponry and fled.

Though shaken, Gormr stubbornly prepared
to marshal his attack, but heaven's Master
loosed another crackling, dazzling shaft,
revealing to the Dane's reluctant awe,
raised among the horrid, obverse troop,

a mailed ruler nailed to glowing studs,   *hæra* (OEN)
the one-eyed steersman of those blackened spirits,   *sturimatr, *traukar*
who Gormr thought resembled buried Alfred.   (OEN)

Arriving on his right, the rower reckoned   *Godrum / Gormr*
a mob of miners, Mendip men, the same
he'd pressed to trench his ditch and heap his ramparts,
appearing suddenly on Polden's brow
as though they'd scooped shallow graves in the hillside
awaiting their Redeemer's call to arms.
Assembled and commanded by young Bucca,
they wielded mattocks, picks, and whetted spades,   *mattucas, beccan,*
and Somersetan swordsmen steeled their line,   *scofla* (OE)
for Saxon thanes, unlike the haughty Franks,   *nobles killed peasant*
saw no disgrace in leading loyal churls   *leaders 859*
to slaughter and expel the northern oarsmen.   *reðran* (OE)

Godrum felt the wet west wind swing north
as the spring shower turned to clattering hail,
but he and his grim Jutlanders stood fast
despite the godly terror in their hearts,
for they had heard the history of those heroes,
including hallowed Hrothulf, Halga's heir,
a hero other heroes gladly served,   *Saxo bk. ii*
among them warlike Beorra, the werebear.
The tale told how Hrothulf and his hall-guards,
paying the price for Halga's match with Ursa,
his half-Saxon daughter, Hrothulf's dam,   *totur* (OEN)
in a drawn-out, nighttime, nightmare fight at Leire,
succumbed to the unslaughterable host   *þikliþi* (OEN)
that Scyld, the king's half-elfish sister, gathered
to raze her brother's band and seize his throne.
No matter how hotly the heroes hewed,
how many liches mislaid limbs, they soon   *lik* (OEN)
reformed and fought as fiercely as before,

until each fellow fell and gnawed the soil,   *filak (OEN)
including Beorra, in human form.

They knew, as well, of Harald War-tooth's doom
at Bravellır, where Woden, in the mold
of Bruni, Harald's charioteer and friend,
bumped the unsuspecting *rex* from his cart   *uakn (OEN); *Saxo bk.*
and stove in his skull with his own club.   *viii*
So they stood fast, the master and his crewmen,
the irritated stranger recollecting   *Godrum / Gormr*
that the bastard West Saxon athelings numbered
King Scyld among their mottled ancestors.   *Saxo bk. i*

"Woden!" Gormr bellowed from his lungs,   *Open (OEN)
but just as he released his staggered throng,
the one-eyed specter sprang down from his scaffold,
for Alfred counted on the Lord to quell
the Danes as when he stunned the Midianites
by night with Gideon's lamps and jarring trumps.   *Jud. 7:19-20*

But Gormr and his crews, despite the thunder,
despite the onset of exulting corpses,
despite the troll toiling under his token,   *takn (OEN)
the White Christ under his battle-standard,   *Hoitakristr, *hærkubl
came on, and Alfred knew his plan had failed.   (OEN)
He saw his Saxons faced an enemy
superior in numbers, craft, and arms,
as if the Savior had forsaken him
and his inspired men—as if he'd spurned
their faith to let them perish on that ridge,
forgotten in a year, a month, a day,   *gear, monþ, dæg* (OE)
though fame for any man, Augustine says,
is brief, an instant in eternity,
and published only in a narrow tract
of this small star, this stone, this mustard seed.   *stan, senepsæd* (OE)

Some days before, the lesser light had masked
the sun, a sign, said Werwulf, waxing vatic,
their slender corps would quench the northman's candle,
but now, the Saxon saw, the omen meant
the newly risen foe would quell his folk.   *fah, folc* (OE)

So Alfred fought, and men around him fought,
closing with Gormr's rowers face-to-face,
like wretches who'd lost everything of worth,   *wreccan, cildru,*
their children, cattle, lands, their wives, their lives,   *feoh, land, wif, lif,*
their weapons whetted by impending death.   *wæpen* (OE)
Then Alfred knew the Lord was not in the wind   *wind* (OE); *1 Kings*
that clamored like the voice of many waters;   *19:11-12*
was not in the rain or the helm-rattling hail   *ren, hægel* (OE)
that baptized Saxon men in Adam's ruin;
was not in the blinding lightning he sent down
as if to carbonize them with his Ghost,   *Gæst* (OE)
but in the wordless spell that held its peace   *spell* (OE)
amid the scraping blades and grunts of hatred
uttered by men wielding and shunning judgment.

So Alfred fought, encouraged by his angel,   *engel* (OE)
carving the necks and limbs of heathen fiends,   *fiend* (OE)
severing hands defiled with every sin,   *handa* (OE)
breaking teeth with his hefty jeweled hilt,   *teþ, gimmisc, hilt,*
(which housed a tusk of Peter's, brought from Rome),   *tusc* (OE)
and piercing, with his point, the plaited wire   *herepada (war-shirts),*
in which the Danes believed as in their gods.   *godu* (OE)

Sherborne's lord commanded on the right,
where Polden's height fell gently towards the north,
his *guþleoma* guiding the Dorset men,   *war-lamp* (OE)
while on the left, the thane of Somerton   *Dornsæte, þegn* (OE)
led Somersetan men along the rim
of the pale pit that yawned beyond the ridge.

But where the sailors saw a stubborn scrum
of Saxons holding back their crowding lines,
the Saxons, though condemned to pain and death,
discerned that high among the glaring clouds
the heroes of our risen Healer's host,   *hæle, Hælend* (OE)
archangeli, virtutes, potestates,   *archangels, virtues,*
throni, principatus, dominationes,   *powers, thrones,*
equipped with godlike arms, fought on their side,   *principalities,*
and as the Greeks and Romans held a god   *dominions*
might don a shipmate's or a kinsman's features,
the Saxons saw angelic radiance,
steadfastness, fighting spirit, strength, and love   *soþfæstness, ellen,*
shining beneath their neighbors' iron helms,   *eafoþ* (OE)
as if familiar friends had been revealed
as our Redeemer's warlike choristers.   *Onliesend* (OE)
They saw, moreover, that the Lord of Hosts,
Dryhten weroda, Dominus sabaoth,
by lending them his troops, had multiplied   *truman* (OE)
by twenty, fifty times their tiny body   *corþer* (OE)
and promised them eternal victory.   *sige* (OE)

Gorm observed the one-eyed, mailed scarecrow   **treman* (OEN)
storming among his oaks with hellish force,
his cross behind him, bright on the black hill,   **krus* (OEN)
and felt it only just that heaven's Lord   **Ifnatrutin* (OEN)
should show himself to unbelieving Danes   **untroaþir, *Tanir,*
before he broke their board-burg, snapped their oars,   **borþburk* (OEN)
and sentenced them to everlasting flames.
But by God's grace, the captain's spirit turned   **ont* (OEN)
to salvaging such men as might be spared.
Today, he saw, his sailors would not scatter
Saxons sheltered by their Savior's wings,   **Saksar* (OEN)
but they might yet evade the killing edge-play   **eklaikir* (OEN)
by backing under his consoling shadow.

Lord Halga also sensed that Ymme's Lord
had opted to espouse the Saxon cause.
Contented to do penance for the shame
of Hrothulf's nonappearance in the field
and on his own account, for the longstanding
shame of having shunned his uncles' God   *Kuþ* (OEN); *Harald &*
despite his fair apostle, whom he'd failed,   *Eric ss. of K. Hemming*
he formed a rearguard of his Slesvig men
and Frisians to secure their chief's retreat.
They balked the Saxons' center and their *alfr,* *elf* (OEN)
but on the left, some oarsmen broke and bolted *Edington* (OE);
downward across the kind, inclining mead   **kraskarþar,* *hus,*
towards Eþandun's dear gardens, halls, and barns. **laþar* (OEN)

But in their rear, which now was Gormr's van,
the Jutlanders' reserves withdrew unhindered,
on foot and horseback, painted boards intact, **hiltiborþ* (OEN)
past Chilton Polden, down the welcome grade
past Cossington, and down the ridge towards Knowle,
until they heard that Ymme's man had fallen   **uar* (OEN)
and Alfred's men were menacing their shoulders
and Athelheah's Dorsetans and the men
of Somerset, its swordsmen, monks, and miners, **trekiar,* *mokar* (OEN)
were slashing at their hocks and downing stragglers.

Then the rearward stream became a flood
as fiends were seized with terror of the Lord   *Jud. 7:22-25; 1 Sam.*
who lashed them into a stampede, like beasts,   *14:15*
and now the sodden, trodden turf was burdened
with loose limbs and bloody trunks of men
and dumb faces gaping up at the clouds
as Danes feebly parried the Saxons' fury
with bent blades and mutilated shields.   **skialtir* (OEN)

Men died and horses died as Godfred's grandson   *Godrum / Gormr*
and Hrut's two sons and other steers- and crewmen
struggled to mount and quit the slaughterfield,
but hacked Halga's Slesvig men and Frisians
and other thinning threads of champions,
instructed in the iron law of war,
stayed on to hold the wind-whipped, rain-whipped   **rukr* (OEN)
                                        ridge
and pay the debt of death that all men owe—
and not men only, but the lovely gods
like Balder, bored by oathless mistletoe,
like him the harried Christian herd adored,
the gibbeted magician, now their Lord,   **Trutin* (OEN)
who fell headlong to hell but re-upwelled,
a life-giving spring for those who love him—

and now the downpour transformed to a snowstorm,
stinging and blinding those who fled the fight
as when, after a night of tears and prayer
and visits by two armed and mounted saints,   *apostles John and*
the emperor, the first called Theodosius,   *Philip; Emp.*
ambushed by Arbogast, the Frankish count—   *Theodosius I d. 395*
who fought to keep Eugenius on the throne
whereon he'd placed the rhetor as his puppet,
likely having hanged poor Valentinian—   *Emp. Valentinian II d.*
in a steep notch of the so-called Julian Alps,   *392*
broke out of his forlorn encirclement
when the Lord loosed a whirlwind that wrenched   *Sept. 6, 394; Orosius*
the rebel legions' shields from their arms   *bk. vii*
and blew their arrows back in their own eyes.

Some fellows galloped through the villages   **kumnar* (OEN)
and rushed into the reeds that rimmed the moor,
but most lumbered heavily down the road,
half-maddened, with the Saxons at their heels,
too hurried to discard their ponderous mail,

and now the sun cut through the silver cover
and the green hillsides shone like emerald walls   *grønar, *brenkur,
or emerald surges menacing the shore   *ranir, *stront (OEN)
against the iron-gray of the lingering storm,
as fat, untiring flakes, as white as wool,   *ul (OEN)
cascaded down from heaven's crowded towers
and boiled upwards from below the ridge
like flocks and herds and companies of spirits,
converging, swarming, yearning to observe
a struggle for the destiny of men.

"Another wonder," Godfred's grandson groaned,   *untr (OEN)
careering on his worried horse among   *uik (OEN)
the reckless rout of foreign fugitives.
His forward force was tumbling towards the fort   *treburk (OEN)
like swine running screaming into the sea.
"Another miracle!" acknowledged Alfred.
Not far ahead, the bishop called, "Behold!"
and pointed skyward with his two-edged staff.
Uplifting his good eye, the *guma* saw   man (OE)
the wheel of the *Wuldorcyning*'s war-car   Glory-King (OE)
coruscating with his exorbitant glory,
enfolded in the flying, fiery feathers
and flaming flanks and haunches of his team
victoriously trampling down the turmoil.
"I—H—S," cried Alfred, *"in hoc signo!"*

They neared the devils' dike, which bulked above   *dic* (OE)
the swamped heap of tents, to find a mortal
trial underway along the ramp.
The seed of Sceaf saw from where he sat   *Alfred*
that his small force now held the fort's approaches,
but also that some foes yet hoped to win
the mouth of safety, fanged like Paradise.

He kicked his mount to order back his men   *eh* (OE)
before the Danes drove them into the ditch
and slaughtered them like surplus hogs in autumn.
Too late: he heard a steersman shout, and crowds
of arrows spitted his astonished friends.   *stræla* (OE)
Men grunted and fell dead, while those who lived
waggled their gnawed shields left and right.
The *rex* rode on, exhorting uselessly,
exhausted, impotent, and void of hope,   *meðig, mihtleas* (OE)
while arrows, stones, and beams beat down his force
as unwanted hail murders wheatfields,
and saw the stronghold's jaws pushed open wide,
though Saxons set their shoulders to the boards.
And now the wet west wind, with whelming power,   *westanwind* (OE)
scourged the invaders' eyes with whirling ash,
baffling them and blackening their hearts
so cruelly that they cursed the *cræft* of spells   *power* (OE)
and raved and roared in terror at the swarm
of hornets armed like Grecian cavalry,   *Rev. 9:7-10*
with eyes like men's and women's whipping hair,
and the milk teeth of juvenile wolves.

And all the sons of Cerdic saw this work: *K. Cerdic d. 534*
the gusting snowstorm turned into a mass
of little, chalk-white butterflies that flew   *fifeldan* (OE)
into the faces of the fearful fiends   *fiend* (OE)
and flung them, flailing, from their parapets
and quelled the killing counterstroke they'd launched
to countermand and cross our Judge's doom.   *Demend* (OE)
And now the sun broke through anew and drenched
the grassy slopes and level beds of reeds
that swayed among their elders' skeletons
with a clear glare, the splendor of his glory   *gleomu, witga, templ*
the prophet witnessed soaring over the temple.   (OE)*; Ezek. 10:18;*
And *Sigedryhten*, our Redeemer, drew   *Victory-Lord* (OE)

the jeweled and vaulted bow of righteousness,   *rihtwisnys,*
which only he, the Most High, can bend,   *Heahgod* (OE)
and hung it on the slate-gray eastern sky,
a pledge, it seemed, the Saxons would regain   *wedd* (OE)
their sway over the eastern underkingdoms.

The blinking, racing creatures of the breeze
surged in a churning pillar from the fort
and, incandescing as they came about,
hovered, churning, over the Saxons' heads,
now bright as chalk, now dim, dim, bright,
                                    dim, bright,
before descending into an orchard, where,   *æppeltun* (OE)
alighting on the flowering apple trees   *æppeltreow* (OE)
(the breed of beam on which our *Cyning* hung)   *King* (OE)
that blanketed the knees of the green hill   *cneow, grene, hylde*
in a rose billow, like a virgin snowfield   (OE)
blushing at dawn or hurrying the gloom,   *glom,*
the cloud of creatures marshaled by the Spirit   *wolcn, wynsum,*
turned the winsome, glowing wood one white.   *hwit* (OE)

XI.

"This Lytle War"

༄

Under siege, the Danes debate their next move. Alfred and his chiefs hold a like discussion. The Danes propose single combat between Guthrum and the ghostly Saxon chief.

The waters you collected into seas
bear many a vessel launched with noble hopes.
Sometimes you supply a following gale,
clear sailing under a cloudless tiled dome;
but sometimes wayward breezes thwart our passage,
incursions of the powers of the air,
forcing us to beach on foreign sands;
or buried shoals will tear away a keel
and Aegir's daughters, hungry for new lords,
will clutch the choking oarsmen to their dugs;
or veering squalls will whip the shredded web,
whip flying sheets from the shying, plunging yard,
and running seas pummel the straining sides
till nails pinning pine strakes to ribs
of oak work loose, and pitch and hair work loose,
and biting brine pours in, a load like lead,
swamping the stogged hull, goading the hands
to heave the cargo, even their blood-bought loot,
into the smoking hollows shot with foam.

Then men mistrust the steersman who has failed   *sturman* (OEN)
to slip their hides past your unsleeping eye.
They look around to see which passenger,
which fellow farer, wears the mark of Cain;

they search the hold, they search their shipmates' eyes
for some ill criminal to glut your fury,
when all you hunger for, dear Thunderer,
is every man's unmoored, unguarded heart,
that every man might harbor in your bosom.

Seven days and nights of cold and rain   *rægn (OEN)
reflooded Parrett mouth and drowned the moors.   *miurar (OEN)
The rowers' stores were gone, their fodder gone,
and men were hacking shards from barracks timbers
to broil horseflesh. Worse, the Saxon trolls
(or were they Welsh?), laboring out of bowshot,
had trained off the stream that fed the fort.

In council, Gormr, features drawn, declared,
"We've sent out writs to fetch our absent friends.
I say we wait, for now, to see who shows.
The grip of Alfred's God weighs heavy on us.   *krib, *Kuþ (OEN)
Attack now, we'll squander half our might   *maht (OEN)
while Wulfhere watchdogs the royal throne."   *stal (OEN)

"Respectfully," said Wiga, Sigfred's friend,   *uinr (OEN)
"Our numbers double theirs, not reckoning
the Danes' superiority in battle.
But while the Saxons feast beyond these walls,
our people yield to fever, cramps, and dread—   *liuþir (OEN)
all night, they hear the troll-steeds mourn our fallen."   *hesta flahþa (OEN)

Gormr acknowledged Theodric, who asked,
"What if we fled by night, screened by a feint
at the clear spring that sweetens Down End pill?
With speed, we'd reappear in Chippenham
before Lord Wulfhere knew we'd left this refuge."

Their leader studied his surviving steersmen.   *stilir, *sturnmin (OEN);
He missed young Ymme's lord, his loyalty.   Halga
He missed Siward's truthfulness and strength,   *Sikurþr, *Haraltr,
and Harald's, for whose sake he'd launched this struggle. *kab (OEN)
He felt his soul had fled with his dead boy's
or that it called for him through all nine worlds.   *niu haimar (OEN)

"Ne," said Gorm, "this force, this staggered legion
is all our strength, our kingdom, and our hope.
We must not risk our costly gains to date
on a rash sally, a mad dash to Wiltshire.
You forget, these West Saxons purchase peace,   *Uestsaksar (OEN)
unlike their unyielding ancestors.
And you forget what happened to us here
on Polden ridge, the visionary awe
that mastered us, some cunning man's strong spell
or something wholly irresistible,
a demonstration by their Victory-God.   *Siktiur (OEN)
Rally your rowers. Each of them, though ill,   *reþar (OEN)
is worth a dozen Christian husbandmen."   *Kristn (OEN)

Escorting Godfred's grandson to his hut,   Godrum / Gormr
Earl Hrut, his senior counselor, observed,
"Our Jutlanders suspect the Mercian lady,   *froia (OEN)
the snow-white foreign frow you carted here,   *snaehoitu snot, *hafta,
your prisoner or your hostage or your bride,   *kisl, *kuin (OEN)
has unmanned you with her foreign glamour.
They say she raised the corpse of her late lord. *nar (OEN)
You run the risk she'll stick you in your sleep, *Lakbarþ (OEN)
as Rosamund the Gepid stuck the Lombard   K. Alboin d. 573; *sumbl,
after he made her drain the toasting cup   *kalkan, *faþur (OEN);
his craftsmen fashioned from her father's skull." K. Cunimund d. 567

201

"Fear not," said Gormr, waving his bare hand,
"She's Mercian, as you say. A Jutlander.
She needs me to install her cub as king."   *kunukr (OEN)
The northern chieftain ducked into the hut.

⁕

Next morning, when fresh pickets had been set,
young Alfred mustered all his men in hope
of stemming the effusion of desertions.
Food and fuel were short, men missed their homes,
and Somersetans feared Froda would fall
on Athelney and massacre their families.
Ingeld's seed, aware he must inspire   Alfred
his worn compatriots to hold their ground,   geleodas (OE)
remembered holy Gregory's instruction   larboding (OE)
on governing diversities of men.
The Lord God alone, the *Heahgæst*   Holy Ghost (OE)
that blazed on holy heads, hirsute and bald,
in David's city, in that roaring room,   Acts 2:2-4
could find the words to fortify his levy   fyrd (OE)
against their starving, unforgiving foes.   fa (OE)
But just as Alfred mounted the low stool,
young Athelm, Wiltshire's junior alderman   ealdormann (OE)
beckoned to him, begging for a word.

"Lord," he said almost inaudibly,   hlaford (OE)
"my lord's lady's here, in Godrum's *loc*.   compound (OE)
Your daughter's with her. Solemn Athelflaed."
He said no more. The Saxon chief stared through him,
as if he saw two spirits watching, standing   sawla (OE)
small and precise, on Godfred's grandson's shoulders.

"*Hæfdingas*, companions," Alfred cried,
"our *Heahgod* has granted us the victory,   High God (OE)

for he alone dismayed the pagan Danes
and drove them tumbling headlong down the ridge,
where scores of corpses feed the birds and wolves.
Our trickery, our spirit, came from him.   *searu* (OE)
Shall we pull back and let the Danes retreat
because we lack the pluck to finish them?
My faithful friends, you've weathered this campaign."   *freondas* (OE)

"To Athelney!" men shouted, "Athelney!"
and Athelred's successor understood   *æftergenga* (OE)
his army's banked, smoldering heat was fading.

"Your women and your children," cried the *cyning*,   *wifmenn, cildru* (OE)
"are on the chopping block, and so are mine!
My darling Edward's kenneled on our island,
while Ealhswith, sweet intellect incarnate,   *gesceadwisnys* (OE)
is old Gormr's prisoner in that fort!"
He waved an arm, widely, weakly, behind him.

"Old Gormr's whore!" a coarse *beorn* charged.   *hero* (OE)
The king fell silent, and a silence fell
on all the Saxon churls, monks, and thanes.
Only the homely birds pursued their music,
connubial whinchats weaving their low nests,   *nest* (OE)
buntings hectoring their brooding brides,   *bryde* (OE)
and out of sight, among the sodden tents,
interpreting between the Son and Father,
two steel-plumed, purple-gorgeted doves,
tu culufran or *cuscutan*, in Saxon.   *doves, ringdoves* (OE)
Perpetually renewing vernal hymns,
the avians laced the smoky air with prayers
beyond the sphere of men, just as the choirs
at Glastonbury and great Ambersbury,
Ambrosius Aurelianus' home,   *British chief, late 5th c.*
sang all day every day, all night each night,

tendering him who made the angelic host   *þreat* (OE)
and made all flying things our debt of love.

Without a word, the king stretched out his hand.
Athelnoth stood next to him, and Garulf,
who handed Athelnoth his horn-tipped bow
and a smooth shaft capped with whetted iron.
The seed of Ingeld nocked the black-fledged missile,   *Alfred*
the throng dividing like the piled tides
before the Prophet's rod, uncurtaining
thin-bearded Finn, a fighting Wiltshireman.
The *stræl* struck him through the throat, and Finn,   *arrow* (OE)
dazed and swaying where he stood, dribbled red
blood from his lips and choked. Sickened, Alfred
thrust the bow on Athelnoth and said: *cwæþ* (OE)

"We will not flee to Athelney, companions.   *geferan* (OE)
Nor will we squander blood and life and hope,
rushing the ditch like stampeding lambs.
All Somerset, all Wessex is our larder,   *spechus* (OE)
and we may harvest all our Lord affords
while gaunt marauders gnaw their horses' ribs.   *wicg* (OE)
We've cut their water, just as Hezekiah
stopped up the streams around Jerusalem,   *2 Chron. 32:3-4*
afflicting the Assyrians with thirst.
We've sent for Berkshire's and for Devon's levies.
Deserters will be hanged. We'll win this war   *hereflyman* (OE)
by the Lord Creator's sole grace and favor."   *Ordfruma* (OE)
The gathering dispersed, dissatisfied,
but understanding who was in command.

King Alfred, Athelnoth, and Athelheah
set out to walk the pickets' outer ring.
"We should be gone from here in seven days,"
said Ingeld's son, still trembling, to his friends.   *Alfred*
"Not everyone, dear bishop, can survive,

come springtime, on his last winter's *fætnys.*   *fat* (OE)
His fellows laughed as churls turned their heads,
eager to share a feeble ray of cheer.

⌾

Another week of rain had chilled the troops   *ren, truman* (OE)
when game Deormod, red-faced and soaked,   *georn* (OE)
entered Godrum's *tabernaculum,*   *tent* (L)
which Alfred, as the conqueror, occupied.   *oferswiþend* (OE)

"Frea," said Deormod, the limpid drops   *Lord* (OE)
that trimmed his cheeks mimicking sad tears,   *tearas* (OE)
"our scouts report an army fast approaching
Bridgwater from the south. Five hundred strong."   *fíf hund* (OE)

A burden pressed the worn commander's chest.
"Fetch Athelheah," he said, "and Athelnoth."
"So we fight, flee, or come to hurried terms,"
he said when they were seated in his presence.

"Attack," said Athelnoth, "it's not too late.
But first detach a force to hold the bridge."   *brycg* (OE)

"Bring Godrum here to bargain," said the bishop,
"and when you give the word, we'll cut him down."   *word* (OE)

"Ia, we owe poor Finn," the king declared,   *yea* (OE)
"and all who bought this lodgment with their blood.
We'll bet on both approaches, and our *Beorn."*   *hero* (OE)

La, Heahgod, la, Hælend, guard your sons   *High God, Savior* (OE);
from Satan and the pagan mariners.   *ealiþend* (OE)
Defend your sworn friends, who oppose your foes,   *freondas, fa* (OE)
from bloodlust, which the enemy employs   *deofol* (OE)
to lure men who love your name to sin.   *synn* (OE)

205

The thane of Somerton and Sherborne's ruler   *þegn* (OE); *rector* (L)
led Sceaf's scion and a score of swords   *Alfred*
through the east-facing gate of their trenched billet
and up the gentle slope to no-man's-land.
The Athulfing, his features hot with soot,   *Alfred*
recognized old Gorm and his supporters
as they descended the elf-shining lea,   *ælfscienene leah* (OE)
accompanied by twenty mailed Danes.

The embassies stopped short, some rods apart,
and Jutish Hrut and Aldhelm's eighth successor   *bp. of Sherborne*
stepped forward, each to state his army's terms.   *here* (OE)
Each legate had lost kinsmen. Each had led
to death men who'd trusted in his care,   *deaþ* (OE)
but each was trusted by his peers to master
his hatred and assert the nation's will.   *þeod* (OE)

"The Saxon bear emerges from his lair,"
the Jutlander began, "to lead a crew
of starveling thieves too poor to wear a sword.
If Your Grace hates their gruel, our ring-giver   **riktrifr* (OEN)
will gladly share his roast stag and boar
to resurrect your famed episcopal girth.
You called this conference. What will these knaves pay
to ransom their doomed limbs from Frankish steel?"   **stal* (OEN)

The prelate saw and raised Hrut's mockery.
"With reverence," he said, "for Hrut's clear spirit,
unclouded by the fumes of meat and mead,
the West Saxons offer peace as follows: *friþ* (OE)
the Danes shall quit this kingdom for all time,
give hostages, return their prisoners,
and for their own souls' benefit, not ours,
consent to serve our everliving Savior."

The earl, granting nothing with his eyes,
disclosed the rowers' opening position.

"I hope my lords enjoyed their fantasy
of safety and unending, unchecked power.
First, you'll pay a thousand silver pounds   *þusinn, *pund, *bot,
bot and wite for this beggarly riot;   *uiti (OEN)
second, you'll pledge loyalty to our throne;
and third, you will disband this pack of thieves,
as vile as Tunni's slave host or the black   crushed by K. Froda
slave rout that thrashed the Persian caliph.   6th c.; Zanj Revolt
If Somerset lies quiet for a year,   869–883
you may select a Saxon alderman,
yourself or Athelnoth, or that burnt ghost."

The churchman was diverted by the patter
of rapid hoofbeats hurrying from the camp.
A messenger dispatched across the river?
Had Froda's men already forced the bridge?   *Fruþa (OEN)

Both headmen huddled with their countrymen,
then both without delay regained mid-field,
Lord Athelheah hauling a mottled sack.
He drew a mass therefrom and held it up.

Purpling with fury, Hrut declared,
"Lord Froda's noble blood will blast this land.
You err, priest, in publishing this crime."   *brestr (OEN)

The bishop handed Hrut the bearded shape,
then thrust his arm in the sack's mouth and seized
a second trophy by its red-gold cable.

The jarl jeered. "Who claims his due reward
for ridding Gorm of this swaggering clog?
King Hrothulf of the Heruli attacked   *Ruulf (OEN)
the Lombards merely to prove his misprised manhood. 508; *Lakbarþi
He lost his helm, his standard, and his life.   (OEN)
Our state is now the steadier, distraitored."

Athelheah conveyed the second head—
high Halga's seed, in case you hadn't twigged—
dug in his bag again, and hoisted high
a clotted bundle of black matted locks
that half-concealed hurts to cheeks and nose,   *hleor, nosu* (OE)
which all-revealing time would never heal.

"You persecute us Jutlanders," said Hrut,
as coldly as our risen Lord, on doomsday,   **tumstakr* (OEN)
will sentence those who scorned his sovereignty,
"although we placed a Christian on our throne   K. Harald Klak; Emp.
and made the Christian emperor our ally.   Louis; **kristn,*
Lord Wan was our War-Father's faithful thane,   **Ualfaþur, *þiakn*
a votary, like Starkad, of the ways   (OEN); Saxo bk. vi
of our plain-living, godly ancestors.
This relic that you flaunt will draw the rage
of Woden on you West Saxon vermin."   **Oþen* (OEN)

"Lord Toca has surrendered," Sherborne's lord   Bp. Athelheah
replied, unwilted by the leader's heat.   *wisa* (OE)
"Our offer to redeem your people stands."
He proffered Wan's grim legacy. The earl   *laf* (OE)
secured it with his wrists against his chest.
Again the two ambassadors turned back,
Hrut with three heads, the bishop with his sack.

"My lords," shrilled old Hrut from among the earls,
his voice half-muted by intruding gulls,
"the former kings would spare their folk from war
by staking a campaign on one sole champion.   Saxo bk. iv; **kabi,*
Forget this paltry trading. Fiolnir's priest   **kuþi* (OEN); Woden
will fight your one-eyed Christian troll alone.
He owes you southerners at least one death   **suþrmæn, *lif,*
for murdering his boy, his only son."   **mogr, *sunr* (OEN)

The Saxon masters turned to Athulf's seed.   *Æþulfs sæd* (OE)
"A Danish dodge, no doubt," said Athelnoth.

"I say we gore old Gorm, as we agreed."

King Alfred probed a cloud with his blue eye.
"We do not fear their stratagems," he said,   *searu* (OE)
"which our hatred pierces like clear air.
Nor do we fear their weapons or their gods.   *wæpen, godu, gesithas*
Companions, there's a summons from the Spirit   (OE)
in Godrum's unconvincing invitation.
Tell the criminals we'll take their challenge   *sceaðan* (OE)
but only if they swear to serve our Savior,
should he deliver me from heathen steel."

The fiends agreed. A level ground was marked
with hazel wands between the hostile works.
When the foes faced each other, Gormr saw   *fa* (OE)
a charcoaled, one-eyed demon, Mervyn's ghost,
who called to mind, again, King Athulf's runt—   *Alfred*
while Alfred saw a grizzled people's chief,   *þeodguma* (OE)
on whose broad shoulders seemed to perch the figures,
remote and small and clear, of his dear *domina*   *ides* (OE)
and their dear *filia,* her diminished image.   *dohtor* (OE)

"Prepare your soul, devil," Alfred said,   *sawul, deofol* (OE)
"to join your heathen ancestors in Hades,   *hæðen* (OE)
where you will feel the fallen angels' forks—"   *forcan* (OE)

"I've heard that burden," said the northerner,   *Godrum/Gormr*
"but who are you to threaten heaven's wrath?
My servant Mervyn? Damned Alfred's phantom,   *⋆traukr* (OEN)
come to avenge his shame on living men?"

Like lightning traveling from east to west,
the seed of Ingeld launched a storm of strokes,   *Alfred*
which Godrum, backing, parried with his blade.
The Saxon recognized the clanging ring
of Offa's gift, from Charles, of Hunnish steel,   *K. Offa of Mercia*
and recognized the cunning of a foe   *acc. 757*

209

who meant to husband fighting strength and breath— *eafoþ* (OE)
or had the Healer humbled Harald's sire,   *Hælend* (OE)
dulled him with hunger, harried him with grief?
A feint at Godrum's eyes brought up his buckler,
which Alfred used to screen a kneeward sweep,
but the fiend hitched and wheeled to his right.

They separated, each to catch his breath,
and each to hear, in his own thumping blood,
the martial thunder of the Lord of Hosts,
whom men have known as Mars or wounded Tiw,
how he collected in each soul the tale
of dread at failing those who needed him,
of grief at losing those few that he loved,
of joy to own the honor of the fight
in sight of men and deathless ancestors—
in sight of Christ himself, who would decide
whom to spare and who would burn forever—
and yet, as men mark off a fighting ground
with sticks or stones, excluding friend and foe,
how he relieves the swordsman's mind of all
the joy and grief and dread that burden him
and bids him meditate his fatal craft
as though his thrusts and blocks were humble prayers.

Again the men exchanged quick testing strokes
and sudden flights of dragon-patterned blades
as each endeavored to provoke his rival
to waste his strength in angry, empty blows.
They fought, and Godfred's scion drew first blood   *Godrum/Gormr*
incising Alfred's thigh, but he replied
with a quick flick that nicked the oarsman's ear.
The long moments passed, and having spent
long days in the field, on irregular fare,
each *guma* glimpsed the bottom of his cup   *man* (OE)
and the frail thread of dregs that beckoned there.

Then each lord's allies, knowing that their portions
hung on their representative's success,
began to shout, drowning the shrieking steel—
from which the fencers took less heart and vim
than respite from the imminence of death.   *deaþ* (OE)

Then Gorm bungled a stroke that should have struck.
Alfred, drawn by a feint at his left knee,
flung his shield down, opening up
his left arm, shoulder, cheek, and temple,   *earm, ceacban,*
but Offa's weapon whistled overhead.   *þunwange* (OE)
Had the Lord jogged his arm, or had the sailor
gone high to expiate his heinous sins?
The Dane's shaded eyes and sagging features   *hleor* (OE)
said nothing of his spiritual state.

By mutual consent, the gladiators
regained the peaceful boundary of the field.
Both bled, both blew, hearts hammered in both breasts
as cupbearers brought them bread and beer.   *byreleas, beor* (OE)

"Can Alfred hear me?" Godfred's grandson called,
"from where he perches now, in purgatory?
Pure pride pushed him to disperse his troops
and post himself, exposed, in Chippenham.
This troll or bogey here will not prevent
the consummation of his failed reign,
which is to see his people kneel to Grim."   *★Krimr* (OEN)

Sufficiently refreshed, the Saxon chief   *Alfred*
attacked across the ring, enveloping
the fiend in a bright whirlwind of steel.
Defending, counterstanding, to a pitch,
Gormr recalled how Starkad searched the earth   *Saxo bks. vi, viii*
for someone worthy of the sober work
of disencumbering him of evil deeds

amassed across three lives of common men,
such as the gibbeting of his own king,
ring-giving Wicarus, at Grim's command.
He parried, plodded, played for time, repaired
his meager vigor while the Saxon toiled.
As if by inspiration, he discerned
the swinker's every swing before he swung.

Soon Ingeld's seed had so indulged his ire,   *irre* (OE)
the robber's blocks forestalled his lagging stabs,
which seeing, Godrum launched a fresh assault,
subtracting additional fractions from his shield.
Depleted, lacking sap to check the chap   *secg* (OE)
and disconcerted by his blurting subjects,
the Athulfing fled thrice around the fence   *Alfred*
and, hooted by his enemies, surrendered
to horror such as Abraham endured   Gen. 15:12
the time nighttime's benightedness engulfed him.   *þeostru* (OE)
Then Charles's gift to Offa whiffed his nape,
and Sceaf's scion knew, with certainty,   *Alfred*
the sailor meant to liquidate his sins,   *lida* (OE)
or else the Lord, again, had turned his edge.   *ecg* (OE)

Athelred's successor turned and stood   *æftergenga* (OE)
face-to-face with the fiend, a fathom off.   *fæþm* (OE)
Instructed by the Comforter, he bowed
into the Dane, abandoning his brand,   *brand* (OE)
and grappling with him, bore him to the ground.
They wrestled in the grass, grunting and straining, *wraxledon, gærse* (OE)
and Alfred choked the *ælf* with bleeding fist,   *elf* (OE)
and beat his bleeding mouth and snout and eyes *muþ, nebb, eagan* (OE)
but the tough devil bucked with fearsome force,
the love of life implanted in each creature,
and scrabbled, wan and weaponless, to safety.

"Lord," cried Wiga, who was Sigfred's spy,   *hæra, *Uiki, *Sihfriþr
"the drengs have brought refreshments! Come   (OEN)
                   and drink!"
The fighters clambered to their feet and picked   *cempan* (OE)
with trembling fingers at their helmet strings.
Swimming in sweat and blood, the pair inspired   *swat* (OE)
remorse among their men, both old and young,
who ought to have come forward for their lords
to fight as deputies or substitutes,   *speliend* (OE)
but shame and awe debarred their tardy offers.
And rightly so: for in this *lytel* war,
waged by weres who wagered their worn souls,   *sawla, blod, cynedom,*
their blood, their sovereignty, their peoples' fortunes   *folca sælþa, wæpen,*
on their right arms, their weapons, and their gods,   *osas* (OE)
only a lord who delved the purest ore
could rightly seize, or yield, the victory-prize.   *sigelean* (OE)

Their mail-coats weighed on their molten limbs   *hringlocan* (OE)
like stones bound to a man condemned to drowning.
Godfred's grandson shucked his clinking sheath   *Godrum / Gormr*
and shocked his jarls with the awful sight
of his uncovered bruised and bloody trunk,
a barked boar bear's sad, manlike carcass,   *biarntiur* (OEN)
as Alfred, like a snake sloughing its case,
wriggled fitfully from ruptured rings
and felt the salt breeze astringe his hurts.
Without a word, he gripped his mottled bill,   *bill* (OE)
his grandfather's parting gift from Charles,   K. Ecgbert acc. 802
and entered on the island hemmed with wands   d. 839
where Eric's bane, brandishing his blade,   *bani* (OEN)
prepared to bring the battle to an end.   *beadu* (OE)

Bare as their ancestors, the pair converged,   *ealdoras* (OE)
acclaimed by none but caroling yellowhammers.
The Saxon felt new valor fill his limbs,   *ellen* (OE)

the *Beorn*'s blessing on his blessed thane,   *hero* (OE); *þegn* (OE)
and roughly rushed the rugged alien,
but Gormr jinked his onset, forced a parry,
and purling rapidly, attacked his back

The nib bit, and Alfred felt his blood
ooze in a tepid runnel down his spine.
He knew how brief an interval remained
for him to spare his family and folk
from slavery and death at heathen hands.   *þeowdom* (OE)
He'd die for them right now, without a thought,
but now his charge was not to die, but heal
the people of this plague by bleeding one
single vicious, unrepentant devil.
The king rushed the rower yet again   *reþra* (OE)
and passing, whipped his tip at Godrum's top.   *copp* (OE)
The brunt would have blown his brains from their box
had not the nimble knave canted his crown,
but nonetheless the Saxon's lancet flayed   *æderseax* (OE)
a flap of fell from the fiend's faltering poll,
threading a row of rubies down one ear.

"You're tonsured," taunted Athulf's youngest son,
"like Childeric the Frank, monasticized,   *K. Childeric dep. 751;*
with papal leave, by short-snooted Pippin."   *K. Pippin acc. 751*
The Saxon king did not complete his boast
but fainting, failed, and woke at Godrum's feet,
darkly, through his blinded eye, perceiving
the blur of Offa's worm-dyed file-leaving   *wyrmfah fela laf,*
fixing to pin his ribcage to the turf.   *turf* (OE)
Writhing, Alfred wrapped the rower's shanks,
shirking steel that slit his seeping side,   *side* (OE)
and thinking, Now he's paid for all his crimes,
levered the slippery brigand to his back.
Just as he thumped the thirsty earth, the thurse,
contorting to absorb the impetus,

felt Alfred's greasy claws unclinch his grip
and crib the Mercian monarch's gift from Charles.
And now the bloody babe from Osburh's belly   *belg* (OE)
(that's Alfred, as Osburh was Oslac's girl)   *Alfred's gdf.*
straddled murdered Godfred's prostrate seed   *Godrum/Gormr*
and pressed the weapon's neck to the thane's throat.   *þegn, þrotu* (OE)

"Grandfather Grim," the seed of Ingeld growled,
"frets where fiends exfoliate his hide.
Will you surrender to your *Sigedryhten?*"   *Victory-Lord* (OE)
When Alfred got but hard stares from his foe,
he rolled the quaking balance of his weight
forward against the edge that nipped the devil.
He would have cut his gullet to the bone,
avenging all the kings the fiends destroyed
and all the Saxon spearmen bled in battle,
but the nicked, lacquered implement he clenched
between his bleeding fingers wouldn't budge—   *betwux, fingras* (OE)
(his bad eye caught a hand—he mashed it down)—
nor would his joints or ligaments obey
the urgent lust to push the steel home.

As if the Lord had dulled his sinful will
or a *dry* droned a rune to blunt the blade,   *wizard* (OE)
the hilt halted, much as the Lombard's lingered
over the nape of Sanctulus of Norcia,   *Gregory,* Dialogues
and Alfred felt, beneath his sticky palm,
the urgent legend graven in the metal,
"go, sell your coat, and buy a sword"—
tunicam suam vendat, emat gladium—   *Luke 22:36*
which Alcuin gilded as an allegory,
interpreting the parable for Charles,
the Lord's "sword" being his two-edged "word."

So unlike rigorous Ingwar, who broke open
Aella at York and Edmund after Hoxne;   *867; 870*

unlike Theodoric the Ostrogoth,
who clove King Odovacar as he supped   *493*
and took his title, King of Italy
("He's boneless, men," the princely killer quipped);
unlike deceitful Simeon and Levi,   *Gen. 34:25-29*
who drowned defiled Dinah's shame in blood;
and unlike Cain, who spilled his brother's life;   *Gen. 4:8*
but just as anointed Saul the Benjamite   *1 Sam. 15:9*
acquitted the Amalekitish king,
and David, Judah's heir, spared drooping Saul,   *1 Sam. 24:4, 26:9*
the seed of Ingeld spared King Godfred's spawn,
if only through the Lord's misericord.

"*Volo*," Godrum whispered timidly,   *I will* (L)
inaudibly to any but himself.
"*✶Iak uil*," as if he'd seen a christening   (OEN)
and heard the baptizand pronounce his vows.
"*Ic wille*," said less faintly than before,   (OE)
"submit to Christ and serve him faithfully
and lead my host under his light yoke."   *✶liþ* (OEN)
He didn't utter all he had in mind.
He didn't claim that Christ had ransomed Grim   *✶Krimr* (OEN)
or would do so when he renewed the world.
He didn't ask whose helpmeet Ealhswith
would be in the new earth of the Eighth Age
or ask to be vouchsafed a Frankish bride
or urge his long-held need to speak with Harald.   *Guthrum's s.*
Nor did he remonstrate with Athulf's seed   *✶saþ* (OEN); *Alfred*
for muddying his soul with ugly hate—
such thoughts were likely snares laid by the devil.   *✶fiati* (OEN)

The Saxon stared, uncertain what he'd heard.
He leaned, he heaved, he thrust, he punched,
                              he plunged;
he jolted, jerked, and jumped, to no avail.
King Eric's bane, a lightness in his breast,   *✶bani* (OEN)
despite the weight of Alfred crashing on him,

desiring to pursue the thing, declared,
"We'll yield, deed, and quit these western hills
to regain the agreeable Anglian fens."
The seed of Ingeld failed to reply.   *Alfred*
"We offer peace," the northmen's chief affirmed.   *friþr* (OEN)
"What will you give to sweeten our submission?"

Young Alfred recollected Godrum's oath,
sworn on his ring and swiftly disavowed.   *Wareham 876*
He recollected treacherous Exeter,   *Exanceaster* (OE)
the pact of peace they'd pledged, repealed, struck
the night the Persians hailed David's *nefa.*   *descendant* (OE)
But Gormr grinned, and Alfred knew his man.
Though Saxon counselors would look askance   *ealdras* (OE)
at bargaining away King Edmund's *regnum,*
the king saw merit in the devil's tender.

"The Anglian nation craves a Christian *cyning,"*
he said. "You shall be baptized with your men
and proceed hence to East Anglian lands.
Return your prisoners, but keep your loot—
we know a shepherd needs to feed his sheep.   *hierde* (OE)
Our *Heahfrea* will correct your sins   *High-Lord* (OE)
as he has punished ours so grievously,
but he will never spurn or swindle you."

Contented with the running tide of grace,
the sailor smiled, and his smashed face shone   *Godrum/Gormr*
as Alfred backed the wrecked edge from his neck.
"I know this peace is good," said Godfred's seed,
"approved by Athelnoth and Sherborne's lord
and Saxon sailormen and mead-bench bears—   *skibarar, *siotulbirnir,
for you are Athulf's boy, restored to men."   *barn, *men (OEN)

XII.

Baptism by Water

⁓✲⁓

Guthrum and his men are baptized at Aller. The Saxons and Danes celebrate the chrisomloosing for twelve days and nights.

"Hosanna," roar the thrones and cherubim
and all the chorus of our Savior's host   *þreat* (OE)
in praise of his impending victory
over *principes et potestates,*   *Eph. 6:12*
and by his mercy, those tremendous hymns,
resounding through the crowded room of heaven,   *rum* (OE)
rain down in the pert airs of birds,   *regnaþ* (OE)
the feathered ones, the angels' messengers,   *ærendsecgas,*
filling our ears, our hearts, our hungry souls   *earan, heortan, sawla,*
with wonder at the Father's steadfast love.   *Fæder* (OE)

Therefore, when Godrum and some thirty men   *þirtig menn* (OE)
threaded their way among the clumps and sallows   *weg* (OE)
where marigolds and purple loosestrife bloomed
and irises that pastured butterflies   *glædenan, buterflegan*
(but where no godhead lay in wait for Ilia,   (OE); *Aeneid bk. i*
the grieving vestal who brought forth the twins),
and waded through the rushes' waving blades
that symbolized new life, and neared the verge   *lif* (OE)
of Parrett's living course, escorted by
the thane of Somerton, confirmed as *dux,*   *þegn* (OE)
and thirty sturdy youths, no trumpets blared,   *beman* (OE)
no timbrels rattled, and no reed-pipes hooed   *pipan* (OE),
but warblers, yellow wagtails, yellowhammers,
chiffchaffs, and blackcaps blew their blended tunes,

while mallards gabbled low among themselves
and other silent witnesses looked on,
two swans afloat downstream, a dark-legged heron   *hragra* (OE)
examining the river's wrinkled skin,
some ravens tumbling high in the upper air,   *hræfnas* (OE)
and higher still, the hanging hawks and kites.   *hafecas* (OE)

The Saxon king and Sherborne's shire-bishop,   *scirbisceop* (OE)
accompanied by Christian priests and soldiers,   *wigan* (OE)
plodded into the slow, soft-bottomed flow.

Unlike the seventh bishop, Ealhstan,   *Ealhstan 7th bp. of*
who with great Eanwulf of Somerset,   *Sherborne cons. 824;*
when Alfred's father, Athelwulf, was king,   *Eanwulf ald. of Som.;*
downriver from that spot, at Parrett mouth,   *848; fæder, muþ,*
had hewed retreating sailors in the surf   *lidan, brim* (OE)
and fed their carcasses to crabs and gulls,
his after-goer greeted Godfred's seed   *æftergenga, sæd* (OE)
and stood with him in water to the waist;
and when the candidates were in position,
and Christian witnesses, dear Ealhswith,   *witnesmenn* (OE)
dear Ymme, Wulfthryth, and the local folk,   *Halga's wid.; K.*
were all in place in bunches on the banks,   *Athelred's wid.*
the bishop, voice diluted in the breeze,
began to question thankful "Athelstan,"   *þancful* (OE)
the name the king had given Harald's father—   *Godrum / Gormr*
for Ecgbert's younger son, King Alfred's uncle,   *sunu, fædra* (OE)
so named (as Alfred's grandson would be named),
had likewise been assigned the Anglian kingdom,
and wielding his father's Frankish rod,   *c. 825; K. Wuffa of E.*
had ransomed Wuffa's people from the Mercians.   *Angles*

That cub killed Beornwulf, the Mercian king,   *K. Beornwulf d. 825; K.*
the seed of Offa's rival, Beornred,   *Beornred d. 757; K.*
and kin to Beorhtwulf, who later ruled   *Offa acc. 757; K.*

when death arrested Wiglaf's second reign—   *Wiglaf d. 840; K.*
killed Beornwulf, and thus repaid the death   *Beorhtwulf acc. 840;*
of Athelbert, the Wuffing Offa martyred,   *deaþ* (OE); *K. Athelbert*
it's said, on Lady Cynethryth's command.   *d. 794; w. of K. Offa*
King Ecgbert's youngest later governed Kent   *Athelstan s. of Ecgbert*
as underking to brother Athelwulf   *undercyning* (OE)
and won immortal glory from the Danes
when once, off Sandwich, with Lord Ealhhere,   *ald. of Kent*
he took nine ships and massacred their crews.   *851*

His forehead horned with light, Lord Halga's friend, *heafod gehyrned,*
though shivering in Parrett's mild chill,   *freond* (OE); *Ex. 34:29;*
pronounced the bold *responsa* he had learned,
as did his thirty would-be Christian men.   *þirtig, cristen menn,*
The bishop blew three tepid puffs of breath,   *biscop* (OE)
to drive off devils, on his mouth and eyes,
and crossed him, fed him salt, laid heavy hands
on his broad, grizzled crown, decreed the fiend
cast out, crossed him again, and cordially
declaimed the lesser creed. Young Alfred stood   *læssane credan* (OE)
with newborn Athelstan and shuddered with him
as Aldhelm's eighth successor exorcised,   *Bp. Athelheah*
again, all unclean spirits from the Dane,
crossed (thrice) and breathed on Parrett's shining
                                        surface,
and sprinkled it with sanctifying chrism.

The bishop then took spittle from his tongue   *tunge* (OE)
and touched it to the catechumen's ears   *Godrum / Gormr*
and nostrils (as when Christ the Healer cured   *Mark 7:35*
a deaf-mute among the garrulous Greeks),
and exorcised the enemy again,   *feondulf* (OE)
and called on "Athelstan" to abrenounce   *Godrum / Gormr*
Satan and all his works and all his pomps,
anointing him with consecrated oil   *ele* (OE)
on *pectus* (chest) and shoulders (*scapulae*).

221

The sailors and their Saxon sponsors trembled,
and yet the light-clad Danes felt spots of heat
where oil held the sunlight and repelled
the gamesome gale's frigerating touch.
The thirty heathen fiends affirmed the creed,
the Trinity, the Church, eternal life;　　　　　　　*eilif lif (OEN)
then Sherborne's ruler, in the Father's name,　　　nama (OE)
lowered Godrum into the gliding current
and, glancing at his *guþwine,* held him　　　　　war-friend (OE)
under the moving wave, until the *cyning,*　　　　king (OE)
stationed at his side and made in his image,
almost invisibly inclined his head,
when Athelheah raised glistening Athelstan,　　　*Godrum / Gormr*
sputtering, into the cloudless, sunlit day.

"And of the Son," the bishop cried and pushed
the man a second time beneath the flood,　　　　*flod* (OE)
and his collected clerics did the same　　　　　　*preostheap* (OE)
with the drenched drengs given into their hands
as Athelheah observed the Athulfing　　　　　　　*Alfred*
again to glean his will in this affair.
The Saxon nodded, and his prelate plucked　　　　*Alfred*
their former foe into the wholesome light.　　　　*Godrum / Gormr*

A voice of waters joined the choiring birds,
and a low dark bound appeared downstream.
The locals recognized the tidal bore,
which made its way from Parrett mouth twice daily.
The bishop dunked, before he caught his breath,
the dripping *dryhten* under the green-gold tent　　lord (OE)
a third time, in the Holy Spirit's name,
and Gormr, unresisting, felt the pour
nip at his wounds and summon him to heaven.

"Into thy hands I commend my spirit,"　　　　　*komændo mina
he said, convinced his son would join him there　*ont i þinar hontur*

as he descried the undulating sky   (OEN)*; Luke 23:46*
above the turbid, rippling element.
He saw, and felt, a swell of shadow pass
that seemed at once to lift and press him down
and felt the brine burn in his nose and eyes
pickling him, as for eternal life.
Lord Athelheah saw Alfred look away
and drop his one good eye, as if in thought,
before he turned his weathered, whiskered cheek   *wange* (OE)
and thrust his arm through the stream's slippery visage
to hale the heathen airwards by the hair.   *hæþen, hær* (OE)
The Saxon Christians on the riverside
observed a shining crop of Christian sailors
arise, like new green reeds, from Parrett's grave
and watched the priests, including Denewulf
as Winchester's new bishop, cross their crowns   *biscop* (OE)
with second unction, per the Roman rite,—
and bind their living skulls with linen bands—

for Saxon priest and king did not debase
the sacrament, as Father Jacob's sons,   *fæder, bearn* (OE)
to purge their sister's plundered maidenhood,
degraded the Lord's oldest, holiest rite,   *Gen. 34:13-31*
viz., *circumcisio, ymbsnidennys,*
to a stratagem of sanguinary vengeance;
nor as Count Stilicho, the half-Vandal
general who upheld Honorius' throne,
defending Italy from Alaric,
made Easter Day a festival of mayhem   *Apr. 6, 402*
when at Pollentia he attacked the camp
where Christian Goths revered their inferior Word   *Waurd* (G)
(spelled *uuinne, aza, uraz, reda, daaz*);   *meadow, god, aurochs,*
nor as Count Ingo did when he ran through   *wagon, day* (G)
King Oscytel, still streaming from the font,
after the Franks thrashed him at Montpensier.   *892*
"I'll never trust a Dane," the count explained,

"nor baptized, nor staggering under his sins."
The Saxons in the water and on land
erupted in a heartfelt shout of joy
that overwhelmed the willow warblers' lays.   *leoþ* (OE)

⁓∞⁓

The toasting hall at Wedmore had been swept,   *winsele* (OE)
and rushes carpeted the whitestone floor
when on the octave of their baptism day
King Athelstan and thirty newborn northmen   *þirtig* (OE)
(who knew the place from former toasting sessions)
entered with sixty Saxon witnesses.   *sixtig* (OE)
Briskly brandishing his brief blade, the bishop   *biscop* (OE)
had worked the liturgy in Alfred's church
by which the fiends, transmuted into limbs
of God the Son, had shed their linen bands
and stepped, blinking, into the waiting time
where men prepare for his surprise return.
The Athulfing now feasted his new friends,   *Alfred*
whom Ealhswith and Athred's widow served,   *Wulfthryth; widwe,*
joined by Ymme and the neighboring ladies.   *cwene* (OE)
When all the guests had eaten, Alfred rose.

"To murdered Edmund's heir," the king exclaimed,
"who by our Savior's unsearchable grace,
despite the flood of Christian blood his sword
has poured on this tormented, groaning land
where Christ himself, like Abraham at Ur,
observed the evolutions of the stars
and blessed the flocks of waterfowl that shared
their speckled patch of sodden moorland with him—
to this cursed man of war, in Christ reborn,
who shall mount Wuffa's smutched throne and rule   *K. Wuffa of E. Angles*
the gull-eating Angles in his name,
we raise the overflowing cup of life!

For who dares judge our Judge's punishments?
This merman has forgone an excellent son,   *mereman, mære magu,*
whom we may call the firstfruits of the war;   *frumwæstm* (OE)
he has lost Halga, always a brother to him;
and has lost friends than whom a man would rather
lose his God-given limbs, by his own sin—
at least he must affirm so to *Frea*.

"So drink up, my friends, to Athelstan,   *drincaþ, freondas,*
our son to whom we've given precious gems,   *sunu* (OE)
the gems Saint Bede identified in Scripture,   *Bede d. 735*
on which he will rebuild the Anglian kingship.
No doubt your puppet, Oswald, will resign,   *K. Oswald ca. 870;*
and Eadwald, we promise, won't expel you.   *Eadwald, K. Edmund's*
But it would be unseemly for our son   *br.*
to marry our lamented brother's relict,   *Wulfthryth da. of*
his spiritual aunt, bereft again.   *Wulfhere*
Therefore she'll wed Lord Theodric, a Saxon,
while her two boys, my royal brother-sons,   *broþorsuna,*
will be esteemed the heirs of Athelstan.   *Æthelstanes irfan* (OE)

"For all their sakes, and for our father's father's,
her father shall not perish for his shame—   *Wulfhere; Wulfheard*
her bold brother bought his life with his life.   *his s.; blot,*
Each folk shall dwell in its own territory   *þeodland* (OE)
under the fruitful law our *Frea* framed.   *Lord* (OE)
Godson, you shall wed a foreign frow,   *godsunu, frowe* (OE)
the Frankish princess Mervyn urged on you,
young Ymme, and stand life-guard to her babe,   *lifweard, lytling,*
called Eric, after Zealand's people's king.   *Selunds leodcyning*
Her spiritual *sweor* I shall be,"   (OE); *K. Eric I d. 854*
by which he meant her ghostly father-in-law,
"and she, my spiritual *snoru*"—
his daughter-in-law, spiritually considered.
"King Athelstan," said Alfred, "schooled by this lady,
shall age in knowledge of our Savior's law   *Nergend* (OE)

and judge all men beneath the Anglian dome.
This miracle the King of Glory wrought. We say,   *wundor, Wuldorcyning* (OE)
Hodie est Deus in Israel—   1 Sam. 17:46
There is a God in Israel this day."

Now Godrum rose. "You can't imagine, friends,"
he said, "the buoyant joy of being saved
from devils who have dogged you day and night.
I pray you never know the weight of sin
a man can labor under and still breathe,
still fight, still spout his nonsense every hour.
But there it is. He did it. I am freed
beyond all hope known in my old life,   **hopa* (OEN)
freed from my faults, my sins, and my foul hatred,   **sakar, *sutir, *fion*
as if those ills were not one and the same.   (OEN)
So to our host, our Alfred, Ingeld's seed,
the sole survivor of your native kings,
we Christian Danes lift up our brimming horns!   **Kristn* (OEN)
For injuries received, he grants us lands
we've already purchased with our steel
based on the Roman road King Ecgbert carved   K. Ecgbert d. 839
through the whole island fifty years ago.

"But we accept our own, with our new name,   **nafn* (OEN)
and pledge to govern as a Christian king   **kristn kunukr* (OEN)
where once we murdered monarch, monk, and man— **man* (OEN)
though even if our reign brings wealth and peace,   **friþr* (OEN)
and we deserve men's praise, we'll never earn
the fame our friends have carried to the grave.
They're gone, those men. But no grief at their loss
can quell the joy that heaven's Lord has poured
upon my head on this most holy day—   **hofoþ* (OEN)
such joy as would itself convince my heart
of our incarnate God's unbounded power,
had he not driven off the devouring fiend
when I lay helpless, pressed by my own weapon,
even before you, bishop, spoke your spell.   **biskub* (OEN)

"I pray my Lord will never leave my side,
although I understand the Holy Ghost,
the third part of the Holy Trinity,   *þriþiukr, *Hailak;
which blesses us with knowledge of the wonders   *Ðrenik, *untar,
the Lord has done in this uncertain world,   *Trutin (OEN)
recedes and flows according to his will,
much as the moon looses and binds the tides—
for even he, the Lord, went down to hell,
where he endured the torments of the damned
and knew, with God's capacity for woe,
eternity in two nights and a day—
thus paying our steep passage to this hall.   *hal (OEN)

"When I and my companions, years ago,   *altþoftar (OEN)
voyaged to the Beormas' land, beyond   Saxo bk. viii
Halogaland, beyond the northmost cape,
beyond the barren shores where Finns and Terfinns
trap and fish, and guard their antlered herds,
and beyond the Cwen Sea, named for a nation   *Kuin Sia (OEN)
that cruel matrons rule, we came to a place   *kunur (OEN)
of dismal woodlands, mist, and biting chill.   *uiþir (OEN)
Beaching our steeds, we heard and felt a sob
convulse the air which so oppressed our breasts
that each of us believed his heart would crack.
A giant took us home and offered us   *iatun (OEN)
rare feasting and the pleasure of his daughters,   *totur (OEN)
then ferried us in darkness through the fog   *þoku (OEN)
across the vast black river to a town,   *burk (OEN)
a walled town, that sprawled along the bank.

"When we set foot on land, we heard again
that terrible, soul-disabling sob,
and voiceless dogs mobbed us as sad heads,   *huntar (OEN)
the heads of heroes, staked, guarded the walls.   *halir (OEN)
A clinging stench enveloped us, and mire,   *sar (OEN)
a stinking, unclean sludge, sucked at our shoes.
We entered unopposed and found the street

swarming with ghosts, then forged on to a hall,   *hal* (OEN)
whose crudely chiseled stones exuded filth.
Beyond the vestibule, we found a feast
in progress where repulsive devils drank   *diaflar* (OEN)
and brandished bones and tossed a goatskin ball,   *ballr* (OEN)
and there we found the source of those huge sobs—
for mounted on the grimy, looming high seat,
a ravaged, wizened, one-eyed giant slumped,
his head and neck mottled with putrid wounds.   *undir* (OEN)

"Beside that battle-Tyr, to left and right   *hiltr Tiur* (OEN)
lay other sickly forms, both bearded lords
and smaller, slimmer ladies, necks and backs   *froiur* (OEN)
prodigiously dislocated or broken,
their once enchanting throats and bovine brows   *halsar* (OEN)
corrupted with black sores. We didn't stop
to contemplate the view, but rushed to loot
the unattended hoard off to one side.
But when we touched the devils' precious plunder—   *diaflar, *ualraubar,*
huge swords, a purple cape, some lumpish rings,   *suiarþ, *kapa,*
a gilded aurochs horn crusted with gems—   *ringænæ, *ur,*
a sentry shrieked, the devils thronged, and all   *gimstæinar, *fiatur* (OEN)
but thirty of my men were torn to shreds.
The rest of us escaped, by heaven's mercy,   *hifns miskun* (OEN)
though unremunerated for our trouble.

"For many years, I foolishly assumed
that miserable king of fiends deplored   *kunukr* (OEN)
his fetters, sores, and loss of worldly might.
Later, I guessed he wept for his lost son,   *Baltr* (OEN)
the manly incarnation of his purpose,
murdered by a hateful thurse's guile.   *Luki* (OEN)
But now I know he grieved for his own sins,
his crimes of fraud and lust and treachery,
towards friend and foe, in peacetime and in war.
For he had understood, our fleshly father—   *faþur* (OEN)

the son of Frithuwald, for it was he—
though from what Alfred says, it might as well
have been Theodoric or Chlodovech,
or great Karl, suffering for his crimes
as Frankish poets boldly postulate—
for he had understood, our ancestor,
each sin of ours pierces the Father's heart
and lays another stripe on his dear Son
and on each man and woman in his church.

*Open (OEN)

K. Clovis d. 511; K.
Theodoric d. 526; Emp.
Charles d. 814

*Sunr, *karl,
*kuna, *kirkia (OEN)

"Wherefore the troll laments, with boundless sorrow,
the squalor he distributed on earth.
We cannot save our fathers or our friends—
that work is for the Holy Ghost alone—
but we can love and praise the Most High God,
the *Hæstr As, *Hærian, *Hifnitrutin,
and bless him for the punishments he sends,
the hammer-blows with which he steels our souls,
over and over, in his living forge;
the hissing pool in which he quenches pride;
and the harsh file he plies to whet our courage
to make each one of us a two-edged flame
to wield against his enemies on doomsday.
Then even evil angels will be healed,
not to mention our godlike ancestors,
for everything our Father made he loves
and shall redeem, all in his own good time.
For he is everything. So say the Franks
as taught by John the Scot, the Irishman
who tutored royal Judith and her brother,
and so says Athelstan."

*Hailak Ont (OEN)

Lord of Hosts, Lord
of Heaven (OEN)

*tumstakr (OEN)
*iklar (OEN)

*Faþur (OEN)

John Scotus Erigena d.
877

He raised his horn,
surveyed the festive crowd, and shared a glance
with his converted men, with Athelheah,
with Alfred, Ealhswith, and Lady Wulfthryth,

and bellowed, jubilation in his eyes,
"Friends and enemies: hail our living Lord!"   *uinir, *uuinir (OEN)
"Our living Lord!" they thundered with one tongue.

∞

Young Alfred led young Ealhswith to bed.   geong, bedd (OE)
A room had been prepared, a marriage bower—   bur (OE)
fresh rushes strewn, small blossoms from the moors   riscas, blostman,
crowded in jars on windowsill and chest,   moras, cyst (OE)
and clean fleeces heaped on a plumped-up pallet— fliesu (OE)
for Alfred's wedded woman had refused,   rihtwif (OE)
after his reprieve of "Athelstan,"
to lie beside her mutilated husband   rihtwer (OE)
until their enemy had gone his way.

"We hail the Lord of Hosts," said royal Alfred,   Dryhten weoroda (OE)
"for not since Oswy clobbered pagan Penda,   Nov. 15, 655
by Winwed's flooded banks, with his small band;
not since King Alaric abandoned Rome,   410
limiting the intemperance of the Goths
to three days and nights of rioting;
and not since Hector's sons reconquered Troy   A.M. 2858
has our almighty Lord, the Holy One
of Canterbury, Winchester, and Rome,
Constantinople and Jerusalem,
performed a more blessed miracle than this,
suppressing the envenomed heathen horde
and purging them, like Pharaoh's furious host,   Ex. 14:27-28
in the cold gush of his preserving flood.

"Now wheat and barley ripen in the fields;   bere, ripaþ, felda,
apples swell on the trees; pigs, calves, and lambs   æppla, lamb (OE)
grow day by day in meadows, woods, and folds;   leas (OE)
and brooding mothers nurture swimming babes,   modru, cild (OE)
while fathers calculate how to provide.   fæderas (OE)

And now we pray *Frea* will heal our scars   *the Lord* (OE)
as he healed his, although he wore them always,
apparent hurts to vulnerable flesh,   *flæsc* (OE)
such as you see in me here, here, and here,
and hidden damage to our qualities
which only the Holy Ghost can renovate.   *Halga Gæst* (OE)
You seem well, lady, but I pray he'll cure   *frowe, sindolg,*
the stubborn wounds you suffered as a prisoner."   *hæftling* (OE)

Kneeling down, he met her lowered eyes.
A tear fell from her chin. It stung his hand.   *cinn* (OE)
"My husband has a kingdom to restore,"   *bonda, rice* (OE)
she said, constricted, salt glazing her cheeks,
"so I won't overload him with old sorrows.
Like those who slew our *Cyning,* whom he pardoned,   *King* (OE)
we know not what we do. Such is our fate.   *Luke 23:34*

"Suffice to say, no day or night has passed
since my dear husband thrust me from his hall   *Pega sis. of St.*
that one of our Lord's ministers, Saint Pega,   *Guthlac; Eadburh d. of*
Saint Eadburh, or Werburh, or our Mother,   *K. Penda; Werburh d.*
has not sustained my lacerated heart.   *of K. Wulfhere; Modor*
I didn't slit our poor children's throats   (OE)
or nail Gorm's helmless head to the floor,   *Jud. 4:21*
nor have I stuck our loving people's king   *leodcyning* (OE)
for damning me to hell among the Danes.   *næddran* (OE);
With faith, *Frea* says, we can handle serpents."   *Mark 16:18*

"The half-converted fiend will burn in pain,"
the Saxon interjected bitterly,
"who knows how many years, for all his crimes
and misconceived beliefs I warned him of.
The Father overflows our orthodoxy,   *Fæder* (OE)
but heresy betrays a sullen soul.
But now I pray," he said, scrawling a cross,
"his glorious might will keep me in the joy   *mægenþrymm* (OE)

he poured on me when he redeemed the Dane.
The Holy Spirit, blowing where it pleases,
has summoned peoples via grievous errors.
The Vandals, Goths, Burgundians from Bornholm,   *Wendlas, Gotan,*
the Lombards whom our Father Sceaf ruled,   *Burgendes,*
they first received our loving Lord deformed,   *Langbeardas* (OE)
horribly deformed by the Arian teaching
that Christ our risen Savior is not God.
Not so the Angles, Saxons, or the Jutes,   *Angle, Seaxan,*
or the Franks who federated with King Clovis,   *Iotas, Francan* (OE)
all baptised into the plain Roman creed.
In time, the Arians put away their knavery.
Maybe he will save everyone, in time."

"In gratitude for *Heofoncyninges* mercy,"
said Edward's mother, Alfred's wedded half,   *modor, hæmedwif* (OE)
"I promised him, as soon as I was free,
to enter a community and live
and die under holy Benedict's rule—
perhaps in holy Ealhburh's house at Wilton,   *K. Ecgbert's sis.*
or one in my own land, if any stand.
You need not stare, my dear. I do not choose,   *leof* (OE)
now, without your leave, by my own will,
to spurn the nuptial vow that comprehends
obedience to heaven and my husband.
I'll stay or go, my friend, as you command."   *freond* (OE)
She stopped. So many things she couldn't tell him,
how she'd subverted Godrum's strength and courage, *cræft, ellen* (OE)
keeping him up all night before the battle
and then again before their single fight—
a stratagem for which she'd win no fame.   *searu* (OE)

The Athulfing let fall the *freo's folma*,   *lady, palms* (OE)
his stricken features purple, then flood-pale.
A surge of hatred shook his weakened frame.
He thought of how the Prophet purged his horde,   *Ex. 32:27-28*

punishing those who turned their backs on God.
But he would not accuse her of the crimes
King Lothar heaped on his rejected lady,   *K. Lothar II d. 869;*
misdeeds only a devil could conceive,   *Teutberga d. 875*
or those Procopius lavished on the empress,   *Emp. Theodora*
the bear-keeper's daughter, Theodora.   *d. 548*

"Kneel with me, lady," Alfred said,   *ides* (OE)
"the adversary has me by the throat.   *wiðerbroca* (OE)
We pray you, *Brego*, break, burst his grip. *King* (OE)
Please kneel with me, my Mercian mediator."   *midligend* (OE)
She slid down and found his grasping hand.
"Almighty Lord of Hosts," the Saxon said,   *Ælmihtig Dryhten,*
"you kept our mother Sarah uncorrupted,   *duguþas, modor,*
although her husband loaned her out to Pharaoh. *bonda* (OE)
You spared her from Lucretia's sin, who slew *Gen. 12:15, 20:2*
herself, sinless, the nation-hater's prey.   *leodhata* (OE)

"Now spare me from the Levite's bloody labor— *Jud. 19:29*
we owe it to our dead, including Finn—
and teach me how a king, without your Spirit,
is just another servant of the devil's,
at war with every man and with your law.
Send us your saints and soldiers, *Sigedryhten*, *secgas, eard* (OE);
to help us hold and cultivate this homeland   *Victory-Lord* (OE)
and shield us from devils day and night."

The pious lady added, Alfred's consort,   *ides, efning* (OE)
"Grant us a double portion of your Ghost
that we may soon forgive old enemies,
Mercian and Saxon, foreign prince and pledge,
one flesh disjoined by misery and sin.   *syn* (OE)
Grant us your blessing, *Frea*, that we may   *bletsung* (OE)
love each other as you, despite our crime
in torturing and killing you, love us."

Unlike their bleeding *Beorn* on his tree,   hero (OE)
they knew their God had not forsaken them.   *Matt. 27:46*
They knew he bore the marks of martyrdom,
the tally of the ransom he had paid,
and knew they, too, would always own their sorrows,
the difference being, their scars were their own,
while his are yours and mine and everyone's.
They felt repenting tears burn in their eyes
(in Alfred's case, one clear, the other dull),
the salty flood that would engulf their sins,   *sealt flod* (OE)
and, blinking at each other through the swells   *yþa* (OE)
that rolled across their vision, they beheld
a miracle too wonderful to utter:

each saw the other in eternity
transfigured, changed, as we will be that day   *dæg, þeod* (OE); *1 Cor.*
when every nation stands before the throne   *15:52; Rev. 7:9*
from under which the living river springs
that pours from heaven, parting in four heads,   *Rev. 22:1*
the Pishon, by whose banks the best gold grows;   *Fison, Gion,*
the Gihon, which surrounds Ethiopian land;   *Tigris, Eufrates* (OE)
the Tigris, which butts up against Assyria;   *Gen 2:10-14*
and the fourth famous *flumen*, the Euphrates—   river (L)
they saw each other as we'll see each other,
surrounded by his bloody company   *fyrdgetrum,*
fresh from the last battle with the dragon,   *draca* (OE); *Rev. 12:7*
for in their gleaming, salt-stained faces burned,
like candlelight glowing through shaven horn   *candelleoht* (OE)
or the hushed heaven-dweller, vapor veiled,   *heofontungol* (OE)
the glory of our risen *Guþcyning*.   *warrior king* (OE)

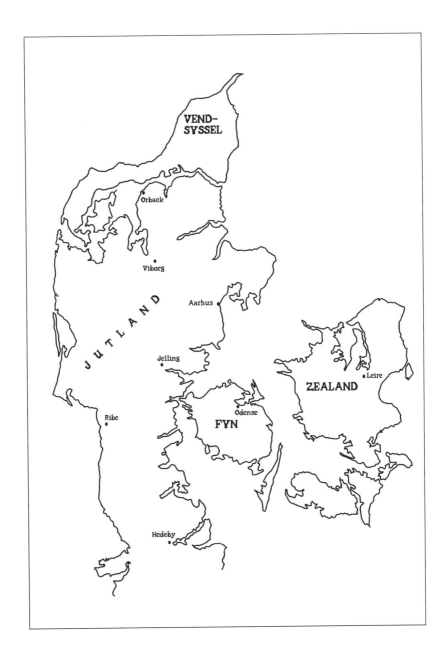

The West Saxon Kingdom

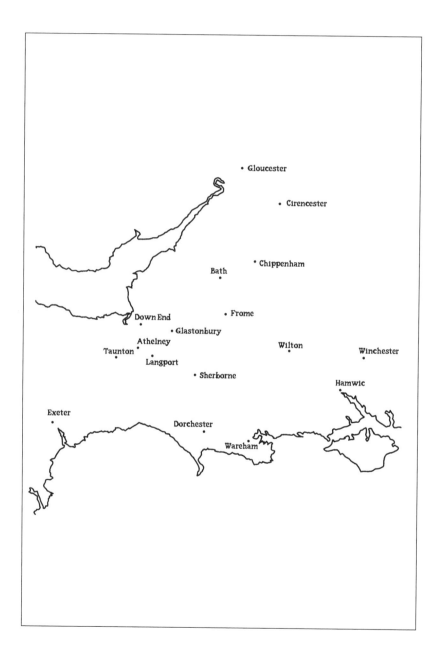

- Gloucester
- Cirencester
- Chippenham
- Bath
- Frome
- Down End
- Glastonbury
- Athelney
- Taunton
- Wilton
- Winchester
- Langport
- Sherborne
- Hamwic
- Exeter
- Dorchester
- Wareham

The Four Old English Kingdoms in the Ninth Century

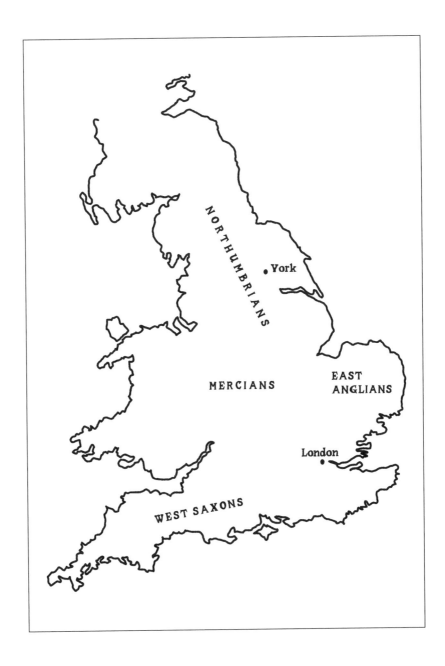

NORTHUMBRIANS

• York

MERCIANS

EAST
ANGLIANS

London
•

WEST SAXONS

Glossary

ABBA   Jutish gleeman, father of Samson and Edith (ahb´-ba)

ABOTRITES   Slavic people on Baltic coast east of Jutland (ahb´-o-trites)

ADDI   Alfred's senior hall-guard (ahd´-dee)

AELLA   king of Northumbrians d. 867 (al´-a)

AENEAS   ancestor of Julius Caesar who led Trojans to Italy (a-knee´-us)

AGAG   king of Amalekites spared by Saul (ah´-gog)

ALARIC   king of Visigoths who sacked Rome d. 410 (al´-a-rick)

ALCUIN   Northumbrian monk who became master of Charles the Great's palace school in Aachen d. 804 (al´-quin)

ALDHELM, SAINT   West Saxon monk who founded monasteries of Frome and Bradford on Avon; first bishop of Sherborne d. 709; author of *De lauda virginitatis, Carmen de virginitatis,* and *Aenigmata* (Riddles) (ahld´-helm)

ALFRED   king of West Saxons d. 899 (al´-fred)

ALFSTAN   alderman of Dorset (alf´-stan)

ANDERNACH   site of battle in 876 between Louis the Saxon and Charles the Bald (on´-der-knock)

ARTORIUS   Latin name for Arthur (are-tor´-ee-us)

ATHELBALD   king of West Saxons and Alfred's brother d. 860 (a´-thul-bald)

ATHELBERT   king of Kent d. 616; married to Bertha daughter of King Charibert of Paris (a´-thul-bert)

ATHELBERT   king of West Saxons and Alfred's brother d. 865 (a´-thul-bert)

ATHELFLAED   daughter of Alfred d. 918 (a´-thul-flad)

ATHELGEOFU   daughter of Alfred (a´-thul-yay-a-fu)

ATHELHEAH   ninth bishop of Sherborne (a´-thul-hay-a)

ATHELNOTH   thane of Somerton, later alderman of Somerset (a´-thul-noath)

ATHELRED   king of West Saxons and Alfred's brother d. 871 (a´-thul-red)

ATHELSTAN   king of East Angles and Alfred's uncle (a´-thul-stan)

ATHELSWITH   Alfred's sister d. 888 (a´-thul-swith)

ATHELWEARD   Alfred's youngest son (a´-thul-way-erd)

ATHELWULF   king of West Saxons and Alfred's father d. 858 (a´-thul-wolf)

ATHELWULF   alderman of Berkshire d. 871 (a´-thul-wolf)

ATTILA   king of Huns d. 453 (at´-til-a)

ATTILA   Danish warrior under Godrum (at´-til-a)

AUGUSTINE OF CANTERBURY, SAINT   Italian monk sent by Gregory the Great to proselytize the pagan English kingdoms d. 604 (a-gust´-in)

AUGUSTINE OF HIPPO, SAINT   North African bishop d. 430; his *Soliloquia* were included in Alfred's translation program, along with Orosius' *Seven Books of History Against the Pagans*, Boethius' *Consolation of Philosophy*, Gregory the Great's *Dialogues* and *Pastoral Care*, Bede's *Ecclesiastical History of the*

English People, and the first fifty
Psalms; Augustine's *De civitate
dei* (*The City of God*) was a
favorite of Charles the Great's
(a-gust´-in)

BALD   one of Alfred's hall-guards
(bald´)

BALDHILD,
SAINT   consort of Clovis II and regent
during minority of his son
Chlotar; said to be of East
Anglian royal line, sold into
slavery as a child d. 680 (bald´-
hild)

BALDWIN   count of Boulogne d. 879;
married Judith daughter of
Charles the Bald and widow
of Athelwulf and Athelbald
(bald´-win)

BEDE   Northumbrian monk, his-
torian, scientist, and biblical
commentator d. 735 (bead´)

BEDRICWORTH   monastery where King Ed-
mund's remains were preserved
(bed´-rick-worth)

BENEDICT,
SAINT   Italian monk who founded
monastery at Monte Cassino
in 530 and instituted rule; life
recounted in Gregory's *Dialogi,*
which was included in Alfred's
translation program (ben´-a-
dict)

BEORMALAND   area on southern shore of
White Sea (bay´-orm-a-land)

BEORN   Norse chieftain and adventurer
(bay´-orn)

BEORNSTAN   one of Alfred's hall-guards
(bay´-orn-stan)

BEORNWULF   swineherd of Selwood Forest
who accompanies Alfred after
invasion (bay´-orn-wolf)

BEORHTHELM   one of Alfred's hall-guards
(bay´-ort-helm)

BEORHTRIC   king of West Saxons d. 802
(bay´-ort-rich)

BERENGAR   count of Bayeux and Rennes,
father of Poppa (bear´-en-gar)

BERKSHIRE   shire northeast of Wiltshire and
north of Hampshire (berk´-
sher)

BOETHIUS   Roman senator and philoso-
pher d. 524; author of *De con-
solatione philosophiae,* which was
included in Alfred's translation
program (bo-eath´-ee-us)

BONIFACE, SAINT   Saxon monk from Devon,
apostle to the Germans, killed
by Frisians in 754 (bahn´-if-us)

BRAVELLIR   site of battle between Harald
War-tooth's allies and his
enemies (brahv´-a-leer)

BRUNHILD   daughter of Athanagild king
of Visigoths d. 567; married
King Sigebert I d. 575; mother
of King Childebert II d.
596; grandmother of King
Theudebert II d. 612 and
King Theuderich II d. 613;
great-grandmother of King
Sigebert II d. 613; sister of
Galswintha d. 568 who mar-
ried King Chilperic d. 584 and
was murdered by Fredegund
Chilperic's mistress d. 597
(broon´-hild)

BRUTUS   Roman ancestor of Britons
(brute´-us)

BURGRED   king of Mercia and husband of
Athelswith; expelled by Danes
874 (burg´-red)

CANTABRIANS   Celtic people in northern
Spain defeated by Romans ca.
19 B.C. (can-tahb´-ri-uns)

CEADWALLA   king of West Saxons d. 689
(chay´-add-wall´-uh)

CENWALH   king of West Saxons d. 674
(chen´-walk)

CERDIC   king of West Saxons d. 534
(cher´-ditch)

CHARLES
THE BALD   king of West Franks, king of
Italy, Emperor of the Romans
d. 877; son of Emperor Louis,
father of Judith and King
Louis II of West Franks

CHARLES
THE GREAT — king of the Franks, king of the Lombards, Emperor of the Romans d. 814

CHARLES
THE HAMMER — mayor of the palace d. 741; father of King Pippin, grandfather of Charles the Great

CHERUSCI — people of northwestern Germany who fought Romans under leadership of Arminius (cher-oos´-key)

CHILDERIC — last Merovingian king of Franks; deposed by Pippin 751 (chil´-der-ick)

CHIPPENHAM — town on Bristol Avon in northwestern Wiltshire (chip´-uhn-um)

CHURN — river that runs through Cirencester and empties into Thames at Cricklade (churn´)

CIMBRIA — people of Jutland who fought Roman Republic at end of 2nd century B.C. (kim´-bree-uh)

CIRENCESTER — town on River Churn where Godrum stages attack on West Saxon kingdom (siz´-i-ter)

CLOVIS I — king of Salian Franks d. 511; converted to Roman Christianity 496 (clove´-iss)

CLOVIS II — king of Neustria and Burgundy d. 658; fathered three future kings by Baldhild, a slave said to be of East Anglian royal parentage (clove´-iss)

COLCHESTER — town in Essex (coal´-chest-er)

CREDITON — town in Devon, reputed birthplace of Saint Boniface (Wynfrith) (cred´-it-uhn)

CWICHELM — king of West Saxons d. 636 (quitch´-helm)

CYMA — a Wiltshire thane (cue´-muh)

CYNEGILS — king of West Saxons d. 643 (cune´-a-gills)

CYNEWULF — king of West Saxons d. 786 (cune´-a-wolf)

CYNEWULF — one of Alfred's hall-guards (cune´-a-wolf)

DAN — legendary ancestor of Danish kings (dan´)

DAVID, SAINT — Welsh bishop of Mynyw d. 589; grandson of Ceredig ap Cunedda king of Ceredigion

DENEHILD — daughter of Denewulf (dane´-a-hild)

DENEWULF — swineherd in Selwood Forest, later bishop of Winchester d. 908 (dane´-a-wolf)

DEVON — shire southwest of Somerset and east of Cornwall (dev´-uhn)

DORSET — shire south of Somerset and Wiltshire (door´-set)

DRUSUS — Nero Claudius Drusus Germanicus d. 9 B.C. (droos´-us)

DUMGARTH — king of Cornwall (dumb´-garth)

EADBALD — king of Kent d. 640 (ay´-ad-bald)

EADBURH — daughter of King Offa, wife of King Beorhtric of West Saxons; fled to Charles the Great after accidentally poisoning her husband (ay´-ad-burk)

EADWULF — alderman of Berkshire (ay´-ad-wolf)

EALHSTAN — seventh bishop of Sherborne (ay´-alk-stan)

EALHSTAN — a Wiltshire thane (ay´-alk-stan)

EALHSWITH — Alfred's wife d. 908; daughter of Mercian alderman Athelred Mucel and Eadburh of Mercian royal blood (ay´-alk-swith)

EANMUND — monk at Breedon on the Hill (ay´-an-mund)

EAST ANGLIA — kingdom comprising shires of Norfolk and Suffolk

ECGBERT — king of West Saxons d. 839; Alfred's grandfather (edge´-bert)

EDMUND | king of East Angles d. 870

EDWARD | eldest son of Alfred, king of West Saxons d. 924

EDWIN | king of Deira and Bernicia d 632; converted to Christianity in 627

EGLON | Moabite king assassinated by Ehud judge of Israel by means of feigned embassy (egg´-luhn)

EHUD | Hebrew judge who approached Eglon king of Moab by means of feigned embassy and killed him with a two-edged blade concealed on his thigh (ay´-hood)

ELFTHRYTH | youngest of Alfred's three daughters; married Baldwin II of Flanders (elf´-thrith)

ELIZABETH, SAINT | mother of Saint John the Baptist and kinswoman of OUR LORD

EOMER | West Saxon nobleman sent to assassinate King Edwin by means of feigned embassy and stabbed him with poisoned blade (ay´-o-mer)

ERIC (HORIK) | Danish king d. 854; son of King Godfred d. 810

ERIC (RORIK) | count of Dorestad and ally of Emperor Lothar d. 855; son of King Hemming d. 812, brother of Halga's father Harald

ERMANARIC | Gothic king d. 376 (air-man´-a-rick)

EXETER | town in eastern Devon on River Exe where Alfred besieged Godrum 876–877

FONTENOY | site of battle in 841 among sons of Louis the Pious, Louis the German and Charles the Bald defeating Lothar of Italy (later emperor) and Pippin of Aquitaine (font´-a-noy)

FREYA | Norse goddess of fertility (fray´-uh)

FRODA | Danish chieftain under Godrum from Ribe River area of Jutland (fro´-duh); OEN *Fruþa

FROME | town in eastern Somerset where Saint Aldhelm founded abbey (frome´)

FURSEUS, SAINT | Irish monk, first Irish missionary to Anglo-Saxon England, preached in Frankland d. 650; visions described in Bede's *Historia Ecclesiastic Gentis Anglorum,* which was included in Alfred's translation program (fur´-see-us)

GEWISSE | early tribal name of West Saxons (yeh-wiss´-uh)

GLASTONBURY | abbey in northeastern Somerset; in later legend reputed to have been founded by Saint Joseph of Arimathea, kinsman of OUR LORD

GODFRED | Danish king d. 810; father of King Eric d. 854; Godrum's grandfather

GODRUM | also Guthrum, Gormr, Guþormr; Danish chief who invaded West Saxon kingdom in 871, 876, 878; defeated by Alfred at Eþandun in 878; King of East Angles (gode´-rum)

GREGORY THE GREAT | pope who sent Augustine the Italian monk to proselytize the Anglo-Saxon kingdoms, subsequently known as Saint Augustine of Canterbury d. 604; Gregory's *Dialogues* and *Pastoral Care* were included in Alfred's translation program

GRIM | god revered by pre-Christian Saxons, also known as Woden; OEN *Krimr, *Oþen

GYRTH | Bishop Athelheah's cook (girth´)

HAESTEN | Norse chief who accompanied Beorn on voyage to Africa and Italy (hast´-en)

HALFDAN | one of chiefs of Great Army of 865; reputed to be son of Ragnar Lodbrok (half´-dan)

HALGA | Danish chieftain under Godrum; father of Hrothulf, son of Harald, grandson of King Hemming d. 812 (hal´-guh); OEN *Helki

HALMUND — one of Alfred's hall-guards (hal´-mund)

HAMPSHIRE — shire bordered by Dorset and Wiltshire to west, Berkshire to north, Surrey and Sussex to east (hamp´-sher)

HARALD — Godrum's deceased son (hair´-ald); OEN *Haraltr

HARALD — Godrum's deceased father (hair´-ald); OEN *Haraltr

HARALD — Halga's deceased father, brother of Eric count of Dorestad (hair´-ald); OEN *Haraltr

HARALD KLAK — Danish king acc. 812, 819, 825; baptized 826; d. 852 (hair´-ald clock)

HARALD WAR-TOOTH — Danish king killed by Odin at Bravellir (hair´-ald)

HÆDDA — first abbot of Breedon on the Hill in Mercia d. 721 (had´-uh)

HEMMING — Danish king d. 812; grandfather of Halga (hem´-ing)

HEREFRITH — abbot of Glastonbury (hair´-uh-frith)

HILDA — Ealhswith's companion

HIMMERLAND — region of northern Jutland

HINCMAR — archbishop of Reims d. 882 (hink´-mar)

HROLF — Norse warrior who seized Rouen in 876; granted land on lower Seine (later known as Normandy) by King Charles the Simple (hroalf´)

HROLF KRAKI — Danish king in 6th century (hroalf´ crock-ee)

HROTHULF — Danish chief under Godrum; son of Halga, grandson of Harald, great-grandson of King Hemming d. 812 (hroath´-ulf); OEN *Ruulf

HRUT — Danish chief under Godrum, noble of Hedeby (hroot´)

HUNERIC — king of Vandals d. 484; son of King Genseric d. 470, father of King Hilderic d. 533 (hun´-er-ick)

HYGELAC — Norse warrior killed 515 in Frisia by Theodbert (Theudebert), future king of East Franks d. 548 (hewg´-uh-lack)

INGELD — legendary Norse warrior (ing´-geld)

INGELD — son of Cenred, brother of King Ini abd. 726; Alfred's great-great-great-great-grandfather (ing´-geld)

INGWAR — one of chiefs of Great Army of 865; reputed to be son of Ragnar Lodbrok (ing´-gwahr)

INI — West Saxon king abd. 726 (een´-ee)

ITCHEN — river in Hampshire where alderman Athelwulf defeated Weland in 860

JOHN THE BAPTIST, SAINT — forerunner and kinsman of OUR LORD

JOHN THE EVANGELIST, SAINT — fourth gospeller

JOSEPH OF ARIMATHEA, SAINT — legendary founder of Glastonbury abbey; kinsman of OUR LORD

JOSHUA — Moses' successor as Hebrew war leader

JUDITH — daughter of Charles the Bald; at young age married King Athelwulf, becoming Alfred's stepmother; at Athelwulf's death, married his son King Athelbald, Alfred's eldest brother; after his death, eloped with Baldwin count of Boulogne

JUTLAND — Danish peninsula extending from northwest Germany and forming narrow channel between North Sea and Baltic (ute´-land)

KENT — southeastern kingdom settled by Jutes; ruled by West Saxons after Ecgbert defeated Mercians at Ellendun in 825

LACOCK — village in Wiltshire south of Chippenham

LEO IV — pope d. 855 who invested Alfred as consul of Brittannia; supervised repair and expansion of Roman walls

LIMFJORD — inlet cutting across northern Jutland (limb´-fyord)

LOTHAR I — emperor d. 855; son of Louis the Pious, father of Emperor Louis II d. 875, Charles of Provence d. 863, Lothar of Lorraine d. 869

LOTHAR II — king of Lorraine d. 869; son of Emperor Lothar d. 855

LOUIS THE PIOUS — emperor d. 840; son of Charles the Great d. 814, father of Emperor Lothar d. 855, Louis the German d. 876, Pippin of Aquitaine d. 838, and Charles the Bald d. 877

LOUIS THE SAXON — king of Saxony d. 882; son of Louis the German d. 876; defeated uncle Charles the Bald at Andernach in 876

LUND — chief town in Scania

LUNDENBURG — London

MARIUS — Roman general and politician d. 86 B.C. (mahr´-ee-us)

MARY, SAINT — mother of OUR LORD

MERCIA — central English, primarily Anglian kingdom (mersh´-uh)

MEROVEUS — founder of Merovingian dynasty of the Salian Franks; father of Childeric I d. 481, grandfather of Clovis d. 511 (muh-rove´-ee-us)

MERTON — site of battle in 871 between Danes and West Saxons in which King Athelred was mortally wounded

MERVYN — Alfred's assumed name as Welsh bard

MILDRED — a Wiltshire thane

MITHRIDATES THE GREAT — king of Pontus who fought Mithridatic Wars with Rome d. 63 B.C. (myth´-ri-dot´-ease)

NERO — Roman emperor d. 68 (near´-oh)

NINUS — warlike Assyrian king, mentioned in Orosius (nine´-us)

NORTHUMBRIA — northern English kingdom resulting from union of Bernicia and Deira under one king

NYKLOT — Abotritan chief under Godrum (nick´-lot)

OCCHUS BOCCHUS — Old English water spirit (oak´-us boak´-us)

OCTA — one of Alfred's hall-guards (oak´-tuh)

ODDA — alderman of Devon (oad´-uh)

ODOVACAR — first Germanic king of Italy, having deposed Romulus Augustulus in 476; said to be of Scirian descent (oh´-do-vay´-car)

OFFA — king of Angles in southern Jutland; ancestor of King Offa of Mercia d. 796 (oaf´-uh)

OFFA — king of Mercia d. 796; descended from king of Angles in southern Jutland (oaf´-uh)

ORBAEK — town at western end of Limfjord in northwest Himmerland on Jutland (oar´-back)

OROSIUS — Spanish priest who studied and collaborated with Saint Augustine of Hippo; author of *Historiarum Adversum Paganos Libri VII,* which was included in Alfred's translation program (oar-ohs´-ee-us)

OSBURH — Alfred's mother, daughter of Oslac, said to be of royal line of Wight (ahs´-burk)

OSLAC — Alfred's maternal grandfather; King Athelwulf's *pincerna* (butler), said to be of royal line of Wight (ahs´-lock)

OSRIC — one of Alfred's hall-guards

OSWALD — puppet king of East Angles appointed by Danes after execution of King Edmund in 870 (ahs´-walled)

PAULUS — one of Denewulf's Welsh swineherds (powl´-us)

PENDA — pagan king of Mercia d. 655 (pen´-duh)

PIPPIN I OF AQUITAINE — king of Aquitaine d. 838; son of Louis the Pious d. 840, father of Pippin II the Younger d. 864

PIPPIN THE SHORT — king of Franks d. 768; crowned in 752 after deposition of Childeric in 751; son of Charles the Hammer d. 741; father of Charles the Great d. 814

PIPPIN II THE YOUNGER — claimed crown of Aquitaine; enlisted Norse assistance; believed to have sacrificed to Odin; son of Pippin I of Aquitaine d. 838; died ca. 864 a prisoner of Charles the Bald

PRIAM — king of Troy at time of attack by Greeks under Agamemnon (pry´-uhm)

RADAGAST — Abotritan god (rad´-uh-gast)

RADAGAST — Visigothic chief who invaded Italy in 405; defeated by Stilicho and executed 406 (rad´-uh-gast)

RAGNAR LODBROK — Norse chieftain led attack on Paris in 845; said to be father of Halfdan, Ingwar, and Ubba, leaders of Great Army of 865; invasion said to be retaliation for King Aella's execution of Ragnar by having him tossed in a snake pit (rag´-nar load´-broke)

REPTON — town in Mercia where Halfdan defeated Mercian forces in 874, leading to expulsion of Burgred and appointment of Ceolwulf II as puppet king of Mercia

RINGSTED — town in Zealand

ROMEBURG — Rome

ROMULUS — founder of Rome (rahm´-yule-us)

SALACIA — consort of Neptune (suh-lay´-shuh)

SANCTULUS OF NORCIA — monk whose miracle is recounted by Gregory the Great in his *Dialogi,* which was included in Alfred's translation program (sank´-tewl-us of norsh´-uh)

SAUL — first king of the Hebrews, anointed by Samuel (sawl´)

SCANIA — area across the sound from Zealand; contiguous with Swedish territory but ruled by Danes (skah´-nyuh)

SCEAFA — legendary son of Noah, ancestor of West Saxon kings (shay´-a-fuh)

SEMIRAMIS — warlike Assyrian queen, mentioned in Orosius (sem´-ee-rahm´-iss)

SERGIUS — pope who baptized King Ceadwalla in 689, Ceadwalla having abdicated the West Saxon throne and traveled to Rome (surge´-ee-us)

SIGEBERT — king of West Saxons acc. 756, deposed by Cynewulf in 757 (see´-a-bert)

SIGEWULF — one of Alfred's hall-guards (see´-a-wolf)

SIGFRED — co-king of Danes; OEN *Sihfrithr

SIWARD — Godrum's Scanian captain (sea´-word); OEN *Sikurþr

SMALA — father of Siward, Godrum's Scanian captain (small´-uh)

SOMERSET — shire bounded by Devon to west and southwest, Dorset to southeast, Wiltshire to east, Gloucestershire to north; encompasses Bath, Glastonbury, Somerton, Athelney, Edington, Down End, Aller, and Wedmore

SUEBI — German tribe defeated by Drusus in 9 B.C. (sway´-bee)

SULLA — Roman general, consul, and dictator, served under Marius in Jugurthine War and Cimbrian War, appointed proconsul of Cilicia, successfully campaigned in Social War against Italian allies, elected consul, led Roman forces in First Mithridatic War, defeated Marian forces in civil war, appointed dictator by senate, slaughtered enemies, reformed laws, resigned dictatorship, reelected consul, retired d. 78 B.C. (sul´-luh)

SUSSEX — South Saxon kingdom ruled by West Saxons following Ecgbert's defeat of Mercians at Ellendun in 825

SWANAGE — town on southeast coast of Dorset; Godrum's fleet destroyed off Swanage in early 877 while he waited under siege in Exeter (swan´-edge)

THEODBERT — Frankish prince who killed Hygelac in 515; king of East Franks d. 548 (thay´-oad-bert)

THEODORIC — first Ostrogothic king of Italy d. 526 (thee-odd´-a-rick)

THEODRIC — Nordalbingian Saxon captain under Godrum (thay´-oderich)

THUNOR — Saxon god of thunder (tune´-oar); OEN *Þur

TOCA — Danish chieftain under Godrum from Orbaek in north west Himmerland on Jutland (toke´-uh); OEN *Toki

TUNBERT — nineteenth bishop of Winchester

TYR — Norse god of law who sacrificed his hand to bind Fenris the wolf (tier´); OE Tiw

UBBA — one of chiefs of Great Army of 865; reputed to be son of Ragnar Lodbrok; in early 878, defeated by Odda of Devon at Cynuit in Somerset (oob´-uh)

UTTA — one of Alfred's hall-guards (oot´-uh)

VENILIA — consort of Neptune (vuh-nill´-ee-uh)

VIBORG — town in central Jutland where first king was raised according to Saxo Grammaticus (vie´-borg)

WAN — Danish chieftain under Godrum from Limfjord area in northern Jutland (wan´)

WAREHAM — port town in east Dorset where Alfred besieged Godrum in 876

WELAND — Danish chief defeated by Alderman Athelwulf on River Itchen in Hampshire in 860 (way´-lund)

WELAND — legendary craftsman revered by Norse (way´-lund)

WERWULF — monk in Alfred's service from Breedon abbey, which the invading Danes had destroyed (ware´-wolf)

WHITE SEA — inlet of Barents Sea forming route to Beormaland; Norse Ohtere's description of his voyage to Beormaland was incorporated in Alfred's translation of Orosius

WIGA Zealand chieftain under Godrum, friend of Siward (wig´-uh); OEN *Uiki*

WIGHT island off Hampshire coast settled by Jutes in 5th century; the West Saxons conquered it under Ceadwalla 685–686; Alfred's mother Osburh was said to be of Wightish royal line (white´)

WIGRED a Hampshire thane (wig´-red)

WILLIBALD West Saxon monk and kinsman of Saint Boniface who beginning ca. 722 traveled to Frankland, Italy, Sicily, Greece, Ephesus, Cyprus, Syria, Jerusalem, Constantinople, Naples, and Monte Cassino, where he spent ten years in the Benedictine community; traveled to Germany at request of Pope Gregory III, was consecreated bishop of Eichstätt in Bavaria, and in 742 founded double abbey of Heidenheim am Hahnenkamm (will´-ih-bald)

WILTON town on River Wylye in southern Wiltshire

WILTSHIRE shire bordered by Dorset to the southwest, Somerset to the west, Gloucestershire to the northwest, Oxfordshire to the northeast, Berkshire to the east, and Hampshire to the southeast

WIMBORNE town in east Dorset where King Ini's sister Cuthburh founded an abbey ca. 705; burial place of Alfred's brother, King Athelred d. 871

WINI first bishop of Winchester acc. 662 (wee´-nee)

WODEN god revered by pre-Christian Saxons, also known as Grim (woe´-den); OEN *Open, *Krimr

WODENSBURG town in northeast Wiltshire

WUFFA founder of East Anglian royal line in 5th century (woof´-uh)

WULF one of Alfred's hall-guards (wolf´)

WULFRED a Hampshire thane (wolf´-red)

WULFHEARD alderman of Surrey, ally of King Ecgbert, father of alderman Wulfheard and alderman Wulfhere (wolf´-hay-erd)

WULFHEARD alderman of Hampshire, son of Wulfheard, brother of Wulfhere (wolf´-hay-erd)

WULFHEARD son of Wulfhere alderman of Wiltshire (wolf´-hay-erd)

WULFHERE alderman of Wiltshire, son of Wulfheard alderman of Surrey, father-in-law of K. Athelred, father of Wulfthryth and Wulfheard (wolf´-hair-uh)

WULFTHRYTH daughter of alderman Wulfhere, widow of King Athelred, mother of Athelwold and Athelhelm (wolf´-thrith)

WYNFRITH Saxon name of Saint Boniface (win´-frith)

YMME Halga's Frankish concubine (imm´-uh)

ZEALAND largest island of Denmark, home of ruling Danish house (zee´-lund); OEN *Siulunt

ZULPICH site of battle in 496 between Clovis I and Alamanni and in 612 between Brunhild's grandsons, Theudebert II of Austrasia and Theuderich II of Burgundy (zool´-pick)

Bibliography

Abels, Richard P. *Alfred the Great: War, Kingship and Culture in Anglo-Saxon England*. London: Pearson, 1998.

The Anglo-Saxon Chronicle. Manuscript A: The Parker Chronicle. http://asc.jebbo.co.uk/a/a-L.html.

Asser. *Life of King Alfred*. In *Alfred the Great: Asser's Life of King Alfred & Other Contemporary Sources*, edited by Simon Keynes and Michael Lapidge, 66–112. London: Penguin, 1983.

Augustine. *The Confessions of St. Augustine*. Translated by John K. Ryan. New York: Doubleday, 1960.

Bede. *Commentary on the Acts of the Apostles*. Translated by Lawrence T. Martin. Kalamazoo, MI: Cistercian, 1989.

———. *Ecclesiastical History of the English Nation and the Lives of St. Cuthbert and the Abbots*. Translated by J. Stevens, revised by J. A. Giles. London: Dent, 1910.

———. *On Genesis*. Translated by Calvin Kendall. Liverpool: Liverpool University Press, 2008.

———. *The Reckoning of Time*. Translated by Faith Wallis. Liverpool: Liverpool University Press, 1999.

Beowulf. Translated by Alan Sullivan and Timothy Murphy. New York: Pearson, 2004.

Biblia Sacra, Vulgata Editionis, Sixti v. Pont. Max. jussu recognita et Clemens viii. auctoritate edita. Tournai: Desclée, 1901.

Blackmore, Richard. *Alfred. An Epick Poem. In Twelve Books*. London: J. Knapton, 1723.

Boenig, Robert. "The Anglo-Saxon Harp." *Speculum* 71, no. 2 (April 1996): 290–320.

Boethius. *The Consolation of Philosophy*. Translated by V. E. Watts. Harmondsworth: Penguin, 1969.

———. *The Old English Boethius*. Translated by Susan Irvine and Malcolm R. Godden. Cambridge, MA: Harvard University Press, 2012.

Bowra, C. M. *From Virgil to Milton*. London: Macmillan, 1945.

Brown, Peter. *Augustine of Hippo*. Berkeley: University of California Press, 1969.

Buczacki, Stefan. *Fauna Britannica*. London: Hamlyn, 2002.

Buxton, John, ed. *The Birds of Wiltshire*. Trowbridge, Wiltshire: Wiltshire Library & Museum Service, 1981.

Byock, Jesse L., trans. *The Saga of King Hrolf Kraki*. London: Penguin, 1998.

Caesar. *The Conquest of Gaul*. Translated by S. A. Handford. Harmondsworth, UK: Penguin, 1951.

Campbell, James, ed. *The Anglo-Saxons*. Oxford: Phaidon, 1982.

Carnicelli, Thomas A., ed. *King Alfred's Version of St. Augustine's Soliloquies*. Cambridge, MA: Harvard University Press, 1969.

Chesterton, Gilbert Keith. *The Ballad of the White Horse*. San Francisco: Ignatius Press, 2001.

Cocker, Mark. *Crow Country*. London: Jonathan Cape, 2007.

Cocker, Mark, and Richard Mabey. *Birds Britannica*. London: Chatto & Windus, 2005.

Cottle, Joseph. *Alfred, an epic poem, in twenty-four books*. London: Longman & Rees, 1800.

Darling, F. Fraser. *Wild Life of Britain*. London: Collins, 1943.

De Vriend, Hubert Jan, trans. *The Old English Herbarium and Medicina de Quadrapedibus*. Oxford: Oxford University Press, 1984.

Duckett, Eleanor Shipley. *Alfred the Great*. Chicago: University of Chicago Press, 1956.

Einhard. *The Life of Charlemagne*. Translated by Samuel Epes Turner. *Medieval Sourcebook*, Fordham University, https://sourcebooks.fordham.edu/basis/einhard.asp.

Fitchett, John. *King Alfred: A Poem*. London: Pickering, 1841-1842.

Frohawk, F. W. *British Birds*. New York: Abelard-Schuman, 1958.

Gibbon, Edward. *The History of the Decline and Fall of the Roman Empire*. 6 vols. New York: AMS Press, 1974.

Godman, Peter. *Poetry of the Carolingian Renaissance*. Norman: University of Oklahoma Press, 1985.

Gregory of Tours. *The History of the Franks*. Translated by Lewis Thorpe. Harmondsworth: Penguin, 1974.

Gregory the Great. *Dialogues*. Translated by Odo John Zimmerman. Washington, DC: Catholic University of America Press, 1959.

———. *Pastoral Care*. Translated by Henry Davis. Mahwah, NJ: Paulist Press, 1950.

Greswell, William H. P. *The Story of the Battle of Edington*. Taunton, Somerset: Barnicott & Pearce, 1910.

Hageneder, Fred. *The Meaning of Trees*. San Francisco: Chronicle Books, 2005.

Heath-Stubbs, John Francis Alexander. *Artorius: A Heroic Poem in Four Books and Eight Episodes*. London: Enitharmon Press, 1974.

Hollander, Lee, trans. *The Poetic Edda*. Austin: University of Texas Press, 1986.

Horspool, David. *King Alfred: Burnt Cakes and Other Legends*. Cambridge: Harvard University Press, 2006.

Huneberc of Heidenheim. *The Hodoeporicon of St. Willibald*. Translated by C. H. Talbot, *Medieval Sourcebook*, Fordham University, https://sourcebooks.fordham.edu/basis/willibald.asp.

Jefferies, Richard. *Wild Life in a Southern County*. London: Thomas Nelson & Sons, n.d.

John Scotus Eriugena. *Periphyseon*. Translated by I. P. Sheldon-Williams and J. J. O'Meara. Montreal: Bellarmin, 1987.

Jones, Glyn. *A History of the Vikings*. New York: Oxford University Press, 1968.

Keynes, Simon, and Michael Lapidge, trans. *Alfred the Great: Asser's Life of King Alfred & Other Contemporary Sources*. London: Penguin, 1983.

Mabey, Richard. *Flora Britannica*. London: Sinclair-Stevenson, 1996.

Margary, Ivan D. *Roman Roads in Britain*. London: Phoenix House, 1957.

Marren, Peter. *Battles of the Dark Ages*. Barnley, Yorkshire: Pen & Sword, 2006.

Marsden, Richard, ed. *The Old English Heptateuch and Ælfric's Libellus de Veteri Testamento et Novo*. Oxford: Oxford University Press, 2008.

Nelson, Janet L. *Charles the Bald*. London: Longman, 1992.

Nennius. *Historia Brittonum*. Translated by J. A. Giles, *Medieval Sourcebook*, Fordham University, https://sourcebooks.fordham.edu/basis/nennius-full.asp.

Oman, Charles. *The Dark Ages*. London: Rivingtons, 1949.

———. *A History of England before the Norman Conquest*. London: Bracken Books, 1994.

Orosius, Paulus. *The Seven Books of History against the Pagans*. Translated by Roy J. Deferrari. Washington, DC: Catholic University of America Press, 1964.

Palmer, Eileen M., and David K. Balance. *The Birds of Somerset*. London: Longmans, Green & Co., 1968.

Peddie, John. *Alfred, Warrior King*. Stroud, Gloucestershire: Sutton, 1999.

Plummer, Charles. *The Life and Times of Alfred the Great*. Oxford: Clarendon Press, 1902.

Powicke, F. Maurice, and E. B. Fryde, eds. *A Handbook of British Chronology*. 2nd ed. London: Royal Historical Society, 1961.

Pratt, David. *The Political Thought of Alfred the Great*. Cambridge: Cambridge University Press, 2007.

Pseudo-Dionysius. *The Complete Works*. Translated by Colm Luibheid. Mahwah, NJ: Paulist Press, 1987.

Pye, Henry James. *Alfred, an epic poem in 6 books*. London: J. Wright, 1801.

Roesdahl, Else. *Viking Age Denmark*. Translated by Susan M. Margeson and Kirsten Williams. London: British Museum Press, 1982.

Saxo Grammaticus. *The History of the Danes, Books I–IX*. Edited by Hilda Ellis Davidson. Translated by Peter Fisher. Cambridge: D. S. Brewer, 1996.

Scandinavian Runic-text Database. Department of Scandinavian Languages, Uppsala University. http://www.nordiska.uu.se/forskn/samnord.htm.

Searle, William George. *Onomasticon Anglo-Saxonicum*. Hildesheim: Georg Olms, 1969.

Smyth, Alfred P. *King Alfred the Great*. Oxford: Oxford University Press, 1995.

Stenton, Frank. *Anglo-Saxon England*. 2nd ed. Oxford: Oxford University Press 1947.

Tacitus. *The Complete Works of Tacitus*. Translated by Alfred John Church and William Jackson Brodribb. New York: Random House, 1942.

Tilyard, E. M. W. *The English Epic and Its Background*. New York: Oxford University Press, 1966.

Turner, Frederick. *Epic: Form, Content, and History*. New Brunswick, NJ: Transaction, 2012.

Virgil. *The Aeneid*. Translated by Robert Fitzgerald. New York: Random House, 1980.

Wallace-Hadrill, J. M. *Early Germanic Kingship in England and on the Continent*. Oxford: Oxford Univeristy Press, 1971.

Whitelock, Dorothy. "The Importance of the Battle of Edington." *From Bede to Alfred: Studies in Early Anglo-Saxon Literature and History*. London: Variorum Reprints, 1980: vii, 78–93.

Whitlock, Ralph. *Somerset*. London: B. T. Batsford, 1975.

———. *The Warrior Kings of Saxon England*. New York: Barnes & Noble, 1993.

———. *Wiltshire*. London: B. T. Batsford, 1976.

Widukind of Corvey. *Deeds of the Saxons*. Translated by Bernard Bachrach and David Bachrach. Washington, DC: Catholic University of America Press, 2014.

Williams, Gareth. *Early Anglo-Saxon Coins*. Botley, Oxfordshire: Shire, 2008.

Wilson, David. M. *The Anglo-Saxons*. London: Thames & Hudson, 1960.

———, ed. *The Archaeology of Anglo-Saxon England*. London: Methuen, 1976.

Wormald, Patrick. *The Making of English Law: King Alfred to the Twelfth Century*, vol. 1, *Legislation and Its Limits*. Oxford: Blackwell, 1999.

Acknowledgments

Many friends have contributed to this poem. Tom Dahlberg, Ted Olsen, Bob Hanten, and Erick Kaardal have listened to sections at Tom's cabin, surrounded by bear trophies. Their sympathy with Alfred is a continuing inspiration.

My wife, Susan, has listened to and read the poem, contributing from her store of northern lore.

The poets of the Eratosphere online workshop have provided help and encouragement, especially Katie Hoerth, Andrew Frisardi, Richard Meyer, Edward Zuk, Ed Shaklee, Don Jones, and the late Tim Murphy. David Mason and Tom Cable were generous readers at West Chester. I am grateful to Professor Calvin Kendall, translator of Bede's commentary on Genesis, for reading and commenting on the poem. My friends in Converse Allstars have contributed their responses to several readings.

Through his epic poems, *The New World, Genesis,* and *Apocalypse;* his *Epic: Form, Content and History*; and his comments and encouragement, Frederick Turner has been a guide at every stage.

My thanks to Katie Hoerth at *Amarillo Bay* and to the editors of the *Copperfield Review* for publishing excerpts.

Finally, my thanks to Lily Coyle and Laurie Herrmann of Beaver's Pond Press for bringing to bear the talents of Miko Simmons, Jim Handrigan, and Kellie Hultgren.